Spencer Hill Press

Contact: Spencer Hill Press, PO Box 247, Contoocook, NH 03229, USA

Please visit our website at www.spencerhillpress.com

First Edition: May 2012.

White, Emily. 1980
Elemental : a novel / by Emily White – 1st ed.
p. cm.
Summary:
Ella has been imprisoned for most of her life. Once she escapes, she needs to figure out who she is and why she was taken. Is she the prophesied Destructor... or will she be the one who is destroyed?

Cover design by Victoria Caswell.

ISBN 978-1-937053-04-8 (paperback)
ISBN 978-1-937053-05-5 (e-book)

Printed in the United States of America

A NOVEL BY

EMILY WHITE

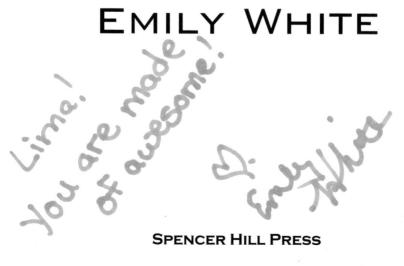

SPENCER HILL PRESS

To Jason—for inspiring me to work harder.
And to Victoria, whose constant support helped me
get through the worst moments of doubt.
Thank you both.

Chapter One:
Escape From Hell

I closed my eyes again and hovered in that empty world between sleep and waking. In sleep, I could ignore the silence and pretend it felt right. In the world of dreams, the darkness released me rather than tortured me, and I could be alone because I wanted to be and not because solitude had been forced upon me. Sleep was like a drug to my soul.

My dreams were mine, the place where I refused to be a prisoner. *Sho'ful*, the ship that floated through space carrying untold numbers of souls and sucking the life out of each and every one of us, failed to torment me in that one place alone.

"Get up." A voice in the darkness ripped me from the edge of slumber and pierced my ears with its sudden harshness. I gasped, clawing at my ears as the itch of newness burned at the base of my jaw. "Open the door and leave."

The voice seeped away like a dream, or a memory of a dream. It'd been ten years since they'd forced me into cold darkness. *Ten years.* I'd stopped asking why a long time ago. Either they didn't know or they didn't want to deal with the fact they'd put a child in a locked cell.

Leave? I burst out laughing for a precious split second before I clamped my mouth shut. No one left *Sho'ful*, and only fools thought to try. No light gleamed at the end of this tunnel. I lay there, refusing to get up. The voice had been nothing but my imagination. It could be nothing more than that.

A creaking sound broke the silence. And then something large, cold, and hard pushed against me, sliding me across the rusty floor. When I stopped moving, I grabbed hold of the thing that had pushed me and ran my fingers along its exterior. Parts of it were rough and chipping away, and all of it was ice cold.

1

I lay there running over and over in my mind the probability that what I held in my hands was the open door. Impossible. Yet… maybe. *Something* had pushed me. It could've been the door.

I reached up and grasped the thing I was growing fairly certain was indeed the door, and pulled myself up. I moved my feet to find some purchase on the floor. They slid along its smooth surface, throbbing with pain. I groaned in frustration.

With my teeth clenched, I laid my feet flat against the floor and forced my shaking legs to lift me. It'd been twenty-three atmosphere cycles since the last time I'd eaten, and moving was a challenge. I leaned my weight against the door and let out the breath I didn't realize I'd been holding.

It was time to walk out of here and leave *Sho'ful*, so I clenched my right leg and prepared for my first step out of my cell.

And froze.

The hounds.

The guards' precious pets kept watch over the halls to instill terror in the prisoners and dare us to come out. A chill ran up my spine as I thought about all the times I'd pressed myself against the back corner of my cell, getting as far away as I could from a hound that would come sniffing at my door. With perfect clarity, I could still recall the sound of his claws scraping against metal, sharp enough to gouge the hard exterior.

No one in their right mind would leave their cell, even if they could. That didn't stop the guards from dragging inmates out once in a while to feed to the beasts.

I shuddered. They'd done that to the man in the cell next to mine just a few feeding sessions ago. I could still hear his screams, the sound of his flesh being ripped from bone, and the crunch of the hounds' teeth gnawing him apart.

No.

I shook my head, in part to get the memory out and partly in answer to my stupid plan. I couldn't go out there. My heart hammered against my chest in warning. The smartest, the *safest* thing to do would be to close the door and go on living my life the way I'd been living it for the past ten years. A beating heart, safe inside my chest and drowning in depressive nothingness, trumped a beating heart spilling my blood onto the floor to be lapped up by those monsters.

Minutes passed slowly as I struggled to make up my mind. This glimmer, this phantom hope that warmed my chest was the first in living memory. I couldn't just disregard it and lock it away to die like everything else in my life.

The cold truth of what I needed to do hit me then. I'd been dying long enough.

I took my first step toward life.

Several hours and a few bone-bruising falls later, I'd crept through six levels and at least twenty corridors. My efforts had not been rewarded. I was no closer to getting out of this hell than when I'd taken my first step. I started to think I was an idiot for listening to a voice in my head.

No, I *knew* I was an idiot.

I pressed the heels of my palms against my eyes and smacked my head against the wall. Things weren't going so great. I needed to get out. The weight of the black nothingness crashed in around me, suffocating me. I needed to get out. I needed to get out!

Breathe, Ella. Breathe.

I couldn't breathe. What had I done? An interstellar ship didn't have a way off. Why did I ever think it did?

I took a deep breath and let it wash through me. My heartbeat slowed until I could barely feel it at all. The cold metal soothed my forehead. I just needed to stand there for a moment with my head pressed against the wall and my arms dangling at my sides. Things would work out. I'd be all right.

Too bad telling myself that over and over didn't actually help.

I turned my back against the wall and slid down to the floor, resting my head against my knees. Every cell in my body wanted to break down and cry. If I hadn't been so terrified of making noise, I would have. I'd never felt so lost in my life. The hope I'd felt earlier had all but disappeared. If the hounds didn't find me, the guards would, and they'd feed me to the hounds anyway. I'd been such a fool for leaving my cell. A tear burned its way down my cheek, and I clamped my hands over my eyes to stop the rest from gushing out.

Okay, I needed to think this through. I lifted my head from my knees and wiped my tear-soaked hands onto the ragged shreds of my muslin prison uniform. I needed to come up with a plan, if only to keep my mind busy.

If I kept following the stairs down, I'd get to the bottom. What then? Would there be a door to the outside? Is that how spaceships worked? Of course, even if that *was* how spaceships worked, outside was nothing but the vacuum of space. I groaned.

My plan sucked.

I rubbed the blood back into my legs and pulled myself up. A sucky plan beat no plan any day. One, two, three. Step, step, step. After my first initial steps, I found it easier to work in patterns and small groupings to keep track of distances. So far, I'd gone about thirty-eight sets of triple steps and most corridors were forty-three sets long before I hit the stairwell.

Step, step—holy crap!

My face collided with the floor with a sickening crunch. I clutched my head and moaned. *Sho'ful* shook and groaned as my body slammed first into one wall and then the other. I tried to grab onto something to keep from rolling around, but the smooth walls offered no handhold.

This had never happened before. Something was definitely different. During my ten years on the ship, it had been nothing but a smooth ride. Now, *Sho'ful* was shaking to pieces. The grinding and booming ripped through my skull and reverberated through my whole body.

Then the floor fell away from me. Or rather, it dropped so suddenly my body went airborne for a few seconds before crashing back down. Blood pooled in my mouth.

Oh no, not blood. Anything but blood, please. I whipped my head around and strained my ears for any noise other than the rattling metal and booming gears. Though I didn't have any way to know for sure, I suspected the hounds could pick up the smell of blood *really* well.

My pounding heart probably didn't help anything either. Even above all the mind-numbing noise, I could hear it racing in my ears. I tried to breathe deeply to calm myself down.

The ship leveled out and settled. We had landed, somehow I knew. Unfortunately, now that all the shaking had stopped, my heartbeat thundered in the heavy silence.

I swallowed, waiting and listening. A leaky pipe dripped off somewhere in the distance. Even farther away, I heard the muffled voices of guards. The vast, dark, and empty hallway where I sat was silent. I didn't move. Something felt off—like it was *too* silent.

I strained my ears, forcing myself to hear more, but all I got was silence and the drip, drip, drip of the leaky pipe.

Drip, drip, drip…

I drew a breath down to my toes and moved to my knees to stand up. That's when I heard it, a puff of exhaled breath. Blood chilled in my veins.

There wasn't much I could do—I was just as blind in the dark corridor as I'd always been—but now a hound stood somewhere close behind me. I rose to my feet, agonizingly cautious in my slow but steady movements.

I straightened with my hands on the wall. Something scraped against the metal floor—a claw. I took one step forward. A muffled noise like bristling fur filled the silence. I bit back my terror.

Way, way off at the distant end of the hall, something caught my eye, which was odd because I hadn't used my eyes in a very long time. I welcomed the strange sense. I needed all the help I could get. The end of the hall glowed with a weak, pale light that threatened to be snuffed at any moment. But it was *light*, and to me, it meant everything.

The furry, bristling sound moved closer. Razor-sharp teeth slid against each other with a sickening screech. My mind moved ridiculously slowly while my body screamed at me to run. My muscles actually prickled with the need while my brain refused to give the order. And so I was trapped there, waiting for the reality of the situation to settle in, my spastic body having already figured everything out eons ago.

It's too far away, I kept telling myself. *Even if there is something around the corner, you'll never make it.* But my body had had enough, and I ran.

The hound's reaction was immediate. The air rushed past me as he made his first lunge. I cringed, waiting for the blow. It didn't come. The staccato of his claws on the floor came closer—he'd been farther away than I'd thought.

Not far enough, though.

Hot, musky breath blew across my head, whipping my thick and crinkly hair into my face. I spit the strands out of my mouth and ran harder. Sharp fangs closed onto my shoulder, snagging my shirt. I stumbled and screamed. The hound's breath moistened my cheeks, mixing with my tears.

I twisted away and the sleeve ripped from my shirt just as the hound's jaws snapped shut. Foamy slobber hit my arm and neck.

I don't know what I was thinking—maybe I wasn't—but my fist swung out and collided with the hound's jaw, somehow making him stumble back. I took advantage of the opportunity and ran for the end of the hall and the glowing light.

The light—which I'd first thought a miracle—burned my eyes. Each lunge I took brought me closer to its warm promises, but my ill-used sense of sight protested. Actually, it flat out said "no." My eyes and nose burned, tears and snot pouring down my face. To make matters worse, the hound had recovered and started chasing me again, gaining. The light didn't seem to faze him at all.

A room opened up at the end of the hall. I could tell because the light suddenly brightened in the corner of my left eye. I turned, slipping on the floor, but kept my balance. The hound's moist breath hit my neck; his jaws hovered just inches from my head. Claws scraped against the floor.

Hot, sticky warmth oozed from somewhere in the room. The cold ship air battled valiantly with it, but lost. Somehow, I knew I needed to go toward the warmth, just like I'd known I needed to go toward the light. The light and the warmth were connected, and they were the lifesavers I'd been looking for. I just had to get closer to them. Whatever the light was, it was good and protective. It was life. I knew that; I just didn't know *how* I knew that.

Something like a memory flitted across my mind and for a second I imagined sunshine, breezes, and wispy grass, and lying next to a boy—a boy with green eyes.

Then three things happened: I heard the hound's wet chops open wide and felt his steamy breath closing the distance. A claw grazed my back, slicing my shirt and skin open. And I fell through a hole, screaming all the way down.

Chapter Two:
Meir

Pain shot up my legs and spine. With my knees pressed against my chest and my teeth clenched to keep from screaming, I turned and smacked my face right against something hard and freakishly hot—so hot it singed my cheek on contact. I rolled a few inches away and lay flat on my back. I tried to open my eyes far enough to see what the thing was, but the glare burned a thousand times more intensely than before I'd fallen. Stinging wet tears poured down my cheeks.

Snarls ripped through the air above me. I cringed away and covered my face. I waited and waited with my breath held fast. The expected pain from fangs ripping through me never came. I pressed my hands against my lids and forced them open to see. Tears pooled in my eyes, but I wiped them away. Above me, maybe fifteen or twenty feet, the hound stared back at me, teeth bared. He'd pushed most of his nose through a long and narrow break in the ship's smooth exterior. Narrow for him, but perfect for my decrepit little body. A metal limb plummeted down from the break to just beside me, ending in a wide pad—landing gear.

If my face hadn't already been drenched in tears, I would've been weeping for joy right about then. As it was, it felt like my whole body might burst from the sheer unbelievable relief I felt. I knew instantly I was a different person—an Ella who didn't just have a glimmer of hope living inside her, but someone who ran on it like fuel. At that point, I felt utterly invincible. I'd set out to do the impossible and had come out with war wounds to prove my success. In fact, I didn't even care that I was broken and bloody. I was too proud to care.

A little whisper of reason seeped into my mind, threatening to smother my joy. *Time to be smart, Ella. Time to use your head.*

I didn't want to listen to it. I didn't want to do anything but lie there with my eyes closed and feel the hot air blow across my skin—the perfect reversal to the cold death I'd been living through. My skin soaked it up and luxuriated in its sizzle.

I sighed. The reasonable part of my brain was right. I needed to get moving. Circumstances—albeit amazing circumstances I never dared dream of before—had turned me into an ex-con on the run. And an ex-con on the run who didn't get as far away as possible from the prison she'd escaped was an idiot.

I turned over onto my hands and knees and pulled myself up. Something stirred the air by my head. I looked up to see the hound's long front limb stretched through the narrow hole, trying to grab me. His head pressed through the hole and he snapped at me. I smiled back at him before turning away.

Pavement scorched my bare feet. I didn't care. I gasped for breath through the sticky, thick air that stank of rot and fumes. Searing pain ripped through my back and shoulder and yet despite all this, I felt happier than I could ever remember being. I'd made it off of *Sho'ful*.

Somehow, I'd made it off.

But I was still blinded by the brightness, and for that reason only, my joy was cut short. The glare didn't ease up at all. If anything, it became worse. My eyes burned worse than my back as they tried to function in daylight for the first time in a decade.

I pressed my hands above my eyes and forced my lids open again. They fought against me, but my will was stronger. It worked... kind of. Since I'd left the shade of the ship, I had no protection from the sun. A lot of little dark blurs bunched together to my right and left. Ahead of me blinding blue light splintered into blinding white light—open land, I assumed. I decided to try my luck by going straight. The blurs probably indicated some sort of settlement, and that was precisely where I *didn't* want to be.

With one hand shielding my eyes and the other babying the stitch growing in my side, I started running again. I had gone maybe a dozen precarious feet when something to my right caught my attention. I stopped and turned. Ahead of me, a tiny light flashed—a beacon. Unfortunately, it came from the dark little blurs, and I still had no intention of going that way. I started to head back to the open land when I heard it: the voice.

"Follow the light."

My heart pounded in my ears. The voice wasn't in my head. It echoed through the air around me and whispered in the wind. Despite the heat beating down on me from the sun and the burn of my wounds, I felt cold.

Invisible hands grabbed my shoulders and pushed me toward the beacon. I stumbled a few steps before regaining my footing, and then whipped my head around.

There was no one there. I pursed my lips and clenched my fists to rein the terror in.

I knew I had a choice to make now. I could listen to the bone-chilling voice a second time and go toward the beacon, trusting I'd be all right. Or I could continue on with my original plan to get as far away from this place as possible. The latter option was tempting. In fact, it was *very* tempting.

I looked back at *Sho'ful* and shuddered. The hulking monstrosity loomed like a creature out of a nightmare, bigger than I'd ever imagined. The dark shape rose higher than I could see with the sun glaring behind it and stretched across the horizon. No, I definitely didn't want to stay anywhere near that.

But I couldn't deny that the voice had helped me so far. If not for its urgings, I would still be sitting in my cell, waiting for death and doing nothing about it. I bit my lip and looked back at the flashing light.

All right, voice. Lead the way.

I stumble-ran the short distance to the flashing light.

"Get in here, *now*." A man pushed me through a doorway. His rough manner didn't exactly soothe my nerves, and I immediately wondered if I'd made the right choice.

Once inside, I froze, no longer blinded by the glare of daylight. The subdued light felt like balm to my sight and I breathed a sigh of relief. The enormous room sat empty except for a red, blue, and gold sofa and a small, round table. And yet, it didn't *feel* empty. It felt alive, but it also felt cold and dark after the scorching heat outside. Goosebumps popped up all over my skin. I blinked my eyes and wiped away my tears.

The man closed the door, plunging the room into even more darkness, and brushed past me. I recoiled and turned my face away from him.

"I don't think they saw you." He crossed over to the side of the room and drew the shades closed on the only window. "But I think you should hunker down here for a while, regardless."

I gulped. Staying here was not an option. I needed as much distance between me and *Sho'ful* as I could get. I knew it had been a bad idea to come here. I should've followed my instincts.

I turned to leave when the man caught me by the shoulders. I took in a gasping breath to scream just as he clamped one hand on my mouth and pulled me deeper into the room. I twisted and turned, desperate to break his hold.

"Enough of that," he said. "I'm not going to hurt you. I promise."

Promises meant nothing. Everyone in my life had hurt me. Why would this man be any different? In fact, he wasn't. As my eyes adjusted, I took in his black robes and long beard peppered with gray. I'd seen that look before—a long, long time ago, right before I'd been put on *Sho'ful*. They were the garb of the people who had kept me imprisoned. I'd been a fool to listen to the voice. I needed to leave. I kicked at his shins and struggled to pull myself away. His fingers locked tighter around my arm.

"Stop. It." I knew from those two words and the penetrating look in his eyes I would be in trouble if I didn't listen.

My limbs went limp even as my insides shook with terror. I'd walked into a trap.

"That's a good girl." He took his hand off my mouth, but kept his firm hold on my arm. "Now come and sit down."

He dragged me to the plush sofa in the middle of the room. I sank down into the cushions as he sat next to me and let his hands drop to his lap.

The man looked me over as I chewed on my bottom lip and waited for the inevitable beatings to come. It was his duty to punish me. Everyone knew the Mamood—my captors—enjoyed any reason to inflict pain on others.

His black eyes grew sad as he tenderly touched my bleeding shoulder and back. "First, we need to take care of those wounds." He left the room for a moment and came back with a bowl and towel.

After a few more timid glances at my face, he dipped the corner of the towel in the water and washed my shoulder. I winced from the sharp pain.

"Shh," he soothed. "It's okay now. I'm Meir, by the way." He smiled. "Meir Groff."

I nodded and turned away.

"You don't have a name?"

Of course I had a name. What kind of question was that? I just didn't know if I wanted to share it with him.

Meir started humming something after a few seconds and I turned back to stare at him. He looked older than me—a lot older. His salt-and-pepper beard appeared to be just a few short years from silver. Wrinkles, both deep and shallow, swarmed around his charcoal eyes. His ebony skin embraced the wrinkles with love, though. I imagined I could see the pride behind each earned crease, as well as the sorrow.

He stopped cleaning my shoulder and stared at me. I spoke before I had a chance to think it through. "I'm Ella."

Blood rushed to my head at the sound of my voice. Memories swam through my mind again, so clear, so real—memories of spring fields and running with a boy—the boy with the green eyes. He whispered my name to me. His voice rippled like the wind. My eyes rolled back into my head as hot and churning blood flooded my vision.

"Ella? Ella!" Meir shook me and patted the uninjured side of my face.

I looked around, forgetting where I was, and sat up. Everything felt wrong. My body didn't have the strength to do what I'd done today and I knew I was close to crashing—maybe even going crazy. If I didn't get water fast, I was going to black out.

Meir's bowl sat in his hand just inches away. I needed it so badly. I didn't care that my blood swirled around in it like red ribbons. With my eyes closed, I dropped my face in and lapped the water into my mouth. Meir tried to pull the bowl away from me. I grabbed it with both hands and plunged my face deeper into the water to gulp it all down.

"Ella, stop! This is dirty. I can get you clean water."

I ignored him. It was almost gone and I wanted every… last… drop.

When I lifted my soaked face, water dripping down my hair, Meir stared back at me with his same old, sad eyes.

"What did they do to you?"

I shrugged. What didn't they do to me?

He shook his head and wiped my face dry. "I'm so sorry."

My breath caught. No Mamood had ever apologized to me. Tears burned at the corners of my eyes. My lower lip quivered. I would *not* cry in front of this man. I'd sworn to myself long ago that my captors would never see me cry, and Meir would be no exception. I needed to change the subject, and fast.

"Meir, what's a Shadra?"

All blood left his face, leaving his skin like ash. "Why?"

I shrugged and turned away. *Stupid, stupid Ella.* Why had that come out of my mouth? Had I lost all self-control? That name had been haunting my nightmares since the guards had spit it at me at the last feeding session, almost a week ago. I didn't know what it meant, but the sinking weight in my stomach had led me to believe it was bad—very bad.

It didn't help that Meir looked horrified.

"It's complicated," he began slowly, not taking his probing eyes off me. "Essentially, a Shadra is a person sworn to Manoo as a human sacrifice."

"Manoo..."

"The god of the Mamood."

I chewed on my lip again and broke the skin. "Why would someone be called this?"

His eyes narrowed before answering. "Only someone Manoo sees as his enemy would be named Shadra. There is a rumor— one that's spanned thousands of years—that Manoo will be destroyed by someone, someone sent by El. No one knows who this person is." He studied me for several more moments then leaned closer so that his eyes were all I could see. "Now tell me why you asked."

I licked the blood off my lip and looked away. Why *had* the guards called me that? I wasn't anyone's enemy. I was nothing.

Someone pounded on the door outside. I jumped up, sending the bowl to the floor where it crashed into a dozen pieces.

"Open up, traitor!" The man outside pounded on the door again. "Someone saw the Shadra come in here. Bring her out! *Now!*"

Chapter Three:
The Shakai

I looked down at the broken shards of glass and felt all hope shattering to pieces around me. I hadn't been off the ship an hour and they'd already found me. Too close—I knew I'd stayed too close. I cursed myself for listening to the voice that had led me here. And now Meir knew everything. The polite—and maybe even caring—front he'd put up would come crumbling down any moment.

I wiped the sweat off my hands and waited.

Meir grabbed my arm, dragged me through the hall, and opened a door to another room. He did it so fast I practically suffered whiplash. I ripped myself away from him and planted my feet. "What are you doing?" I whispered.

He looked at me like I'd lost my mind. "Getting you out of here."

The man made no sense. Meir was a Mamood. His allegiance rested with the guards outside his door, not with me. He didn't even know me. For all anyone but myself knew, I totally deserved the title Shadra. He couldn't possibly be such a fool. Something else was going on. And then it hit me. Of course—he was waiting for them to offer a reward. I should've known. I shook my head and looked away from him. I didn't want him to know I'd figured it out. As soon as he knew I knew the truth, this show of kindness and compassion would end. A Mamood's true intentions always came out eventually.

I waited until I'd wiped all knowledge from my eyes before I turned back to him and gave a stiff nod. He paused to close the door, and then led me around a large, four-poster bed to the back wall of what must've been his bedroom.

We both jumped when we heard the front door crash open and footsteps cross the threshold into Meir's living room. Oh crap. A small whine *might* have passed my lips—certainly not anything worth noting. Okay, fine. I was terrified. Meir let me go to run his hands along the wall.

I looked frantically behind me, expecting the door to burst open any second and the guards to drag me back to *Sho'ful*. I wouldn't go. I didn't care what I had to do, there was no way I'd let anyone close a cell door in my face again.

The bedroom doorknob turned and I squared my bony little shoulders—ready. Ready to do what, exactly, I didn't know. Maybe I'd do something to force their hand and they'd have to kill me. Kick a few groins, punch a few jaws—whatever it took. I closed my eyes to embrace the darkness… and waited.

An arm wrapped around my shoulder and yanked me off the floor. I kicked my feet out and threw punches at the air, hoping to make contact with flesh and cause some serious damage. The thought was good and the attempt even valiant, but before I knew it, I was falling. I opened my eyes wide to see Meir glaring at me as I hit the floor hard and crumpled. Everything went dark.

At first I thought I'd blacked out. But as every single bone in my worthless little body screamed at me in pain, I knew it was merely wishful thinking. Meir grabbed me and hoisted me onto my feet.

I opened my mouth to yell at him, but he gave me a severe look and pressed his hand across my mouth. Just within my hearing range, muffled voices passed through the stone wall behind Meir's back. I realized we were in a tunnel just outside his bedroom—a secret, cold, dark, and damp tunnel. I looked at Meir as if seeing him for the first time.

My skin prickled in warning. I really needed to get away from him. There was something… off… and not just in the regular, evil Mamood way. Meir had secrets.

The muffled voices died away. Meir hooked his fingers around my arm and pulled me deeper into the tunnel. I thought about struggling against him—in fact, I should have—but I had this sick need to find out what those secrets were. We were both keeping secrets, and from the same people. Maybe that was enough to trust him… and I wanted to trust him, wanted to believe that someone might be on my side. One thing was for sure; there was no longer any way I could leave him without getting some answers.

The questions could come later, though. Right then, I needed to focus. Meir dragged me through the tunnel much faster than I had ever gone before and it was all I could do to remember to breathe *and* put one foot in front of the other. A stitch started growing in my side, burning my lungs and making my muscles spasm.

"How much farther is it?" I coughed. Talking only made it worse—much, much worse.

"It's not too much farther, but we can't slow down. We have to get to Izbet before they have time to set up a blockade. Hurry!" And he started going faster. I should've kept my mouth shut.

After splashing through a few hundred yards of puddles and scraping against the rough, stone walls more than once, we stopped and Meir released my hand. I stumbled to the floor, gasping for air. Hot flames burned my throat with each breath. Despite the chill in the tunnel, sweat poured over my brow and down my neck.

Meir opened another secret door on the ceiling and sunlight poured in. I recoiled from the light—I would have to force myself to get used to it. For now, though, I needed to work on my endurance. That run had nearly killed me. Blood rushed to my face, burning my cheeks and neck. The room spun around me, making my stomach lurch. I heaved, though nothing came up. I tried to breathe through my nose while I dry-vomited, but in my panic, I forgot how. I started gasping and flailing my arms.

Meir wrapped his arms around me, forcing me to stay still. I focused on his breaths and felt his chest rise and fall as something like a memory tickled at my mind. It wasn't a real memory with remembered images, but it felt like one. His strong, protective arms around me and his rough whiskers against my cheek felt so familiar. The smell was wrong, though. He didn't smell like what my memory told me he was supposed to smell like. But that was okay.

As I relaxed into his hold, I realized Meir was like a father. And that was exactly what I needed right then.

Then he let me drop to the floor and the feeling was all but obliterated. I looked up to yell at him for ruining the moment as he climbed into a rusting, bulbous vehicle with a long, thin tail and an open top. Faded paint chips were peeling away from the body, and a few had already scattered on the ground. It did *not* look like something any smart person would be willing to get into. He couldn't possibly expect our getaway to be in that.

"Get in." Apparently he could.

I shrugged my shoulders and climbed in beside him. It was a decision I soon regretted as the tiny speeder sputtered and rocked, knocking me sideways.

"Come on, old girl." He banged a fist on its control panel.

As if wishing to please its master, the vehicle leveled out and issued a soft hum as its electromagnet slowly lifted us up and through the open door. I sighed and patted my stomach to settle it down.

Gasping, I shielded my eyes from the bright, setting sun. The sky was on fire with beautiful reds and oranges. The dry, dead land stretched out before me, and it stopped the breath in my lungs. Years of nothingness had made me forget what beauty truly was.

Meir turned the vehicle and put the sun behind us. A dark blue stretched like velvet across the sky. It was cool and clean, and a comfort to my eyes. The air whipped past us as we sped over the smooth ground, soft and pleasant after the scorching heat of the day. I reclined back in my seat and breathed a sigh of relief.

One hurdle—possibly the biggest one of all—had been passed so far. Now all I had to do was hide out and wait for an opportunity to leave the planet, to get as far away as possible from the Mamood—simple enough compared to what I'd gone through so far. Of course, there was another hurdle I'd been avoiding, something that'd taken a back seat since the guards started chasing me.

Meir knew I'd been named Shadra, and yet he'd said nothing. For some reason, this annoyed me. He must've been hoping for a pretty big reward. No doubt the Shadra would fetch the biggest one of all if what he'd said about me being Manoo's enemy was true. Of course, he couldn't be stupid enough to think he still qualified for the reward. After aiding my escape, the only thing waiting for him was a death sentence.

So what did he want? I looked at him out of the corner of my eye, hoping to glean the truth of the mystery behind Meir. He sat rigid as a stone, not giving me anything to go on. Whatever his reasons for helping me out, he kept them to himself. Too bad I had no intention of letting him.

I turned my body toward him, pushed my hair out of my face, and cleared my throat. He didn't move his eyes off the landscape. This overwhelming urge to grab his face and make him look at me popped into my mind and tightened my arms. I clenched my jaw to keep the thought from turning into action. "Are you just going to ignore the obvious?" I blurted.

"What's that?"

"You heard what the guard said. I'm the Shadra."

A smile tugged at the corner of his mouth. "Yup, I heard him."

"Gah!" I threw my hands into the air and pulled my fingers through my hair.

"Are you angry?" He chuckled.

Apparently, he was amused. I was not.

"Yes, I'm angry. You make absolutely no sense and it's driving me crazy!"

"You've got a bit of a temper." His smile widened. "Besides, who says I'm not making sense? Just because you don't under-stand what I'm doing doesn't mean I don't."

"Then please enlighten me." I narrowed my eyes and waited until he faced me. "What are you doing?"

"I'm saving you."

"Why?"

He turned his gaze to the front of the speeder, and his jaw quivered before answering, "Manoo doesn't deserve my help."

I didn't know what to say to that. "But aren't you a Mamood?" I scanned his robes and facial hair again, making sure I hadn't imagined his Mamood traits.

"Yes and no." He gave me a sideways glance. "I am a Mamood by nationality, but I am a Praeori by faith."

"What is that?"

Meir stiffened beside me and tightened his grasp on the steer-ing wheel. "A traitor."

I watched him carefully as his suddenly wary eyes flitted across the landscape. Every few seconds, he turned his head to look at the setting sun.

We'd been flying over the smooth, tan ground for a while now and when I looked behind me, I saw that the sun was quickly fall-ing below the horizon. It would be dark soon. With each passing moment, the worry lines on Meir's face deepened.

"What's wrong?" Part of me really didn't want to know.

"We need to find a place to hide."

"Why?"

"Not everything on this planet is dead." He paused. "Something lives."

I gulped. "What?"

"Dammit!" He pounded his fist against the control screen and pushed the vehicle to what I guessed was its capacity for speed. The thing rocked and stuttered, yet kept lurching forward.

I pressed my dry lips together and dug my nails into the soft fabric of my seat.

"We're not going to make it to Izbet." He moaned the words, making my heart beat faster.

My head swam. Black spots dotted my vision and my chin dropped to my chest. "What is it, Meir? Please! Tell me!"

He jerked the speeder to the left and headed straight for a small grouping of boulders.

"Meir…" I was way past trying to control the whine in my voice.

He hushed me. I clamped my hand over my mouth. We were coming up to the boulders too fast. I started to worry that my rescuer had gone mad. The crazed look in his eyes didn't help alleviate my fears. But before I could say anything, he jerked the vehicle to the right in a hairpin turn and cut the electromagnet. The speeder dropped and skidded sideways across the ground— sending up a thick cloud of dust and chunks of dirt—until we stopped with a thump against the grouping of rocks that stuck up like a giant's fingers reaching to the sky.

I gasped and rested my head against my knees.

"Sorry," he mumbled. "The brakes went out."

Of course. I'd known no smart person would ever get into this thing.

He jumped out of the speeder and ran around the front to my side. His calloused hands grabbed my arms and I made no move to stop him. I didn't make a move to help him, either. I would've helped if I could've, but my body responded like mush. It was a bad time for me to go into shock, but it was overdue, too.

Meir didn't seem to have any trouble dragging me out of the vehicle and carrying me into the close confines within the outcropping of rock. I imagined my body didn't weigh too much— he didn't even breathe heavily from any exertion.

After he lay me down on the cool ground, he walked back to the narrow entrance of the peculiar shelter to look for something. He fidgeted and pulled at his beard—still worried.

I lifted my head off the ground. "Meir?"

He sighed, but didn't say anything for several long moments. "The sun is almost set."

"And?"

"And the Shakai will come out when it does."

"Shakai." One-word responses were really all my mind could handle at this point. Meir seemed to grasp that and backed away from the small opening to sit by me. He placed his hand on my good shoulder—a gesture that quickly soothed me despite the obvious tension in his muscles.

He sighed again, debating whether or not to tell me. I decided to push him a little.

"I want to know."

He dropped his gaze to the ground and said, "This planet was decimated millennia ago by a meteor. The Shakai are..." His eyes rolled back like he was trying to find the right word and pluck it from his mind. "...insects—the biggest ones can grow to be a little larger than a man's head. They survived the initial blast and thrived through the resulting centuries of settling ash. With each generation, more and more offspring were born that were hyper-sensitive to the severely filtered light. Eventually, those creatures dominated the gene pool because all the others died from starvation and lack of sun.

"When the Mamood came to settle this planet, we set up atmospheric generators all over the surface and cleared away the ash. It was too late for the Shakai. They had lived under too many years of darkness and no longer carried any genes that would allow their offspring to live in the light. So now they only come out at night, preying on their weak because there are no other food sources—except for anyone foolish enough to be out in the dark."

I gulped. "Like us."

"Like us."

"Are they strong?" I didn't know why I asked the question. I couldn't actually think I could fight them off. And yet, I did think that.

"They are many."

Meir's arms shook violently around me—terror—and yet I remained surprisingly calm. My fear from just moments before seeped away and left nothing but a blank numbness. Though my mind tried to reason through the lethargy, it didn't get very far. Instead, happier conclusions of escape and long life seemed the only logical answer. I couldn't have been allowed to escape prison only to become food for some oversized hive of insects. Surely our situation was not as dire as my savior implied. Life just wasn't that unfair.

And then I heard them.

At first, the sound was soft and almost pleasant, like the rustling of dry leaves. If I hadn't known what it was, I might've found it comforting. But after a few moments, the rustling grew into shrieking, ripping, and tearing. The ground shook around me as thousands, possibly millions, of feet clattered along its surface, drawing closer to us.

I wanted to scream, and almost did, but pressed my lips shut instead. The shrieking ripped through the air all around us now—ear-piercing wails followed by grotesque gurglings of death. They were eating each other.

I squeezed my eyes shut and pressed myself tighter against Meir's chest. He responded by clasping his fingers around my arms as if afraid we were going to be ripped apart. I had to admit, it seemed like a possibility.

Then I heard a new sound that sent my heart pounding against my chest—the sound of claws on rock.

Meir dug his fingers into my skin and shuffled us to brace himself on the rock wall behind us.

There were just a few click-clicks of feet at first as the ones in front tested the structure, drawing closer. Something hard brushed my cheek and slid down my neck. It twitched across my skin, feeling, probing. Meir tensed against me, and I shuddered. The hard thing paused and then a screech tore through the air right by my ear. The click-clicks turned into an avalanche as the Shakai swarmed our hideout.

CHAPTER FOUR:
ESCAPE

They crawled on top of us, beneath us, even burrowed between us. Meir's fingers dug into my arms, latching us together. And then he was gone. Dozens of the Shakai crawled all over me, pulling my hair and ripping my skin with sharp-edged pincers.

I didn't register the pain at first. Though their claws dug and ripped through my skin, sending warm blood to run down my arms and legs, my mind moved too slowly. Someone's screams echoed in my ears and I was surprised to realize they were mine. Then the pain rolled through me, and I screamed louder until the Shakai digging at my face choked off my shrieks. Hooked pincers slid in my mouth and tore at my tongue as they fought to get down my throat.

As I swiped my hands at the bugs, ripping one off only to find five more take its place, my body started to warm and tingle. At first, I thought maybe I was passing out, but the tingling turned into a sharp burning. Pain scorched through my veins, charring me from the inside out. I couldn't even feel the Shakai ripping me apart anymore.

I clenched my teeth against it, willing my body to ignore the throbbing—but it wouldn't be ignored. The pain seeped into my head and I screamed, ready for it to explode. My eyes bulged, pushed from beneath by the sheer force of the agony. Too exhausted to fight anymore, I gave in and let the pain have me, praying for death.

The moment I let go of my control, the pain vanished, replaced by hunger—for what, I didn't know yet. All I did know was that every cell of my body ached to *devour*.

My vision changed. Instead of black, creeping shadows in the night, the Shakai turned into bright, pulsing orbs. I could see every molecule in their blood sprint through their veins in a coordinated dance. The air, too, swarmed with bright molecules that dotted the space around me like stars. When I thought to bring my hand up to touch one of the red points of light, the molecule flitted through the sky to my hand before I could even move. I stared in wonder. The others danced in front of me, ready and waiting.

Aware once again of the Shakai pouring over my body, eating my flesh as they went, I ordered the points of light to bend to my will.

Fire erupted in the air and surrounded me. My skin tingled with the power and I moaned in ecstasy as the hunger was fed. The Shakai shrieked and scurried away, dying and burning in the growing flames. Their bodies popped and crisped, sending up hazy smoke in the air.

When I sensed all the nearest fuel for my flames had been thoroughly consumed, I fought to pull the fire back but the hunger was not yet satiated. And so the flames spread, searching and devouring without restraint. The force poured through my veins, sapping me of my wavering strength, and yet also filling me with a sick need for more—part of me *wanted* the destruction. But it was too much, and my legs gave out. I fell to the ground, letting the blackness pour over me.

I awoke some time later on a hard bed with a thin sheet draped over my body. A dim light hovered above my head, casting shadows around the room.

I licked my parched lips, tasting copper, and swallowed. I had no idea how I'd gotten to this room with its whitewashed walls that were almost too clean. The charred remains of my prison clothes sat on the floor at the side of my bed. My eyes opened wide as I realized *my clothes were on the floor*. Heat trickled beneath my cheeks when I thought about what Meir must have seen.

Meir.

Panic fought through my still hazy mind, clearing my thoughts. He'd been ripped away from me by the Shakai. Where was he now? How did I get here? I tried to sit up, but my head swam and nausea swelled up in my stomach before I'd cleared my head off the pillow.

I moaned and swallowed back the bile.

Someone came in then, drawing more light into the room through the open door. I clenched my stomach and turned my head just slightly to see who it was.

My lips pulled up at the sides—an automatic response to seeing my savior alive. I made a quick assessment—he was mostly covered by his robes, but his face was cut up and his hair disheveled. Other than that, if he was in worse shape, I had no way of knowing.

Meir smiled back at me, the most beautiful smile I'd ever seen—gleaming white teeth set against ebony. My heart fluttered. And I knew right then that, yes, not only could this man be like a father to me, I wanted it more than anything.

"I brought you some food." He cradled my head in his arms and pulled me up gently. "I've been so worried, waiting outside your door for hours, just listening for any signs of waking. I wondered if you would make it." His anxious eyes traveled down and up the length of my body until finally resting on my face.

I followed his gaze with my hand and gasped. Nearly every inch of me had been covered in bandages—some of them wet with blood.

"We'll have to get those changed soon, but first, I want you to eat something." He rested a bowl of soup in my waiting hands and began feeding me himself.

It was a simple broth—no sign of solids in sight—but it was delicious, and my stomach ached for it. He couldn't bring the spoon to my mouth fast enough. I lifted the bowl and brought it to my lips, carelessly letting the golden drink spill past the corners of my mouth. Most of it made it down my throat, though, and I ignored the searing pain of the much-too-hot liquid. When it was gone, I smacked my lips and sighed. It was a *very* good soup—much better than my usual diet of stale bread and water.

Meir took the bowl and set it down on a table next to my bed. He dabbed at my neck and cheeks with a cloth, cleaning away what I'd spilled.

I smiled at him again. I couldn't help it—for some reason, having him around made everything feel okay—safe. I knew now that my rescue had been sincere; he had no intention of turning me in for a reward. His eyes grew sad and the crease between his brows returned. I tilted my head at him, questioning.

"What happened, Meir?" My voice barely reached a whisper. "How did we get here?"

He pressed his thick lips into a tight line and shook his head. "I don't really know what happened. After they dragged me past the rocks, I blacked out. I woke up a little before dawn and found you lying on the ground, ripped and bleeding, surrounded by the charred and smoking remains of dozens of Shakai."

I gulped. That part of the evening began to come back to me with increasing clarity.

"I tried to wake you," he continued, "but you wouldn't respond. So I carried you the last few miles to Izbet, snuck past the blockade, and brought you to my friend's home." He grabbed a piece of my hair—a stray that had wound its way across my neck—and pushed it behind my ear. "You've been asleep for hours. The day is nearly over."

"Is your friend a Praeori, too? Does he know I'm the Shadra?"

A dark chuckle passed his lips. "No to both questions, and it's best that he doesn't know."

"How did you convince him to help, then?"

"I saved his life many years ago, and now he is bound to me by an Oath. Of course..." His black eyes went flat. "Never mind." He smiled, but it didn't reach his eyes. "I should get you cleaned up."

Meir left the room, taking my empty bowl with him, and returned minutes later with a large, metal tub of steaming water and a bar of soap. He'd draped a thick, white towel over his shoulder, tied the skirt of his robes above his knees, and pushed his sleeves up above his elbows. He set the tub on the floor at the side of my bed and dropped the soap into the water. He then pulled a package of clean bandages out from the sash around his waist and set it on the table.

I sat myself up and swung my legs over the side of the bed and let my feet skim the hot water. It was euphoric. I moaned as I wiggled my toes and let the velvet liquid lap around my parched skin.

Meir began to unwrap my soiled bandages, starting at my leg. His dark fingers brushed against my sickly pale limb. I blushed, but let him take care of me. He was gentle and careful around my wounds, like a surgeon, skilled and professional. The warm flush of blood in my cheeks seeped away as he continued in his care. I had no reason to be embarrassed. This was not a man who looked upon me as a woman. No, his soft black eyes and tender hands moved over my body much the same way a father's would over his beloved daughter. I smiled. Maybe Meir wanted the same thing I did.

Each wound—and there were many—was scrubbed clean and then coated with a thick, clear gel that smelled of mint and lavender. Instantly, my open sores began to cool under contact with the herbal balm. He placed new bandages on my legs, arms, and waist, scrubbed my face and cleaned the wounds there as well, leaving the balm to soak into my skin. I was glad he chose not to use bandages on my face—I was swollen enough as it was, making movement difficult.

He then handed me a white robe. With my teeth clenched against the throbbing pain, I forced my sore muscles to work and my aching elbows to bend.

When I'd finished putting on the robe, Meir washed my hair. It had been months since my hair had been washed—ever since my yearly washing on *Sho'ful*. My dry and itchy scalp nearly sang with relief as Meir scrubbed the layers of dead skin away. He pulled a bottle of creamy soap from a hidden pocket in his robes and poured a liberal amount onto my head, working it in. The scent of roses filled my nostrils.

I couldn't help sighing. My bliss could not be ignored.

Meir chuckled.

"You're too good to me, Meir. I don't deserve this."

"Hmmm…" He seemed to be thinking, weighing his answer. "I would disagree."

I ducked my head over the bin as he poured hot water through my hair to wash out the soap. He was careful to keep it out of my eyes. When he'd completely rinsed out my hair, he dried it off with the towel, and brushed through my waist-length hair before it had a chance to snarl.

When he had finished, I placed my hand on his arm. "Thank you."

He smiled and pulled me into a fatherly hug. He muttered something I couldn't quite make out.

I pulled away from him and searched his face. The way his eyes took me in with a crease of a smile at their corners, I knew that, for some reason, this man was happy I had come to him.

I chewed on my lower lip and dropped my gaze. There was no way my good fortune could last, and I was terrified of the moment fate would see how lopsided my life had become. I didn't deserve Meir, but I didn't ever want to lose him.

My savior.

He left me then so he could clear away the tub and soiled bandages. Being alone, I decided to brood. I hadn't forgotten the night before. The force that'd built up in my body and poured out of me as a surge of flames wasn't something I could ignore. It also wasn't something I really wanted to think about, either. My ever-logical mind tried to convince me that I'd fallen into hallucinations and what I had seen hadn't really happened, but I couldn't buy it.

Something had happened.

Meir said he'd seen burning Shakai carcasses on the ground where he'd found me. So I *hadn't* been imagining anything. The question was, should I talk to Meir about this? Should I admit to him that not only was I an escaped prisoner, but apparently, I was a freak, too?

I shook my head, partly in answer and partly to get the popping and burning Shakai images out of my head. He wouldn't understand. Who would? *Oh by the way, my mysterious ability to create fire just* might *have something to do with why I'm on a god's hit list.*

Yeah, no.

I'd just have to figure this one out on my own. And in order to do that, I needed to find my home... and the boy with the green eyes from my memory. I smiled for a moment, remembering. But to go home, I'd need to first follow Meir. Meir, who could never know what kind of person I was.

When he returned several minutes later with a set of clothes, I was completely resolved—I would keep my secret. He set the clothes down on the bed next to me and I realized they weren't anything I would've expected. They were black and hard, but they crumpled with each movement, like some kind of flexible body armor. I looked at Meir questioningly and was shocked to see he already wore an outfit like the one he'd given me.

"We're getting out of here tonight," he said. "My friend's son is escorting a cargo ship to Soltak, and it leaves in an hour. We're going as soldiers—Tarmean slaves, charged with guarding the goods."

I gulped. This was going to be a nightmare.

"Go ahead and get dressed."

I realized with a start that I hadn't moved since he'd shared our good news. When he spoke, I pulled myself off the bed and started to fumble with the uniform. With a little help from Meir, I got the pieces on. It fit a tad big on my skeletal form, though it was surprisingly light and airy. I ripped a strip of cloth off of one of the bandages left on the table, tied my hair back, and tucked it into the back of the suit.

Meir appraised me. "Well, hopefully they won't be paying too close attention."

I looked down and realized the uniform was a little more than a tad big. The flexible armor plates hung off my limbs while Meir's fit tight against his muscles. I hadn't realized until just that point how massive Meir was. His long, gray beard and defined wrinkles had given the illusion of weakness, yet out of his loose robes and in this form-fitting uniform, Meir looked more like a war hero than an old man.

I took a deep breath and shrugged. "I guess I'm as ready as I'm going to be."

Meir chuckled and put his hand on my back to lead me out the door. "Come on."

Apparently, our uniforms were not complete. When we got to the shipyard just outside the city limits, Meir's friend, Pallaton, handed us two helmets with grotesque metal faces of snarling mouths and deep, soulless eyes. I shuddered.

Two heads taller than me, Pallaton was about Meir's height, but much paler. His skin was more like a creamy olive and his well-trimmed, black beard had been brushed into glossy waves.

He appraised me with grey eyes—not nearly as friendly and welcoming as Meir's. I put my helmet on to escape his searching gaze. When he didn't look away, I lowered my head and shuffled my feet. I knew I shouldn't have been embarrassed. With my uniform now complete, he couldn't see the guilt written all over my face as if "Shadra" had been tattooed onto my skin. But I was embarrassed, and terrified. I knew right then and there Pallaton was not a man to be trifled with… or lied to.

CHAPTER FIVE:
THE MERIDIAN

Pallaton did finally look away from me, to my great relief, when his son walked down the loading ramp of the smaller, shinier vessel in the yard.

Black robes billowed around the son's muscular form as he joined our small group. He looked very much like his father—the same olive skin, same clear grey eyes—though he'd kept his beard trimmed close to his face and his hair short. His glossy curls pooled tight against his head.

I looked away and bit my lip. This was the first time I could ever remember being in front of someone my own age. Something warm and altogether pleasant broiled beneath the surface of my skin. I wondered if he would think I was pretty. Then I remembered what I looked like—my skin was sallow from poor nutrition and my bones jutted out at every angle. No, he wouldn't find me pretty at all.

But I could pretend.

He had two weapons in his hands that he handed to Meir and me. I took mine and nearly dropped it, surprised by its sheer weight. The boy scowled at me. Although that wasn't quite the right term—he was hardly a boy, but I needed to believe we were equals in some way. I was by no means a woman. The Mamood had taken that away from me when they'd chosen to have me live on nothing but a loaf of stale bread for a whole week. I knew my growth had been stunted. I would never recover.

"You are lucky." Pallaton turned his piercing eyes back to me. "The *Meridian* is the only ship permitted to leave Talia since," he grimaced, "your escape."

Ah, so Meir told him I'd been a prisoner, but Pallaton knew nothing of my being named Shadra. It was a tight line Meir and I were walking. I'd owe him forever.

"It is also lucky that my son, Malik," he gestured to the boy next to him, "will be escorting the crew of the *Meridian* to Soltak."

"We owe you many thanks, Pallaton." Meir squeezed his friend's shoulder, and then put his own helmet on. I recoiled from him, nearly forgetting it was my savior in the suit. With the uniform now complete—the screaming face and ghostly eyes—Meir looked like a monster.

Malik ignored my reaction as he stepped in front of us. "Have either of you ever handled an NK-4 assault laser weapon before?" He pointed to Meir—already guessing the truth.

"Yes."

He turned to me.

"No."

He sighed.

I bit my lip and studied Meir's hold on the weapon. I moved mine, trying to mimic him, but lost my grip and let the rifle fall to the ground.

Malik growled and stooped down to pick it up. "Try to look like you know what you're doing." He grabbed my hands and forcefully—painfully—put them in the correct positions. "You hold it tight against your body, like this, with one hand on the barrel and the other grasping the pistol grip. Whatever you do, do not point it at anyone unless you mean to shoot them."

Indicating a small red button on the side near the trigger, he continued, "Press this to turn it on. Hopefully, you won't ever have to as you aren't actually a real guard." He sneered. "But, if you do, you have to allow the weapon 5.3 seconds to warm up before firing. You'll know it's ready to fire when the switch turns green."

I clenched my fingers around the weapon, completely humiliated and furious that Malik couldn't give me a little leeway. Of course I'd never handled a weapon. *His* people had made sure of that.

"Fine," I snapped at him.

"I'm guessing you know how to pull the trigger?" His lip curled up on one side and he chuckled.

Right then and there my initial attraction to him was completely tossed aside. The only thing my mind could comprehend was a pure and utter hatred for this boy. I wanted to burn the flesh from his bones and desperately wished I could control my newfound power at will.

I leaned my body toward him and concentrated. Nothing happened. So, frustrated from not being able to burn him where he stood, I growled.

He laughed.

I was just about to spring at him to wrap my fingers around his neck when Pallaton stepped between us and put his hand on his son's shoulder. "Enough. The inspectors will be arriving shortly and our friends should be in their places by then." I wondered if Meir had also caught the poison in Pallaton's words when he'd said "friends."

All sign of humor left Malik's face as he turned his dark, furious eyes on Meir. "Just make sure this girl doesn't mess up, or else it's *my* head that's going to need saving."

Meir gave Malik a sharp nod, and then motioned for him to lead the way.

The ramp up the rear of the ship was fairly steep and smooth. I had a hard time keeping my footing while forcing my stick-like legs to push myself forward. Every time I lunged one foot forward, the other would try to slip out from under me. Meir had to wrap his arm around my waist and carry most of my weight.

Malik growled.

I blushed a deep crimson, grateful my face was hidden behind the mask. I knew I was weak, and I hated it. I was tired of Meir having to help me, and of Malik looking at me with such disdain.

It was hard to believe I'd ever found the young Mamood attractive. The little sneer that now seemed a permanent fixture on his face pulled his features down and warped what might've been pleasant to look at into something hideous.

After a few precarious steps, during which Meir had to catch me before I planted my face against the smooth ramp, we walked into what I guessed was the cargo hold of the ship. The small, square room was much darker than outside, but the lenses on my mask adjusted quickly. After just a few short seconds, I could see just as clearly as if I were standing in a well-lit room. Dozens of metal crates littered the hold, piled in random heaps rather than stacked up neatly against the walls. Long, narrow spaces snaked among the piles like aisles in a maze. Each crate was latched to the floor and bore the same "LM" initials, as well as a diamond-shaped symbol.

"Luminarium!" Meir took his hand away from my waist and stroked one of the nearest crates. "That explains a lot. I wondered why the Leaders of Talia would allow *any* ship to leave the planet." He looked in my direction for a fraction of a second.

"Yes." Malik grunted. "Whatever else happens, the Mamood war machine must be funded."

With a warning look to me, he put his hand on Meir's back and led him to the other end of the room. I stayed where I was and turned my back to them, trying to be sneaky. The small room couldn't hide their whispers no matter how hard Malik tried. If he wanted to be that naïve, I'd let him.

I smirked. *So devious.*

When Malik thought he had pulled Meir far enough away, he said, "You know I'm putting my life on the line by helping you... and that... girl." He barely choked the last bit out. Was I that repulsive to him? "I get that my father is bound to you by the Oath, but I am not."

I wanted so badly to turn around and see Meir's face, but then remembered it would be hidden behind the mask. I pressed my lips into a tight line and continued with my charade.

"I'll do it, though," Malik continued, "because my father asked me to and I will not dishonor him through disobedience. However," he paused for emphasis, "if she keeps making these damned mistakes like dropping her weapon and tripping up a *ramp*, I will turn her in myself."

"I'll say something to her." Meir's voice sounded warped and sinister, not at all like his soothing tenor. It was almost metallic. I jumped when I heard it then froze, hoping Malik hadn't seen the movement. "She knows how desperate her situation is. She's trying."

I was completely confused now. Meir's harsh tone did not fit in at all with his calm words. Suddenly it dawned on me. He was speaking through the mask. What with the grotesque face and now the voice, this suit had a greater purpose than just protecting its bearer—it also was meant to terrorize.

Malik didn't speak, and I imagined he was weighing Meir's words. Would my *trying* be enough for him? We'd see.

"Now tell me something," Meir continued. "Since when have the Mamood been willing to ship so much Luminarium to one buyer all at once?"

Malik chuckled. "You're not one of the Leaders anymore, Meir. You are no longer privy to that information."

"Regardless, I'm curious. And it's not like this is exactly top secret."

There was another short pause before Malik spoke. "This is not a shipment the Leaders of Talia are happy to deliver. You're right; even for the Soltakians, it is unusually large, but the Kofra has insisted upon it. It's always about the money with him, anything to fund his army. Nevertheless, the Council remains suspicious. You should know… the inspectors will look for any reason not to send us off."

"What could they possibly want with it all?" Meir was mumbling now and I guessed he wasn't expecting an answer. He got one anyway.

"That is just what the Council wants to know. There are rumors the Soltakians are expanding their fleet."

"All this for their military? Impossible. There must be millions of gems in these crates."

"Exactly. But as I said, the Kofra is hungry for the payload it brings and refuses to listen to the Council."

Another pause. "What do you think our odds are of leaving, then?" I couldn't ignore the worry in Meir's voice. Suddenly, I was filled with hopelessness. If my savior doubted, then how could I not?

Malik's tone turned sharp, like he was speaking through his teeth. "If everything is not done perfectly, we will not leave today and that girl's chances of getting out of here on anything but *Sho'ful* will be severely diminished. But even if we do leave Talia, we still have the checkpoint to get through and that has its own set of problems."

"Tell me."

"Two unknown spacecraft have been seen within the Kofra's territory today."

"Traders?"

Malik laughed. It was dark, and slightly hysterical. "Not unless you know of a planet that outfits its freighters like battleships. Massive battleships."

Meir groaned, or growled. Behind the mask, it definitely sounded like a growl, and I shuddered. "Security at the checkpoint will be doubled, at the very least."

"Yes. But we do have one significant advantage: the Kofra really wants this freighter to get to Soltak as soon as possible. He doesn't get paid until it does. It is my duty to remind the inspectors and the guards of this fact. Speaking of... the inspectors should be arriving shortly. Get the girl ready."

One set of feet started walking back to me and I pretended to be grossly interested in the finer details of my weapon. I heard a door slide open and then close. I went over their conversation in my head, focusing on two little words: "that girl." I knew there was so much more I should have heard. The truth was, I did "hear" it, but I couldn't think of anything but the way Malik spit out his oh-so-special name for me, as if I was nothing. Who did he think he was? I looked at the wide end of my rifle, truly engrossed now, and imagined it had a new purpose—contact with Malik's face.

"We need to talk." I jumped at Meir's metallic voice. I had forgotten all about him during the brief moments of my sadistic fantasies. I really needed to get that under control. I wasn't used to having such an awful temper. Of course, I'd never been around enough people to really have it tested.

When I turned to face him, I nearly jumped again. As it was, my heart just skipped a beat. I had to remind myself it was only Meir.

I peered around his shoulder to where he and Malik had been talking. "Where did Malik go?" I really wanted to say "that boy," but I wasn't about to get snarky with the giant in front of me.

"He has to greet the inspectors and make sure the crew is ready to go."

"Oh."

I bit my lip. Meir stood very still and I was sure he was trying to teach me a lesson. I wasn't taking this seriously enough. I didn't grasp what Malik and Pallaton were doing for me. I dipped my head, letting the shame wash through me. Meir only knew how I was acting outwardly. What would he think if he knew I'd contemplated Malik's murder on more than one occasion in the last few minutes? I was suddenly disgusted with myself.

Had I completely lost my mind? What kind of person was I? Who seriously thinks about murdering someone?

My body folded in on itself. I no longer had the strength to stand. Meir caught me before I hit the floor and leaned me against the wall.

"What's wrong?" His voice was anxious, even behind the mask.

"I'm sorry, Meir." I struggled to choke out the words. It wasn't that I didn't mean them. I just hated admitting I might be a disappointment to my savior. "I've been very awful."

He laughed silently. His shaking body no longer did a very good job of propping me up. I nearly toppled to the floor. "You haven't been that bad. Just a little... awkward."

I shook my head. "Meir, you don't know. I thought about killing him."

Now he really laughed out loud, not the silent little chuckles of before. I pursed my lips.

"Who? Malik?"

I nodded.

He laughed a few more seconds then struggled to compose himself. He coughed. "Well, as long as you're sorry, and you won't have those thoughts again." I was sure I heard a smirk behind all that.

He pulled me away from the wall and led me past the maze of crates to the back of the room, where he and Malik had been talking.

"What is all this stuff, by the way?"

"Fuel, essentially." He turned to face me. "They're gems that react differently when subjected to intense amounts of heat."

"Differently how?"

"I'm not a scientist, Ella. I just know something *does* happen, not *how* it happens."

"So, what *does* happen?"

He chuckled. "They explode."

"This is a good thing?"

"It is when the explosion creates enough energy to power a warship for centuries."

"But doesn't everything else blow up along with it?"

He shook his head and I could hear the smile in his voice despite the distortion. "They have ways to contain it. Now I think it's time I prepared you a bit for the inspectors."

I gulped. I didn't know what Meir thought he could do to prepare me. I was hopeless. We would be lucky to escape with our lives. Well, Meir would be. I was pretty sure Manoo had special plans for me.

"The Tarmeans are slave soldiers—highly trained and efficient." We had reached the rear wall and I noticed a seam in the smooth metal. I wanted to ask Meir what it was, but he continued talking. "It's not likely that the inspectors will pay any attention to us because they're really just here to inspect the goods, but should they speak to you, you must respond immediately. If they ask you something, give them as short of an answer as possible and do so with confidence. The Tarmeans may be slaves, but they are some of the more 'professional' and highly respected slaves."

He appraised my appearance again and mumbled something. I didn't catch most of it, but three words were pretty clear: "…just the goods…"

I knew what Meir was thinking. If the inspectors took one look at me, they'd know I wasn't one of their "respected slaves." I'd be caught and Meir would die.

Blood rushed to my head, clouding my thoughts and obstructing my vision. Black spots started popping up in front of my eyes and I was certain my legs would turn to complete mush long before the inspectors arrived.

"I can't do this. I can't do this."

"Of course you can." He grabbed my shoulders with his broad hands and forced me to look at him. I almost imagined I could see his soft, black eyes through the mask. "Don't forget that I'll be with you the entire time."

"Maybe we shouldn't… Maybe this was a bad idea."

"Shh… I hear them coming." He let go of me and turned with his back to the wall. I mimicked him as best I could and clutched my weapon as tightly to me as possible.

Sure enough, I could hear muffled voices just outside the door. A speaker above my head crackled to life as a voice came over the intercom.

"This is Inspector 443 of the Talian Traders Board. Submit your code, Tarmean."

Meir jerked around to face the wall and punched in six numbers on a small keypad next to the seam I had noticed earlier. The wall slid open at the seam with a soft hiss and three men entered the cargo hold, one of whom was Malik. They brushed past us without a word, and with digital display in-hand, the person I assumed was the head Inspector quickly got to work.

My head started to swim as I clenched my neck and locked my knees. The black spots in front of my eyes grew bigger and began blocking my peripheral vision. *Why is it getting so hot in here?* I wondered.

I swallowed, but as much as I tried, my dry mouth wouldn't moisten and the room wouldn't stop spinning. I wished I could lean against the wall for a moment. Just a moment…

I slammed my foot against the floor to steady myself after I nearly toppled over. The thud echoed in my eardrums for a fraction of a second.

Inspector 443 snapped his head up and with curled lip and piercing eyes, he glared at me, and then turned to Malik.

Panic flashed across Malik's face for a microsecond. It was so fast, I wondered if I'd imagined it. His face was cold when he addressed the Inspector. He shrugged. "Damn newbies. What are they sending out of the camps these days?"

The man wasn't placated. In fact, his face grew suspicious. "Nothing but the best, and *you* know that." He took two large strides to stand in front of me. He wasn't as tall as Meir or Malik, but he still towered over me. I fought back the tears. "What's your number, slave?"

I was speechless. What number? No one had said anything about a number. If I thought I was terrified a few seconds ago, that was nothing compared to the horror I felt as the tall inspector in his dark robes glared down at me with venom in his eyes.

There was no stopping it. I gasped for air as the panic really set in. I was going to die and I was bringing my savior down with me.

I turned to Malik, pleading, but he stood like a cold statue. I then remembered what he'd told Meir. That if I didn't behave better and act like I knew what I was doing, he would turn me in himself. Clearly, he was not going to help. I was dead.

Malik confirmed my suspicions when his frozen face thawed and he moved to stand in front of me. "Speak up, slave!" He drove his fist into my gut, and one of the armor plates sliced into me.

Not what I was expecting, but I didn't have time to think about that. I was far too busy heaving up my insides. I dropped the stupid weapon and followed it to the floor. I was done pretending—let them kill me. After that blow, my burning and spastic body wanted to die. On the bright side—and it was really hard for me to find anything positive at the moment—I didn't have to answer the Inspector. All the air had been knocked out of my lungs. I couldn't speak if I wanted to.

"I said speak!" he screamed louder and hit me again.

The precious little air I had managed to fill my lungs with now went out in a whoosh. Forget what I'd said to Meir, I wanted Malik dead. Though my body jerked out of control as my oxygen-deprived muscles tensed, my mind was still perfectly clear. The weapon I had dropped was just inches away. Five-point-three seconds, huh? I could wait that long.

And all through this calculated plan for Malik's murder, I continued to gasp for air. In fact, little more than a second had passed as I contemplated his demise—no one even noticed. But it was no use. I was still dry-heaving and choking, gasping and wheezing. My insides burned, begging for death.

Someone laughed and as it didn't sound like Malik or Meir, I guessed it was the Inspector. "I didn't know you had such trouble controlling your slaves, Malik." His tone turned serious. "Perhaps we should postpone this trip until you can find more suitable guards."

Malik spoke through his teeth. "I can handle my slaves. You worry about your job and get the inspection done. And don't even think of postponing this delivery. I don't care what the Council says, the Kofra wants this sent to Soltak, and his is the final word."

"Does your father know you're so eager to go against the Council's wishes?"

"Does the Kofra know you are so eager to go against *his*?"

The Inspector mumbled something—a few oaths and curses. He quickly composed himself and continued with ice in his voice, "I don't think it's a good idea to let any ship leave Talia while the Shadra is on the loose."

"Shadra?" Malik hissed.

I strained my head to look up at him. The blood rushed to my head again as my heart worked overtime. He glared at me. The utter rage behind his grey eyes made me gasp. His face turned stone cold and he kicked me in the side. "Get up, you lazy fool."

I was lucky that time. The kick was barely more than a tap. I struggled to my feet, nearly collapsing again a couple of times. My burning lungs started to cooperate. Sweet air moved in and out with ease. I stood up and leaned against the wall. That was all I could do. Malik couldn't expect more, especially not if I was dead anyway.

"The report came in this afternoon." The Inspector grunted. "The felon that escaped *Sho'ful* yesterday had been named the Shadra to Manoo earlier this week. They were going to take her to Kalhandthar for the ceremony when repairs were finished."

Malik said nothing for a long time and it seemed to me like he didn't know *what* to say. "I...I didn't—"

"You didn't know?" The Inspector feigned surprise. It was clear he enjoyed this very much. "Well, I'm not surprised. I am privy to more information than *you*."

Malik's teeth snapped together. "Well, apparently certain information failed to reach you. The Shadra is not on this freighter, and you are supposed to be inspecting the Luminarium, not gossiping about the affairs of the Fiefdom."

"Gossiping?" The man started sputtering again. "If your father wasn't on the Council, I would—"

Malik stepped closer to the man so the Inspector was forced to look up at him. "You would what?"

The Inspector took a step back, doubt written all over his face.

"Sir." The second Inspector interrupted the exchange. "I've finished the inspection. Everything is in order."

The head Inspector turned slowly to face his underling, his eyes still on Malik. "Finished?" His voice dripped with gratitude. "Then by all means, we should go." He nodded to Malik and continued, "We'll see our way out."

The two men left through the same doorway they'd come in by, leaving us alone with Malik.

Malik waited several more moments to say anything. He stared at the doorway with cool calculation. I was suddenly terrified for Meir and me to be left alone with him. I bit my lip, waiting. When he did speak, his voice was dead. "I'll inform the crew we have permission to leave. When we get into hyperspace, I'll bring you something to eat. Make yourselves comfortable in here.

"Oh, and Meir," he continued with venom in his voice, "you and I are going to have a talk when I come back."

CHAPTER SIX:
LOYALTY

Meir and I stood side-by-side; neither one of us moved as Malik left the cargo hold and the door slid closed. *Malik knew.* I didn't even want to think about what this would mean— although, it was pretty clear. Malik already had said he wasn't bound through the Oath.

He was going to turn me in. I only hoped he would let Meir go.

The room started spinning again. I slid down the wall and wrapped my arms around my knees, pulling my legs tight against my chest. This had to be the longest day of my life and it wasn't even close to finished. I found it hard to believe I'd slept through most of it. I prayed Malik would act quickly. I couldn't take any more.

Meir also seemed to sense our situation was hopeless. When his frozen body finally thawed, he didn't even bother to comfort me. He walked off to rest by the open hatch at the other end of the room.

After a few minutes, I couldn't stand the silence anymore, so I walked over to him. His mask rested on the floor next to his feet. He leaned his head against one of the metal crates with his eyes closed. I knew he'd heard me clomp my way over, but he didn't look at me.

I pulled my mask off and set it on the floor next to his. I wanted to break the silence, say something. Meir looked like he wanted to be alone, though, and I was pretty sure I was in no position to be offering any comforting words. Still, I needed to hear his voice. I needed *something* to keep my mind off what Malik was about to do, so I slid to the floor and stared at his too-still face.

I knew he was angry, and very likely angry with me. Fate had screwed him over right along with me. There was no doubt in my mind the invisible hands and the voice from my cell had intended for Meir and me to come together, but my original assumption had been wrong. I had thought I was to be saved and Meir was my savior. Instead, it was pretty clear that Meir's life was meant to be destroyed.

And I was the destructor.

A hysterical giggle escaped my lips. It wasn't enough that everything in my life crumbled around my feet; I had to be the tool to bring everyone else down with me. Well, at least I had a purpose. And here I'd thought my life meant nothing, that I'd waste away in *Sho'ful* and no one would even know. Now it looked like my bad luck might extend to single-handedly bringing about everyone's downfall. All because I'd dared to leave.

I wanted to cry, I really did, but I was empty. The person I'd actually come to care about was the one who would suffer the most. He'd given up everything to help me, and for nothing. Manoo would kill me, and Meir would die for standing in his way. Everything else was meaningless next to that.

The hatch rumbled closed as the ramp slid into the confines of the ship's underbelly. I hadn't even noticed the ship's engines come to life, although they hummed steadily, vibrating the floor beneath me.

I looked at Meir again, and though I didn't think it could be possible, his features were even more frozen. He didn't even look like he was breathing. I stopped breathing as well.

The engines grew steadily louder and soon my bones began to vibrate with the floor. Suddenly—and it happened so fast I didn't even have a chance to grab onto anything for support—the ship took off with its nose pointing skyward. I tumbled along the floor until my body smacked against the closed hatch. That's when I noticed Meir had strategically placed himself against one of the metal crates to avoid what had just happened to me.

We rose and floated above the floor for several seconds before settling back down as the ship leveled out. I crawled back to him. His eyes were open and he was breathing again, with a hint of a smile on his lips.

"I didn't think we were actually going to leave," he said. "I was waiting for the guards to come to take you away." His eyes pierced mine. "I wasn't going to let them."

I gulped. Meir's NK-4 was lying across his lap, and the light was green.

"Meir..."

Meir looked away, his eyes glazed over, staring at something in the distance—something that wasn't in the room. "You know, you remind me of my daughter. She had these eyes that made me think she could see into my soul." His eyes rested on me again. "Very similar to yours."

I couldn't speak. *Daughter?*

Meir sighed. "I wasn't always like this." He pointed to his scraggly beard. "A long time ago, I was one of the seven Leaders of Talia. I was far too ambitious and obsessed with my position. I had a daughter—a beautiful daughter—but she wasn't enough. I was getting older and my line was going to end. Talia had never had fewer than seven Leaders and I was failing in my most important duty: providing an heir."

Meir dropped his head into his hands and started shaking. My hand reached out to comfort him, but I drew it back. I knew somehow his pain and I were related. I didn't want to add to it.

Without looking up, he continued, "Then my wife told me she was pregnant, already pretty far along. She'd wanted to wait to tell me because she didn't want me to mourn if she lost the baby. I knew this was the son I had been waiting for, but I wanted to be sure. So I took her and my daughter to Izbet to see the doctor there. After the ultrasound, my hopes were confirmed: my title would live on. And he was so beautiful. His face... I still remember it."

He groaned. "It was late, but I wanted to go home and celebrate. I thought we could make it home in time. I was wrong."

I gasped and shook my head. I didn't want to hear the rest of this story. I already knew how it was going to end.

"They didn't even touch me. I was ripping them off my wife and daughter, but they ignored me. In the morning..." He looked up at me then, and I saw that his eyes were rimmed red with tears. "Well, the Shakai leave nothing."

"Meir..."

"I can still hear their screams when I go to sleep at night."

I brought my hand up to my mouth to hold back the sobs. I thought I knew what pain was, but in that moment I realized I knew nothing.

Meir's teeth shut with an audible snap. "So you see—I will *never* let anyone touch you."

"You don't have to do this, Meir." I shook my head. "Don't let me be the one to take away what little you have left."

He wrapped his arm around my waist and drew me closer to him. "I was a Mamood when this happened. Now I am a Praeori." He cupped my face in his hand. "Every day I asked El why. Now I know. I lost my wife and children for you. I survived for *you*."

I thought I understood what he meant, that these horrible things had happened for a purpose. All the stuff that had happened the day before surged to the front of my memory. *Sho'ful* landing for the first time ever. The unlocked door that should have been locked. The opening at the bottom of the ship when the landing gear dropped. I wondered why, though. What was the damn purpose in getting me out?

If there was a reason behind it all, I didn't want any part of it. The weight of what it could mean crushed me. I didn't want to carry all that responsibility. I shook my head again. "Who would do this, Meir? And why?"

"Isn't it obvious?"

"No." I wanted it to be obvious. I wanted to know the truth. I wanted it so badly, my insides hurt with the aching for it.

"Then I can't tell you. This is something you need to discover for yourself." He smiled. "Just like I did."

That irritated me. Why couldn't he just say what was on his mind? I wanted to argue with him. I wanted to tell him I had a right to know everything, but Malik's voice came over the intercom.

"Meir, punch in your code." His voice wasn't quite as venom-filled as it'd been when he'd left, but it wasn't quite dead either. It lingered somewhere in between. I guessed he was showing a lot of restraint, and wondered what was going on in his mind.

Meir let go of me and walked through the maze of crates to the keypad. He put in the same six-digit code as earlier and the door slid open. Malik walked through with two silver containers, set them on the closest crate, and walked out the door again. He returned moments later with two folded cots and rested them against the wall.

I stood next to Meir as Malik punched in a different code and the door slid closed. When he turned around to face us, I suddenly wished I had my mask on. I wasn't ready for him to see how I really looked. I knew the disdain he already felt was just a small fraction of what he would feel when he saw my wasted and decrepit face. But I was too late.

His eyes rested on me and he gasped. His reaction only lasted a moment before he turned to Meir, but it was enough. The blood rushed to my cheeks, and tears started welling up in my eyes. I was a hideous wraith, and having that confirmed by Malik was too much. It was funny how my own vanity—or complete lack of self-confidence—could be more important to me in that moment than the fact that Malik knew the truth and my very life was in his hands.

He acted as if he hadn't just nearly vomited at the sight of me and glared at Meir. His face was too stiff as his piercing eyes bore into my savior, and I had the sneaking suspicion that he was trying *not* to look at me now.

A lump formed in my throat.

"Well?" Malik said, ignoring my crumpled and pathetic glare.

"Well what?" Meir had completely regained his composure. His tears had been wiped away, and he stood straight and tall, not the crumpled form of a man he'd been just moments earlier. I almost felt sorry for Malik, having to face this firm and indestructible giant.

"Damn it, Meir. What were you thinking?"

"I was thinking that Manoo must be getting pretty desperate to find enemies if this little girl scares him."

Malik glanced at me out of the corner of his eye for a fraction of a second. He didn't gasp this time, but I could still see his face twitch ever so subtly. "That means nothing. Everyone who becomes even remotely connected to her escape is dead now."

"Only if they find out."

Malik pinched his nose and leaned against the wall. This was the first time I'd seen him break his carefully cultivated façade. It was almost more terrifying than if he were screaming at us. "I've already told my father."

Yes, much more terrifying. Somehow I knew that Pallaton was the last man in the universe who should know that his friend had tricked him into betraying his god.

Meir confirmed my suspicions with a groan.

"What did you want me to do, Meir? I fulfilled my end of the bargain. I got the two of you out of there, but I couldn't let my father find out from someone else. I couldn't do that to him."

"Why bother taking us off of Talia if you're just going to turn her in anyway?" Meir's fists clenched at his sides and his voice turned into a growl. "What? Are you planning to drop her off at Kalhandthar yourself? Claim some type of reward?"

Malik's voice became dead again. "I'm not turning her in. We're going to Soltak."

My heart broke out into a gallop. Malik couldn't mean that. He couldn't possibly be intending to let me go. He hated me.

"Why?" Apparently, Meir couldn't believe it, either.

Malik shrugged. "My father was furious when I told him, and he reminded me to act with honor. His idea of honor and mine differ greatly. He ordered me to turn her into the Kofra, but allowing someone so weak and fragile to become some form of political device is the height of dishonor. I refused him and ordered the crew to leave." He turned to look at me then, his eyes guarded. "You may annoy the hell out of me, but I won't take part in your murder." He paused to look away for a second before turning his gaze back to me. "You shouldn't have to pay for the Kofra's greed."

"Thank you." I wondered then if Malik would ever know just how much I meant those two words. My heart felt like it would burst, it swelled so hard and fast. *Freedom.* I let the thought play across my mind, reveling in the hope it brought.

He nodded, and then smirked. "I'm sorry about earlier. I didn't have much time to come up with a better plan."

I bit my lip. "What happened earlier?"

His smirk fell and he rolled his eyes. I felt very stupid under his gaze, clearly missing something he felt should have been obvious.

"When I punched you?" He shook his head. "You're bleeding—I can smell it. I didn't think I hit you that hard, but then I didn't know just how weak you were."

I looked down at my waist. I'd completely forgotten about that particular incident, which was odd considering how much I had wanted to kill him because of it. A few other, more important, things had come up since then. I hadn't even felt the pain until he mentioned the blood. Now, it was all I could feel.

"Oh." I wrapped my arms around myself and slid to the floor.

Meir was at my side immediately, tearing the suit away from me and ordering Malik to bring bandages and ointment. It was about at that point that my mind and body decided I'd had too much for the day. Fainting two times in just as many days? How pathetic.

CHAPTER SEVEN:
FRIENDS AND ENEMIES

Meir's snores ripped me out of sleep. The last few minutes of my dream had consisted of me running toward a group of un-named—but vaguely familiar—cruisers, come to take me away, with their engines roaring all around me. When I woke up, the engines droned on.

I sighed and sat up. My hand instinctively went to my waist. The black suit had been put back on, so I couldn't see if I was bleeding, but the pain had lessened, so I assumed it had stopped.

I spotted one of the silver containers Malik had brought in earlier, on the floor next to the cot I was sitting on. I picked it up and ripped it open. There was food inside.

I moaned and opened the first vacuum-sealed package I found. It was some kind of sandwich. I didn't care what kind. I shoved it into my mouth before I'd even taken it completely out of its plastic wrapper. I'm sure it tasted good. I didn't really notice because by the time I had gotten the whole thing into my mouth, I was already ripping open the next one. Brown and gooey, it had a sweet taste that overwhelmed my senses.

By the time I'd shoved the contents of the last package into my mouth—some type of bitter drink—my stomach had started protesting. It hit me then. as the acids lurched up into my throat, that I should've taken my first big meal a little slower. I clamped my mouth shut and swallowed. It burned all the way down.

I threw the empty packages to the floor and lay back down on the cot, clutching my very angry stomach. I should've known something as simple as eating would end badly. I lived in Op-posite World. When I expected bad, good happened. When I thought nothing but good could come from something, that's when fate decided to kick me in the butt.

I groaned. My food wanted to come up again—I could feel it—but I refused to let it win. If I couldn't control my own body, how could I possibly control the outside influences of the world around me? No, my body *would* bend to my will. I'd rather suffer than lose this battle.

I groaned again. It seemed my stomach was more than willing to make me suffer. I started concentrating on the purr of the engines and the whoosh of the fans as they recycled the air throughout the ship. And of course, Meir's steady snores were easy to focus on. It helped a little, but my stomach refused to be completely ignored. When it thought it was losing, it enlisted the help of my muscles, which started twisting and pushing at my abdomen to force the food up. When that didn't work, it tried to reason with me.

Just let it out. You'll feel better when you do.

Somehow, I had a feeling this was a typical war tactic: when violence doesn't work, send ambassadors to negotiate terms of surrender. But I wasn't about to succumb. I had earned the nutrients my body now needed to function, and I certainly wasn't about to lie next to my own vomit.

Nope. My stomach would just have to give in and do its job.

I breathed in and out slowly. Meir's snoring aside, sleep had now become utterly impossible for me.

There was a very subtle change in the air pressure around me, and the ship felt like it was slowing down. The little movement, though I might not have detected it otherwise, now made my stomach lurch. I almost lost the war.

The feeling became much more distinct and I was sure we had come to a stop. I remembered Malik mentioning something about a checkpoint to Meir in the conversation I was not supposed to have heard. Perhaps this was it.

My heart started pounding as I also remembered Malik had said we might find trouble here—something about unknown battleships and precautions being doubled. I held my breath and waited. Surely this wouldn't take long. They would confirm that the *Meridian* was scheduled to go to Soltak and let us be on our way, nothing more.

A deep boom shuddered throughout the ship. My quivering stomach rejoiced at its impending success, while my heart skipped a beat and I broke out into an icy sweat.

I fought the urge to run and hide. Instead, I rose slowly with my hand on my waist to shake Meir's shoulder.

"Meir, wake up."

He didn't budge.

I leaned closer and pressed my lips against his ear. "Meir!"

He bolted up then, and nearly sent me flying backwards. "What?" He rubbed his eyes, disoriented. "What happened?"

"I think we're being boarded."

"Boarded? How?" He yawned. "We're in hyperspace." No, he was definitely not all there. I suppressed the urge to shake him. My weak little arms probably wouldn't have done much anyway.

"No, Meir." I shook my head. "We're at the checkpoint."

Another boom resonated throughout the ship. Meir's eyes narrowed as understanding replaced the vagueness of sleep. "What's going on?"

"I don't know. I felt the ship stop and then there was a loud noise, like something was grabbing onto it."

"Hmm…" His eyes grew dark and brooding, but he shook his head and wrapped his arm around my shoulders, leaning me in to press his lips against my head. "We'll be all right."

I didn't know if I could believe that. This wasn't right. I could tell Meir was trying to hide something from me. There was no reason for us to be stopped so long. I didn't dare move as we waited what seemed like hours. Instead, I stayed tight against his chest, feeling his hot, unsteady breath pour across my scalp, saturating my hair.

More time passed… slowly. Too slowly. Eventually, my knees began to shake and I leaned my full weight against Meir, letting him support me. His arms tightened around me in response.

The ship wobbled for a couple beats, and then steadied. I dug my head into Meir's chest to keep from screaming.

He stroked my hair. "It's okay. We'll be all right," he repeated.

I wanted to believe he was right, but…

The intercom crackled to life. "This is Inter-Planetary Escort Malik Abad-i. Submit your code, Tarmean."

Meir set me on my cot and went over to the keypad. The door slid open and Malik walked through. I stifled a whimper when I saw his ashen face.

Malik looked back and forth between the two of us before finally resting his gaze on Meir. He nodded toward the far corner of the room and walked away. As we followed him, I noted with some satisfaction that my stomach had decided to give me a break. My racing heart, on the other hand, was a different story. The blood it sent rushing to my head made me dizzy and I leaned on Meir's arm for support as we wove our way through the labyrinth of crates.

When we had reached the back wall, Malik turned to face us and leaned in to whisper, "Not good."

My heart decided to use my stomach as a springboard as it jumped into my throat.

"What's wrong?" Meir remained composed. That was good. Someone needed to.

"Do you remember what I told you earlier? About… ships?" He raised one eyebrow.

Meir nodded.

"They're following us."

"Why?" He said it slowly, drawing it out. "The Luminarium?"

"We're not sure. Maybe, but it seems unlikely. From what our sensors can pick up, their propulsion systems are not Luminarium-based." He paused, likely pondering how much information he was willing to disclose in front of me. "This freighter is as fast as any Mamood Star Class warship, but they're gaining on us."

Meir murmured something underneath his breath.

I looked up to read his face. He was pulling at his beard and the crease between his brows had returned. The gesture surprised me, actually. I had expected much worse news. Already, I could detect the acceleration of the ship. We were leaving.

Honestly, who cared if we were being followed? My concern was the Mamood, not a couple mystery ships.

But Meir seemed worried, and that was enough to keep me from breathing a sigh of relief. Malik, too, was very much on edge. His eyes were restless as they shifted from Meir and me to the open door at the front of the cargo hold. Even after all that we'd gone through, I'd never seen him this upset. He couldn't seem to stop fidgeting. It was like he couldn't decide if he should stay with us or leave.

"As worrisome as all that is," Malik said, "we've actually got bigger problems."

I should've known. I dropped my head against Meir's arm and sighed.

Malik ignored my little theatrics, and continued, "The spaceport's Delsa-Prime is on the *Meridian* with us. He insisted on accompanying us with two of his fighters. 'Protection,' as he called it."

When I looked up again, Meir's lips were drawn into a tight line. "Not good."

"I'll think of something. The man's not all that bright." He smirked. "Money only bought him the position, not the know-how to wield it."

He started walking back to the door, leaving Meir and me alone and dumbstruck. Before he got halfway through the room, Malik turned around and whispered, "I won't come back here again until we dock. Don't worry about anything until then. Like I said, I'll think of something." His dark robes swirled around his ankles as he turned and left us. The door slid closed, and the sudden quiet in the room became oppressive.

Someone really didn't want me to have a life—of that I was very sure. Malik had tried to act like the change in our circumstances hadn't bothered him, but I could detect the panic seething underneath. Not worry? Impossible.

I crumpled to the floor and let my cheek rest against the cold metal. It felt soothing against my hot, clammy skin—familiar. I groaned. The thought that a cold, metal floor should comfort me with its familiarity absolutely revolted me. Never in my wildest imaginings had I thought I would look back at any part of my time on *Sho'ful* with longing.

Meir's broad arms wrapped around me as he lifted me up and carried me back to my cot. My body draped like some kind of rag doll. I wanted to tell him to put me down so that I could walk, but I couldn't find my voice. He rested me on my cot and backed away to sit on his own.

Time passed steadily, though I don't know how. It was hard to think past my own frozen body, hard to imagine that the universe hadn't frozen with me. But pass it did, and eventually my mind began to thaw. I was able to think again. I forced myself to think of the impossible—the undoable.

Though I had never known the exact plan for my escape, it had seemed pretty clear to me that the original thought had been to just get me to Soltak. Once there, a change of clothes would have been my biggest problem, but easily handled. Now, it was obvious this Delsa-Prime guy wasn't just going to let some Mamood slave escape. Malik was no longer the ranking officer aboard this ship.

That left me with few options. And one of them seemed the only realistic one: I was going to have to turn myself in. The game had gone on long enough and I was a fool to think Manoo would just let me go. I was Shadra—his enemy. Manoo didn't give someone that title unless he really meant it.

A tear slid down my cheek. Could I do this to Meir? I didn't care for myself. My life had ceased a long time ago. It was never right of me to try to reanimate what was already dead. And as time continued to pass, victims would fall at my feet. First Meir, now Malik, and I guessed even Pallaton would suffer for what I'd done. I was the bringer of death, indeed. Better to end it now before the whole universe came crashing down.

I snickered. So much for being a nobody.

I just didn't know how to go about doing it. If I gave Meir and Malik some warning so they could escape, they would try to stop me. Well, at least Meir would. Malik I still wasn't entirely sure about. His honor seemed important to him, but my declaration of self-sacrifice might very well release him from any sense of duty. After all, *I* would be the one making the choice, not him.

That gave me an idea. Perhaps I *could* confide in Malik. I would have to get him alone before they did anything stupid to try to get me away. He could run off with Meir, concocting some story about how they had to go on ahead, and then I could turn myself in to the Delsa-Prime. Meir and Malik would be safe and no one else would get hurt. I knew Meir would be hurt when he found out. I couldn't deny the bond that had formed between us. He was every bit my father now, and it tore at my heart to think of crushing him that way. I had to be strong for him, though. It would be far worse if we stayed together. I wouldn't allow myself to think about just how bad it could get.

I let the tears pour down my cheeks and soak the hard fabric of my cot until I had nothing left. There was no going back now. Though it hurt every tissue in my body to think about leaving him, I knew I could be strong—for him.

Freedom.

The thought no longer brought hope, but a wallowing hole of desolation. It was never to be mine. I had to accept that now.

I turned my body around to look at my savior—memorizing every feature on his face. His soft, black eyes were closed, but I studied the creases along his face. There were laugh lines and ones of sorrow around his eyes and mouth, creating darker shadows in his already dark skin. He was black as night and just as beautiful. His wide nostrils flared with each steady breath and his wide lips were slightly parted. I thought he might be asleep, but without the snoring, I couldn't be sure.

I smiled.

This face, just as it was now, would be in my mind as I took my last breath. I had been given the chance to love someone and know what it was to be loved in return. Manoo could take my life now because I already had everything I'd ever wanted.

A sharp screeching sound, like metal on metal, ripped through the hold, and I was sent flying through the air. The floor was coming up at me fast, but I wasn't going to hit it. No, because the hard corner of a metal crate would hit me long before the floor did. My arms and legs flailed about as if I actually thought I could fly and escape the coming pain. When I saw the sharp edge rising up toward me, I reasoned that I should somehow move, but I instinctively knew that wasn't going to happen.

And then my skull came cracking down on the crate. The corner dug into my temple, ripping the skin wide open. My cry of pain was cut short as my head snapped back, cutting off the air through my windpipe. The floor decided to take its turn then. My legs were below me as I landed and I cringed when the full weight of my body landed on my right knee. But I didn't scream until I heard it pop.

I gritted my teeth and gasped against the agony. Flames of pain shot up my leg and inside my head, but I knew I had to be quiet. Somehow, I had to be quiet. It wasn't time for me to be discovered. Not yet. Not until Malik and Meir were safely away. And I knew no "respectable" Tarmean slave would scream from pain.

Something happened then that made me almost ninety percent sure I'd lost my mind—right in front of me the air began to melt.

I didn't really know how air could melt, but it was doing it. The crates in front of me shimmered at first like on a hot day, but almost immediately that description wasn't even good enough. The air thumped, pulsing back and forth, warping the crates, pushing them toward me, and then pulling them away. It was like everything just a few feet ahead of me was sucked into some center point.

And then I knew I was crazy—beyond a shadow of a doubt, head banging against the wall crazy. Where the air had been twisting and morphing just seconds ago, three men materialized. And yet, they weren't really what you could call "men." Oh no, they were so much more, like something ripped straight out of a dream.

They had wings. Huge, bright wings of colors so vivid, I had to shield my eyes to look at them.

Only one of the winged men faced my direction, but his gaze rested above me. His ivory face was shockingly pale against the bright, pulsing blue of his wings, with waist-length hair only slightly darker than his skin. I stared, frozen in awe at the overwhelming perfection of the clean lines of his jaw and cheekbones and in terror at the thought of what someone so obviously greater than any mortal man was capable of doing to me.

His wings left trails of blue in the shivering air as he twisted to face his companions.

The trapped air in my lungs came out in a silent whoosh. I don't know how he didn't see me, but I thanked whatever deity was out there that he hadn't. El, Manoo—at this point, it didn't matter.

The one who had turned away from me pulled out some kind of flat-paneled device and stared at it. He tapped it a couple of times and said in a watery voice, "I'm picking up a strong radioactive signature, but I can't lock onto it. Whatever's in these crates is messing with the readings. I'm not certain, but I think she's in this room."

She? Oh, crap.

For a split second, I thought about trying to crawl my way to the back corner of the cargo hold and hide in the shadows behind a wall of crates, but as soon as I moved, the shooting daggers up my leg told me that plan was entirely impossible—at least as long as I wanted to keep from screaming.

"Fan out and search." One of the other winged men spoke, this time with a woodsy, airy voice. I couldn't see him, but I guessed by the way he spoke with such authority he was their leader. "I want her found."

Two of the men broke off—the long-haired man was one of them—leaving just the leader to stand so close I could've touched him. I let out a sigh of relief that his back was to me.

If I had been in any way impressed with long-haired man's wings, I now considered them plain and downright boring compared to what was staring me in the face. Delicate, velvety, sea-green folds rippled seamlessly out of the leader's firm, muscle-toned back. My gaze was drawn to the perfect but subtle change from green at the base of his shoulder blades to the deep, twilight blue around the edges. As my eyes absorbed the sheer beauty of the vivid colors, I was blown away at just how massive his wings were. From the leader's shoulder blades, the wings swept to the floor and high above his head, shielding most of his body from me. They were without a doubt the most beautiful things I had ever seen. If I had not been so terrified these strange men would find me, I would've reached out and stroked them. The pull was almost overwhelming.

"There's someone over here." The third man spoke this time, breaking me out of my trance. His tone was much deeper than the other two, almost fiery. "A man. And in bad condition. There's a lot of blood."

Meir.

I stifled a gasp.

"He's unconscious," the fiery one continued.

The leader walked a few feet away and stopped where our cots had been. Meir's bed had been much closer to the crates than mine. When I'd flown through the air, he must've been thrown into the crates and knocked unconscious.

I pursed my lips, furious these men were here and stopping me from going to Meir.

"Stand by him for now," the leader said. "Olorun, have you found anything?"

"She's definitely in this room," the long-haired man replied. "I'm picking up her signature everywhere."

I glanced his way to see what was happening and winced when the movement made my head swim.

The leader turned around to face me. I squeezed my eyelids shut as tightly as they would go, childishly hoping I'd become invisible to him if I did.

"Ella?" Boots shuffled across the floor as he rushed over to me.

I sank further to the floor and let the sobs pour out between my uneven gasps. "Please—please." I didn't know what to say.

Don't hurt me? I didn't even know why they were here or how he knew my name. And where was Malik?

The man grabbed me by the shoulder to sit me up. I screamed as my kneecap ripped further from its socket.

"Oh, no." The man gasped. "Olorun! Get over here."

Another set of boots shuffled over to me. My fists clenched against the floor.

"Steady her leg."

Two hands wrapped around my ankle and calf while another set cradled the top and underside of my knee. I gritted my teeth, prepared for what was coming next. With a quick and steady twist of his hands, the leader put my kneecap back into its proper position. My screams went up an octave for a few short second; it felt as if hot daggers were ripping my leg apart.

The pain started to seep away. My screaming died out into whimpers and my body crumpled from exhaustion. I didn't even have the strength to fight against the leader as he pulled me up onto his lap and pressed my head against his shoulder with his hand on my cheek.

"Shh," he said. "You're safe now."

Safe? I was the furthest thing from safe. He'd found me, and one of his men was guarding my savior. No one was going to be able to help me now.

"We should go back before the others wake and see us." Olorun stood by the leader's side now. I stared at the hem of his grey pants, watched as it slid across the top of his boots with each movement.

"She needs a few more minutes." The leader's hot breath poured over my scalp and brushed along my face to my nose. It was sweet and pleasant. I inhaled deeply and imagined it somehow made me stronger. "We've been separated too long. She's not strong enough for transporting."

"You were without her for just as long." Olorun started pacing back and forth beside us. "Yet you had no trouble with the journey."

The leader's voice turned gruff—almost a growl. "Yes, but I wasn't being starved to death." The hand against my face balled into a fist.

The conversation confused me. Somehow I was connected to the man who now held me and I wasn't entirely convinced that was a good thing. I didn't even want to begin to wrap my mind around what they meant by "transporting." Visions of melting air forced their way to the front of my mind. I shook them away and focused on a new feeling coursing through my body—strength. I was growing stronger; I could feel it. Breathing was suddenly easier for me, though I had never noticed I'd had difficulty with it. But now it came naturally and smoothly, not forced between gasps.

My wounds, too, had stopped burning. I felt wonderful—like the wraith from *Sho'ful* was in the process of transforming into something with substance. My heart beat steadily, not the painful stutters of before.

"Hmm…" The man pressed his lips against my head and inhaled. "I can feel it already. I wasn't aware of how weak I'd gotten." He lifted his head. "Just a few more minutes, Olorun."

"We don't have a few more minutes. That man over there is almost totally healed and will be waking soon. The others on the ship are already stirring."

"Calm down." He spoke with the firm authority of a leader. "No one will see us. The secret of the Auri won't be revealed."

There was a long pause where no one said anything. I felt the man's limbs grow stiff around me.

Olorun broke the silence. "Sir." He grumbled and walked off.

The man holding me relaxed and pressed me tighter against his chest, resting his cheek against the top of my head. "How are you feeling?" he breathed.

I bit my lip and froze. Did I want to answer him? What would happen if I did?

"Ella?" He lifted his head again and grabbed my chin, forcing me to look up at him. He studied me quietly with sad, green eyes. *Green eyes.*

Flashes of a boy in an open field filled my mind. I knew those eyes. They were exactly as I remembered them—crisp jade. The face around them was older, but still the same—the high cheek-bones, the hint of a dimple on his chin, even the honey hair—my memory come to life.

I wasn't in any danger. I almost laughed to think of my earlier foolishness. I was in the best place I could ever be—in the arms of the one who held the key to my past. How silly I'd been to ever think they meant me harm, to even dream of hiding from them.

More of the memory surfaced in my mind. "Cailen." I brushed my fingertips against his face, following the contours of his lips and jaw.

He smiled and dipped his head into my hand. He inhaled and let his breath trail out. "This is good, isn't it?"

"So good." And it was. Everything about his arms around me, his eyes locked on mine, was right.

"I have something for you." He put his hands on my waist and lifted me off his lap. I started to protest, but he put his hand up to stop me and stood.

I stayed on the floor, gazing up at him. I could feel the huge smile spread across my face—my cheeks began to grow sore.

He rummaged through his jacket pocket and pulled out a long, gold chain.

Everything changed very quickly then. One moment, Cailen was gazing down at me with a smile as big as mine. The next moment, Olorun and the other man were at his side, dragging him away.

I was frozen in shock. What was happening? The smile on Cailen's face twisted into pleading rage as the air around them melted and they disappeared.

"Cailen?" I couldn't get my voice above a whisper. The air lodged against a hard lump in my throat.

"Ella." The voice was all wrong—far too deep—but my head whipped to the side anyway, hoping. Meir was leaning against a crate, supporting his weight against his arm. Dried blood caked the whole left side of his face.

I swallowed and blinked my eyes, struggling to get a grasp on reality. Surely, I'd dreamed everything that'd just happened. Winged men didn't exist and there was no man with green eyes to take me home. No Cailen. It all had been a dream.

A tear split through my heart and I gasped for air. Meir was by my side seconds later, patting his hands all over me, checking for wounds. He wouldn't find any, though. My wounds were inside, beyond human eyes.

"Cailen," I called out between my hyperventilating gasps, daring to hope. He had to be real. He had to be.

"Who?" Meir was anxious now. "Ella, who's Cailen?"

Something on the floor caught my eye and I shoved myself away from Meir's fluttering hands. I picked up the gold chain with its round locket and clutched it to my chest.

He was real. I hadn't dreamed anything. He was real.

I studied the delicate workings with my eyes and finger. Red and orange petals rose from the face of the locket and framed a single, clear gem whose facets changed color with each subtle movement. I twisted the locket back and forth, marveling at the beauty of the jewel.

I closed my eyes and wrapped the chain around my neck, fastening the clasp. "So good."

"Ella, who is Cailen?" Meir spoke slowly this time, emphasizing each word.

I didn't turn when I answered him. "Mine."

CHAPTER EIGHT:
MALIK'S STAND

Malik had come in then to check on us. When he saw there was nothing more wrong with us than a few superficial scratches—though I knew they'd been much more than superficial just minutes before—accompanied by what seemed to be a psychotic episode on my part, he left us alone in order to avoid suspicion.

Before he'd left, I'd picked up a few words from Malik and Meir's conversation as I'd lain on my cot. Apparently, those battleships had caught up to us, taken out the two fighters that were supposed to provide us protection, collided with the *Meridian* to pull us out of hyperspace, and then left. Malik assured us there was minimal damage to the ship. We'd still make it to Soltak.

Only I knew the rest of the story. They hadn't just left. They'd almost taken me with them. I was sure Cailen had intended to. But now they were gone. None of it made any sense.

I clung to the locket around my neck as my mind battled with itself. The logical side of my brain kept saying I'd been hallucinating or dreaming, just like it'd done after the attack from the Shakai. But the evidence denied this claim. The first time, there'd been the burning carcasses Meir had seen. Now there was the locket. Logic couldn't argue against that. But what did it all mean? What connection did I have to those winged men? I didn't have wings—I think I would've noticed that. I *could* somehow control fire, which was... odd.

Perhaps there was no connection. Maybe my mind was playing a sick game with me: get my hopes up and dash them. That had to be it.

Physically weak? Here's the ability to control a rather powerful element! But wait, we're not going to let you be able to do it whenever you want. You'll just have to keep getting yourself into sticky situations and see if you're lucky the next time.

Completely alone with no connection to any person or race of people? Here you go! Someone who wants to treat you like a daughter, but we're going to destroy his life in the process. And don't forget the mystery man who makes you feel like you have some kind of sacred bond with a person that transcends time and space. Now he's gone. Deal with it.

I sighed. Hearing voices was a bad sign.

None of it really mattered anyway. I was still entirely resolved in my original plan, perhaps even more so now. The longer I strayed from my destiny—death at Manoo's hand—the more bonds I would make, and the more people would suffer. Now that I knew about Cailen, I *had* to turn myself in. No one else was going to get hurt—I would make sure of that.

I felt us making our descent as I floated above my cot for a few seconds before settling back down and slipping halfway off. I grabbed hold of a crate before gravity and the steep angle of the ship had a chance to send me tumbling against the front wall. Stupid Mamood. I'd have thought they'd put *some* kind of re-straints in the cargo hold for passengers. But maybe they didn't care about their slaves, no matter how "respectable" they were.

The ship landed with a dull thump, and I peeled my eyes open. Other than the descent, I didn't think I'd moved since I'd lain down. Meir had tried talking to me and given up when he realized I didn't have the motivation to answer him. I needed to be alone. It was hard enough thinking about the sacrifice I'd decided to make before I'd met Cailen. Now that I realized just how much I was losing, my mind spiraled down into a foggy, meaningless haze.

Escape had been a bad idea.

I sighed and sat up, swinging my legs off the side of the cot. Although it'd been a bad idea, it'd ultimately been worth it. Knowing what I would sacrifice myself for made me feel almost heroic. I didn't have to be terrified as I stared into Manoo's eyes. He could take my life, but he couldn't take away the person I had become. I wasn't an empty wraith anymore. I wasn't that bumbling little girl who stumbled out of *Sho'ful* out of sheer luck. I was a real human being who loved something more than her-self. And I was strong—strong enough to give myself up and let Manoo do whatever he planned to do to me.

I smiled.

"Feeling better?"

I looked up, surprised. I hadn't realized Meir had been watching me. Had he been watching me the whole time? He must've thought I was going crazy. Perhaps I was. My thoughts were so jumbled I didn't even really know what was going on in my own mind.

Was I feeling better? No, not really. I knew what I had to do, and I accepted it—even found some satisfaction from it—but I still wished there could be another way. I wondered why *I* had to be the one to die, and not Manoo.

Manoo. Dead.

Even though the thought pleased me greatly, I held back my smirk. Meir didn't need to know my violent side. That didn't stop me from imagining it.

He eyed me critically, waiting for my answer. When he realized he wasn't going to get one, he stood up, handed me my mask, and put his own mask on. He started to break down his cot and I did the same, watching him carefully and doing as he did.

Just a few seconds after the *Meridian* had come to a complete stop and all evidence of our stay there had been removed, Malik's voice came over the intercom. He gave the same formal command he had when the Delsa-Prime had boarded the ship. Part of the ploy, I assumed.

Meir and I took our stations beside the door, and I waited as Meir punched in the code and Malik strolled through the open door. My hands wrapped around my NK-4 without any difficulty this time. I marveled at my new strength, shocked to think I had once thought the weapon heavy.

Malik studied us, his eyes lingering on me—likely making sure I played my part. And I would, for now. As long as they were in danger, I would play along. As soon as I'd talked to Malik and gotten Meir away, the charade would be over.

He nodded and turned back to Meir. "I've got a plan." He motioned for us to follow him as he wove his way to the back of the cargo hold. "It requires some skill on your part, Meir. Not to mention your particular knowledge of the city of Co'ladesh."

My heart pounded against my chest. Malik was planning on putting Meir in danger. I needed to talk to him soon.

He stopped at the hatch and pressed a round, red button. The door creaked open, letting soft, gray light stream through. My lenses adjusted immediately to the change. I wondered what time of day it was. The subdued light could have been morning or twilight.

"I have to sign off the cargo," he continued. "It wouldn't raise any suspicions for the two of you to accompany me. While I'm taking care of business with the Ladeshians, I'm going to try to separate us. The girl will come with me, but you'll have to escape the base."

My heart sprinted into full gallop mode now. This was perfect, better than I'd imagined. Meir would be long gone by the time I turned myself in. My plan was going to work.

Malik pulled something out from beneath his sash and handed it to Meir. "Take this communicator with you. It has a locator chip in it. When I'm done and you've escaped, I'll inform the crew and the Delsa-Prime that I'm taking the girl to look for you. We'll pick up some clothes on our way to meet you, but we have to get to your friend quickly. I imagine once inside the Old City, he'll be able to protect us."

Meir nodded. "He will."

"Good." He paused and raised an eyebrow. "Do you think you can get off the base?"

"It won't be easy, but I'll do it."

Malik's lips pulled down at the corners when he turned to me. The scowl was back. "Don't mess up this time."

I gulped. I wondered what Malik thought messing up would be. Turning myself in? Would that be considered a huge flub in his book? Not likely.

I smiled beneath my mask, stifling a chuckle. I was ecstatic. Meir was going to be all right. Doing what needed to be done suddenly didn't seem so bad when I thought about my savior being safe.

The ramp slid out from beneath the ship and Malik descended with us following at his sides. It was far easier for me to walk on the smooth surface than before. Everything was easier for me now—walking, breathing—and I wondered why that was. Just what did Cailen do to me, and how did he do it?

Seven men formed a small cluster a few yards away from the ramp. All except one stood rigid, their hands behind their backs. The man in front seemed ridiculously relaxed compared to the statue-like men behind him, his slouch at total odds with his clean, pressed uniform and razor-straight haircut. He also looked like a giant standing in front of them—a lazy, overly clean giant. I didn't know much about measurements, but I imagined I'd only come up to his waist. The men behind him barely made it to his shoulders. He extended one of his hands and smiled. Malik, as tall as he was, looked like a toddler next to him.

"It is good to see you made the journey unharmed." The giant had a thick, slurred accent, almost like his tongue was too big for his mouth. His eyes flitted past Malik and he chuckled. "Although, not completely untouched."

I suppressed the urge to turn and see what he was talking about.

"You should see the other guy." I could hear the smirk in Malik's voice.

It was then I realized they were talking about the damage to the cargo ship. I sighed.

"I can imagine!" The large man threw his head back in laughter, slapping Malik on the back.

Still laughing, the man motioned to the six men behind him. They filed past us up the ramp to unload the crates of… that stuff. I was pretty sure Malik and Meir had been calling it Lumin-something.

"I'm Base Commander Lastrini, by the way." All pretense of leisure drained away from his formerly open face. What replaced it was hard and guarded. Calculating blue eyes bore into us rather than welcomed us. I shivered. "Come. While they handle inventory of the gems, we will go to my office to take care of the formalities." He turned on his heels and led us a few hundred yards across the length of the tarmac to a large, stone building. We all struggled to keep up with his stride.

The structure was void of beauty and character. With few windows and plain, flat walls, its utilitarian purpose was clear. This was a bunker.

Just as we were about to pass through a narrow, arched entrance, Malik placed his hand on Meir's shoulder. "Go back and guard the ship. Report to me immediately when you get there."

Meir gave a sharp nod and started walking back to the *Meridian*. I knew, though, that as soon as we were out of sight, he'd make his escape. Now I just needed to get Malik alone. It didn't look like I was going to get that chance within the next few minutes. That was all right by me. Meir needed time.

Malik motioned for the Base Commander to continue and I followed them into the dank tunnel. A set of steel blast doors stood closed ten feet ahead of us. Lastrini waved his hand in front of a blue-lit screen and the doors slid to the sides, hiding behind the stone walls.

I almost gasped. The interior looked completely different from the exterior. Where I'd expected to see the same cold, grey blocks, pink and black marble covered the floors and walls. Thick, marble pillars towered above us fifty feet to the ceiling where gilded vines formed delicate patterns. Brightly colored silk banners hung from the walls, depicting battles between glorious, bronzed warriors and pitiful, writhing men.

Lastrini led us through the wide foyer—while I resisted the urge to gawk—to a large wooden door flanked by two creamy white statues of plumed and shielded warriors. The large man waved his hand in front of another blue-lit screen and the door swung open.

We followed him inside. Lastrini sat behind a shiny desk, while Malik took a seat in front of him. I stood by the door. I didn't pay much attention to what they were doing. I was too worried about Meir. My plan would only work if he was able to get away, and I was suddenly afraid that he might not. It was a silly fear, really. I didn't doubt his abilities. It was my own luck I doubted. And Meir and I seemed to have become entwined.

I couldn't help imagining again how shocked he'd be when he found out what I'd done. Would he stay away? Let me make my sacrifice? I hoped so. I didn't need to worry about putting him in more danger. I'd have to ask Malik to keep him here. He certainly didn't owe me any favors, though I doubted he'd decline. I was pretty sure the thought of my death wouldn't bother him.

I was shocked that the thought of my death didn't bother *me*. I would've thought I'd be scared. I was sad about losing the future I might've had with Meir—and maybe Cailen—if I wasn't being hunted, but that future didn't really exist. I *was* being hunted and there were no happy endings for me—only sorrow. I wasn't willing to sacrifice my friends for a few extra moments of joy. Besides, I knew desolation. I knew what it was like to have my life end and to face the nothingness. I could handle it.

"That's a small one."

I blinked, startled. I hadn't been paying attention to them for several minutes, but Lastrini's suddenly louder voice and hard eyes—staring right at me—pulled me away from my thoughts.

Malik peered over his shoulder at me. He assessed the loose Tarmean suit as it hung off my body, turned back to the man, and shrugged. I was small, too small for a Tarmean. No one had seemed to notice, despite the fact that it should've been obvious. We'd been lucky… until now. This Soltakian was too observant.

"I like having her around."

A knowing look came over the man's face. "Keeps you warm at night, does she?" He leered.

Ugh. Apparently Malik didn't think I could pass as a warrior any longer. I guess he decided a lover was a better fit. Disgusting.

"Not exactly." Malik growled. "Strength isn't always measured by size, Soltakian. And I don't keep that kind of slave."

Hmm…maybe I'd misjudged. It seemed I wasn't the only one. Base Commander Lastrini leaned back in his chair with a smug look.

Something chirped in Malik's pocket. He stood up and extended his hand to the Soltakian. "Now that everything is in order, I'll be on my way." There was more than a note of irritation in Malik's voice. He positively seethed. I remembered then how important his honor was to him. Apparently, he didn't like having it questioned.

Lastrini laughed and stood to take Malik's hand. "Please, no hard feelings. You are very odd for a Mamood. I jumped to conclusions and I am sorry."

Malik nodded and drew back his arm. I followed him out the door and through the foyer again to the outside. Lastrini stayed in his office. I felt his eyes on my back.

The soft, grey light had given way to warm butterscotch. Gold rays blanketed everything from the smooth tarmac in front of me to the building behind me. So, it was morning—a new beginning, for everyone but me.

Malik didn't pause as he started walking back to the *Meridian*. I knew I had to act while we were still alone and before he went back to the Delsa-Prime.

"Malik."

He stopped on his heels and spun around. "What?" His face was livid. I guessed speaking out of turn was his idea of messing up.

"Um…well, I just wanted to say that…I've decided—" I bit my lip, "—to turn myself in…to the Delsa-Prime."

He rolled his eyes. "Don't be an idiot."

"I'm not." My hands balled into fists at my sides. "I don't want to be a burden anymore. I don't want anyone to get hurt. So…" I couldn't finish. Malik had turned an alarming shade of red.

He pinched the bridge of his nose and shook his head. "Just stay here while I go tell them about Meir. Obviously I can't trust you to not do anything stupid in front of them."

He spun around again and marched off. So much for that part of my plan.

I quickly revised.

Rows upon rows of enormous metal storage units lined each side of the building we'd just left. In between each row was something like a dark alley, shadowed by the height of the units, and stretching as far as I could see. I reasoned I could easily hide in there while Malik was gone and sneak my way onto the ship when he started looking for me.

Not too hard. Except Malik wasn't a fool. He'd know where I was hiding and find me pretty easily. I'd have to go in deep to have a chance of avoiding him.

I took a deep breath and went into a narrow space, three rows to the left of the building. I reasoned Malik would check the first row, assuming a lack of planning on my part. The compartments loomed like buildings above me and stood so close together they blocked out most of the sun. I'd gone maybe thirty paces down the lane before I started having second thoughts. Malik was going to find me. My whole plan was stupid. I was betraying Meir by leaving him like this.

I had almost convinced myself to turn around when something slammed into my back, pitching me to the ground. I threw my arms out in front of me, but my head dug into the gravel as something heavy sat on top of me.

My mask was ripped off and the stones scraped against the left side of my face. Whoever sat on me pulled at my hair and yanked my head back, tearing strands out of my scalp. I gasped for breath as it was squeezed out of my throat.

"Tarmeans aren't supposed to have long hair, my pretty." Hot breath scorched my ear. "Are you Malik's pet?"

He shoved my head back into the stones. I clenched my mouth and eyes shut, but still dirt and rock lodged themselves inside my lips and eyelids.

Gently this time, he played with my hair. I heard him inhale and groan. "Malik's a little busy right now. So for now, you can be *my* pet."

The man slid his hands along my hips and clenched the top of my thighs, pressing himself closer to me. His breath grew rough and uneven.

I dug my hands into the dirt and tried to push myself up to heave the hulking mass off of me, but that only seemed to excite him more. Stones bit into my flesh as he thrust his groin against my back.

With a quick, jerky movement, he stood up and grabbed me by the shoulders to throw me against the wall of storage units. I cried out and winced when my head slammed against the hard surface.

I knew I wasn't going to get far, but I took a step forward to run anyway. A short, pudgy Mamood was there, shoving his body against mine and pressing me flat against the wall again.

"Tsk, tsk," he whispered in my ear and grabbed my waist. "Where are you running off to?" His other arm came up then and stroked my face. A thick, meaty thumb scraped the dirt and gravel off my cheek. "Mmm... so soft."

His face came close to mine. I could feel his breath pouring from his open mouth. I twisted my head to the side just as his lips dove for mine. I felt his lips curl up into a smirk against my face, and he ran his tongue across my cheek.

I brought my hands up to shove him away, but he pressed himself tighter against me, moving his hips rhythmically against mine.

"Please." I whimpered.

He moved his lips down my jaw to the base of my neck. "Oh yes." His voice grew rough and he twisted his hand into my hair. "Beg for it."

I clenched my eyes shut and struggled to hold back the whine that wanted to escape my lips. That would only excite him more. He took his hand from my hair and pulled up his robes. I gasped. I needed to think of something, and quick. The stink of sweat and cologne lurched its way to my nose, making me dizzy.

When his robes were up, he started pulling apart my suit. That's when I screamed.

He slapped me. "I like it better when you whisper," he growled.

I punched at his kidneys, but he didn't flinch. His thick hands found an opening in my suit and made contact with my flesh.

A deep calm suddenly settled over me and my arms hung limply at my sides. I closed my eyes and let the familiar tingling sensation—that fickle power—wash over me. I no longer noticed his twitching fingers. They no longer mattered. All that mattered now was what I must do.

I opened my eyes and smiled when I saw the blue points of light waiting for my orders. I pushed at them and they obeyed me willingly.

The man flew away from me and slammed into the container just across the alley. Air swirled around us like a whirlwind, picking up the dust and debris from the ground. But I took little notice. My target was clear.

I smirked to see his face twist in terror. He brought his hands up to save himself, but there was no hope. I was in control now. I laughed as I prepared to rip his limbs apart.

A red beam tore through my wall of air and hit the man square in the chest. His body slumped against the ground, a charred hole burnt all the way through.

Dead.

I twisted my head around—enraged—ready to pass my judgment on a new, hapless victim. Malik stood just yards from me with the butt of my NK-4 pressed against his shoulder and his finger on the trigger. He lifted his head to see the damage. After a moment, he pulled the weapon away and dropped it to his side.

He looked at me with flat eyes.

The air died out around me and I took a step back. A lump formed in my throat. I'd almost killed a man. Malik killing someone wasn't nearly as bad. In fact, considering he was a Mamood, it was almost expected. But not me. I was supposed to be innocent—the good guy. But I was turning out to be less and less innocent as each second passed. True, he might've deserved it, but that didn't change the fact of what I'd almost done. I swallowed past the lump and gazed at Malik. "Thank you," I mouthed.

Malik stared back, emotionless. Then he nodded to the body on the ground. "I guess I don't have to worry about you going to the Delsa-Prime anymore."

I brought my hands up to my face and let the sobs pour out. I was shaking and gasping when I felt Malik wrap his arms around me. He didn't say anything, and I didn't want him to. I knew what I was—a monster.

CHAPTER NINE:
CO'LADESH

"You'll need a speeder." One of the guards at the base exit pointed in the direction of the New City Ghetto of Co'ladesh. I hovered behind the Mamood. After a pretty heated argument where Malik displayed his impeccable acting skills, the guards agreed to let us off base to search for Meir. How he'd managed to get out, I had no idea, but he had and now it was time to pick him up. We'd left the Delsa-Prime's dead body to rot in the dark maze of storage units for the moment. "Unless you know the city well, getting around the lakes can get pretty confusing. It's better just to fly over them."

After a bit more arguing where Malik accused the men of letting his slave leave—or possibly abducting him in order to learn Mamood military tactics—they ended up providing us with a speeder and papers good for the day. We were due back by midnight, with or without Meir. If Malik couldn't find his slave, they might be willing to issue papers for the next day, but as they were having trouble with illegal immigrants, they couldn't do more than that. That wasn't going to be a problem, though; Meir's friend from the Old City would take care of us.

"Everyone goes to the Ghetto," the guard had said. As it turned out, they were right. Malik's own communicator confirmed that Meir was indeed in the heart of the off-worlder haven.

We loaded ourselves into the sleek speeder—a much more streamlined and polished descendent of the speeder Meir had flown to get us away from the *Sho'ful* guards—and took off through the city.

The base sat on the outskirts of Co'ladesh; the first stalagmite-looking towers rose in the distance. At first, I was too entranced by the emerald grass as it swayed rhythmically across the plains in the light wind to notice anything odd about the bluish-white buildings. But as we got closer, I could've sworn that they were swaying in time with the grass. Then I noticed that some of them floated above crystal blue lakes.

"They're beautiful," I whispered. Truly, truly beautiful. I couldn't tear my eyes away, even as we entered the city and they towered hundreds of feet above me. "How is it even possible?"

Malik grunted. "They're the product of poor planning."

I sighed and brought my gaze down so I could glare at him properly. Leave it to Malik to ruin my mood.

"I'm being serious. They built their city on the lone hill in the middle of a plain, surrounded by hundreds of lakes. Not only is it indefensible, it makes expansion rather difficult." He shrugged. "Though I will admit it forced them to develop some pretty spectacular technology. There aren't many civilizations out there that have mastered levitation the way the Soltakians have." He nodded to the nearest crystal blue tower, which swayed just out of our reach. "Electromagnetics. The Soltakians can create their own gravity fields. Still, for all their breathtaking technology, you'd think they wouldn't be so dumb."

I rolled my eyes and looked away. He didn't see the gesture through my mask, but I knew I'd done it, and that was enough. Sometimes I respected Malik, sometimes I outright hated him, and other times he just annoyed the crap out of me.

He didn't seem to realize this was my first real experience away from the Mamood in ten out of my seventeen pitiful years. I didn't know anything beyond Mamood architecture, Mamood dress, Mamood military—and even that I'd only seen during the past two days. Seeing something new, something totally different from anything my captors could have come up with, made me realize there was more to this galaxy than I'd ever imagined. It made me realize I really could hope, if even for a short while. It was enough to make my heart want to burst from its cage, just thinking of that hope.

The truth was, the contrasting differences between what I'd seen already of Soltak and the Mamood Fiefdom reminded me of how I'd felt when I'd first stepped off *Sho'ful*—the difference between light and darkness, beauty and nothingness.

Malik could never understand that because his thinking belonged with the Mamood, like a blind man belonged to the darkness. For this reason only, he couldn't appreciate the beauty of the lakes and the plains as we sped over them—wisps of alternating blue and green—or the towers around us, rising up like crystal spikes and swaying in the breeze. He couldn't appreciate the Soltakian's affinity with nature because he belonged to the nation of conquerors.

I almost felt bad for him—almost. He may've been raised with Mamood ideals all his life, but that didn't mean he had to continue in their ignorance when something better was put in front of him. But then, I could no more expect Malik to see the truth than I could expect a blind man to see the sun. Sometimes, the blackness was too heavy, too permanent.

I knew what that was like.

We flew silently for several minutes, weaving past the towers and, at times, flocks of other speeders. Malik seemed content to ignore me, and if I was being honest with myself, I had to admit I preferred the silence. I tried to think of only the sun beating down on my shoulders, the air whipping past my covered face. I was tired, physically and mentally, of thinking about anything else. And I most certainly did not want to remember my... encounter... with the Delsa-Prime, but it crept in there anyway.

I shook my head to shove the images away. It didn't help. I could still feel the ghost of his fingers on my skin, sending chills crawling up my spine.

My body convulsed.

Malik turned his head to look at me. I pretended not to notice.

He returned his gaze forward and took a deep breath. "So... are you going to tell me what that was earlier?"

I cringed. It didn't really surprise me we'd been thinking about the same thing, but I didn't want to talk about it. There was no explanation I could give. I had no more idea of what was going on with me than he did.

I doubted he was the type to let his questions go unanswered, though, so I gave him the truth. "I don't know."

"You don't know."

"No."

He simply nodded his head.

"Look," I said. "I wanted to say thanks for what you did. You saved me... from becoming a monster."

He sighed. "You're welcome."

"I know you hate me, and to be honest, I understand. It isn't like I haven't completely ruined your life since the moment we met, so I know that you killing a man for me is only one of the many things I'm going to have to owe you for."

His hand on the steering console clenched. "Hmmm..."

"What?"

He pinched the bridge of his nose, and then ran his hand through the tight curls of his hair. "I never hated you, Ella." I thought for a second I saw his jaw clench, but he continued on before I could be sure. "I only hated the situation. And as far as ruining my life, well, I did a pretty good job of that myself, so don't take all the blame."

"What are you talking about?"

"Well, my father is pretty furious." He looked at me out of the corner of his eye. His gaze made me jump it was so intense, burning. "When news got around that he'd helped in your escape—" He paused to make sure I was looking at him. "And yes, they *do* know. Our only good fortune is that they'd never guess we'd still head to Soltak. Well, like I said, when they found out my father had helped, he was kicked off of the Council. He's no longer one of the Leaders of Talia. Because I chose you over him," the corner of his mouth twisted up in a half-sneer, "he disowned me. I can never show my face in any part of the Mamood Fiefdom again."

I groaned. The acids in my stomach were churning to punish me. Bringer of destruction... bringer of destruction—that's all I could think of. That's all I was. Every life I touched was going to be destroyed in one way or another.

"So killing a rather high-ranking officer may not win me any points," Malik continued, "but it didn't make my situation any worse, either."

I wanted to close my eyes and pretend I was back on *Sho'ful*, that I hadn't escaped, that all of this was only a horrible nightmare—except my dreams were never nightmares. How many more would have to suffer? How many more would have to die?

"So that's why you wouldn't let me turn myself in." As ironic as it was, it seemed those I was destined to destroy were willing to give up everything for me. How odd. Why couldn't they have picked someone a bit more deserving to be on the receiving end of their heroics?

"If I ever hear that idiotic idea come out of your mouth again," he growled, "I swear I'll keep you locked up myself. I didn't give up my life to save yours just so you could throw it away."

I didn't answer him. There was no point. Obviously I couldn't tell him my plan hadn't changed. Part of me was exceedingly glad I'd get to see Meir again, but the other part was drowning in the guilt of what it would mean for him. I wouldn't prolong this any longer than I had to.

Paved streets started dotting the ground as the lakes thinned beneath us. Malik zigzagged past a growing swarm of pedestrians as we entered a shopping district. Storefronts littered with golden trinkets and other delicate pretties lined a broad avenue filled with hundreds of people in robes and dresses. Some of them sported manes of feathers that glowed on and off with colored lights. I couldn't help but wonder which planet they'd come from. Malik parked the speeder at the corner of the avenue and a narrow side street packed with similar vehicles.

As I hurried along behind Malik, trying desperately to keep up with his quick pace—and admittedly proud of myself for not becoming winded like I would've just a day ago—I became aware of the fact that I didn't like crowds. With each brush of a passing stranger's shoulder against my arm, my skin crawled and my stomach twisted into a knot. When a group of twenty or so children pushed past me with their grubby little hands out in front of them to clear the way, I started hyperventilating. I had to stop and bend over with my head between my knees.

I don't know how long it took for Malik to notice that I no longer followed him—I was too busy listening to the drumming of my pulse in my eardrums—but eventually, I felt his hands on my arms, lifting me up. He walked more slowly this time with one arm around me and guided me through the crowd, limiting my physical contact with anyone. I would be forever grateful to him. Already, I began to forget how much I'd previously hated him.

We stopped near the end of the boulevard near a tiny shop that was less ostentatious than some of the other marble and gold-trimmed stores that had sharply dressed men waiting to open the door for customers. No one waited here and, to my great satisfaction, no crowd of customers pushed to get in.

I took in a deep breath and pulled it all the way to the tips of my toes. Jasmine and musk wafted its way to my nose as Malik held the shop's door open for me. I smiled at him as I walked through, and then rolled my eyes when I remembered that—duh—he couldn't see my face.

I shook my head and chuckled, and then looked at the inside of the shop. I stopped dead in my tracks, partly out of shock and partly because there was no more room for me to walk. The tiny shop was packed full of dresses, shirts, pants, skirts, scarves, and every other manner of clothes in more colors than I'd ever seen. Items on the shelves and racks were almost completely hidden by articles of clothing piled on top of them and falling to the floor. It looked like someone had broken into the shop, ransacked it, and left without taking a single thing. I wondered how many hours it would take for me to find anything in all the mess.

Malik nudged me forward so he could enter the store. I had to kick a pile of men's pants out of the way to give him room.

"Welcome, welcome," a high-pitched, babyish voice called. The words came out muffled, like the speaker was buried some-where beneath her own wares. I couldn't locate her until some clothes on the racks swung back and forth in the middle of the shop. She made a straight line for us through the mess, carelessly letting her wares fall from the racks to the floor as she passed. She was nearly to us before I could see her bobbing grey head. She was shorter than the racks of clothes, and round.

When she stopped in front of us, her hands started fluttering over her flowery dress, smoothing the wrinkles and reposition-ing it where it was twisted to the side. From the big grin that stretched across her face, I guessed she wasn't accustomed to many customers.

I smiled back, forgetting the mask for the second time.

"Is there anything in particular you are looking for?" she asked in her babyish voice, looking at Malik. "I have many se-lections of men's clothes." She frowned. "Though no Mamood robes." Her face brightened again. "I do have Mosandarian and Deluvian outfits, which I've been told by many Mamood custom-ers are just as comfortable as robes. Perhaps you could come to the back and I could take your—"

"I'm actually looking for something for my slaves," Malik in-terrupted. "A simple dress for this one," he rested his hand on my shoulder, "and a pair of pants and a shirt for my other one."

The woman's lips puckered as she looked me over. "Hmm... I *may* have something small enough for you." Her eyes sparkled in one of those *a-ha* moments people sometimes have. "I know just the thing! Come with me, come with me." She shuffled her way through the sea of clothes to the back of the store and I followed reluctantly behind.

The back storeroom made the front entrance look almost tidy. She'd stacked reams of unused cloth against the walls with leg-less mannequins crowding in front of them. As small as I was, I had difficulty blazing a trail through all the stuff, and I wondered how the portly little woman managed it. But manage it she did, skillfully pushing her way through unhindered as if there were nothing there. I sighed with relief when we finally stopped in front of a small wooden platform in front of a floor-to-ceiling mirror.

"Just step up there and I'll go find the dress." She started to skitter away, but stopped suddenly and spun around. "Go ahead and take off your clothes. I'll be back in a minute!"

I tugged at a piece of my uniform while avoiding eye contact with the imposing mirror in front of me. I'd seen my decrepit body in small glimpses here and there, though I'd never seen it all together, and never had I seen my face. I wasn't ready to now. I knew if I really looked at myself, the horror of the past ten years would flood over me. I wasn't prepared to face my own reality. The theory of what I looked like was enough to disgust me. I remembered perfectly well how Malik had reacted when he'd first seen me. The shock, the pity, the care he took to not look at me again.

I peeled my Tarmean armor off one section at a time, saving the mask for last. I yanked it away from my head and tossed it to the floor. My eyes stayed shut. After a few seconds, deep curiosity began to war with my terror. I could chance a peek. No harm would be done. A little, tiny peek…

No.

I clenched my eyes even tighter. Nothing good could come from seeing what I'd become. I was vain enough to care. Of course I wanted to be beautiful. It would've been nice to know I had creamy skin like Malik, or bright eyes like Cailen—something to make me feel like not everything about me had been corrupted and ruined by the Mamood. Such hopes were frivolous, though.

The shopkeeper was back and pressing something against the front of my exposed body. "Hmm… yes, I think this will do. Perhaps a little too short around the ankles, but your weight isn't exactly proportionate to your height. Go ahead and try it on, dear."

I had to open my eyes now. The woman stood there, waiting for me to take the dress from her to put it over my head. I knew I wasn't coordinated enough to fumble my way through dressing myself blind.

I took a deep breath, pulling it all the way to my toes again. I just needed to relax. I could manage to do this without catching a glimpse of myself in the mirror. And if I couldn't, who cared? That's what I tried to convince myself, at least, because I knew that I *would* care. I'd care very much.

I took another breath. Better to just get it done and over with. Stop the procrastinating. I popped my eyes open, ready to be assaulted with an image out of a nightmare. What stared back at me was very sad. Anxiety was written on the creature's face in the crease between her brows and tightness of her lips. Her body looked… skeletal. There really was no better explanation. She had no woman's chest to speak of, and her stomach was sunken rather than flat.

I bit my lip and the creature did the same. It was hard to reconcile the image in the mirror with me. In all honesty, I knew that it *was* me, but having cold, hard proof that I really was wasted and decrepit was hard to accept.

I couldn't pull my eyes away. I needed to find something beautiful, something to love in this creature. The feelings of disgust raging through me could not be my final, lasting impression.

I sighed.

There was… something there. The skin wasn't as sallow as I'd remembered it. The creamy ivory of her—my—complexion hinted at a rosy undertone. My eyes, too, were bright blue, almost sparkling in their intensity. And my hair cascaded down the length of my back in golden waves, not stiff and dry like straw as I'd thought.

So there was beauty I could grasp at. It wasn't completely overshadowed by the hideous way my bones jutted out beneath my skin. I almost smiled.

"Is something wrong, dear?"

I looked down at the woman who still held the dress out for me and shook my head. No, there really wasn't anything wrong. Not like I'd thought there would be. I could live with this. There was nothing a few good meals couldn't fix, no damage that was permanent.

I smiled at her to calm the anxiety building on her face. She smiled back and offered the dress again. I took it this time and pulled it over my head.

There were no frills to the dress. It was light and plain, but the sky blue brought out more of the pink in my skin. The sleeves were short, so I was a little upset my stick arms would be exposed. All in all, though, it was pretty. The waistline tried to accentuate the curves I didn't have, and the skirt fell down my legs like running water. I could see why the woman had so many clothes around her store. Though she didn't seem to have many customers, she was very good at what she did, and by the way she pulled at the cloth and smoothed it over my body, I could tell she really enjoyed her work.

She was behind me when her hands froze. "Hmm... that's odd."

"What is?"

"Well, it's just that you have very pronounced shoulder blades." She ran her fingers over my skin. "They even extend down half your back! Amazing..."

I twisted my torso around so I could see what the woman was talking about. There were two long, slender mounds just where the woman had described them. The shopkeeper reached her hand out to touch them again and the skin indented beneath her poking finger. I flinched away.

"Amazing..." she said again.

"Will the dress still fit?" I turned my back away from her, uncomfortable and eager to cover up this new discovery. I felt naked and exposed beneath her dubious gaze.

"What? Oh yes! Let me just... there we go!" She flitted behind me again and buttoned up the opening. I smiled in relief.

I forced myself to relax as I enjoyed the new image in the mirror. The girl staring back at me looked almost feminine in her pale, blue dress. I smiled.

My eyes roved over my reflection, delighting in what they saw, and finally settled on the gold locket Cailen had left for me. The red and orange petals were vibrant against my ivory skin, almost on fire. As I stared at the gilded flower a whispering voice tickled at my ears. I couldn't understand what it was saying, but each hiss and drawl made my back ache and thrum.

Open... Open... Open...

That one whispered word became clearer with each utterance. And each time the "p" popped, whatever was underneath my skin by my shoulder blades bounced and crawled. But I didn't know what it wanted or what to do, so the blood in my veins started to tingle like it had with the Shakai and the Delsa-Prime. I closed my eyes to control it, to stop it, but it wouldn't be stopped, it wouldn't be controlled. Searing pain ripped through my back, sending scorching heat through my body. I gasped. I needed to give the voice what it wanted, but I didn't know how…

I didn't know how.

My vision turned red and my body arched back as I fought against the ravenous power erupting inside me. I didn't want to hurt the woman, but a sudden and unbidden rage—an absolute need for destruction—choked off all my senses. Only one thought was clear, only one truth was above all truths. I was the—

"Destructor."

Fire erupted above the tips of my fingers and spread out to consume the room and everything in it. My cells oozed with euphoria as the hunger was fed and the woman's screams added a high-pitched cadence to the thunderous roar of the burning tempest. I smiled.

Let it burn. Let it consume everything.

The girl staring back at me glowed in the halo of flames dancing a finger's width above her skin. She looked happy. She looked complete. But there was something she craved, and I knew what that was. She wanted to release the burning ache in her back. She wanted to give in and let it all out. And I wanted to give it to her more than I wanted to pull breath into my lungs, but I still didn't know how.

Some new sound distracted me then. The woman's screams had ceased, but above the roar of the fire, I heard someone call to me. I turned my head to the voice, letting the power play through my veins, ready to bend it to my will against the one who would dare to divert my attention, ready to send it out to eat through more life and fill my body with its strength.

Malik stared back at me. And just as he'd calmed me during my encounter with the Delsa-Prime, reason burst through my mind like a tidal wave. What I was doing was wrong, horrible. I pulled the power back inside of me and quenched it. It burned every cell in my body as it sought new life to quench, but I extinguished the flames around me and fell face-first to the floor.

CHAPTER TEN:
FULFILLING PROPHECY

I'd killed her.

I'd really killed her. There was no avoiding that reality. Her burned and wasted body stood as evidence to the fact that I was a monster. *Destructor*—that's what I'd said in the back room of the shop. That truth was more evident now than it'd ever been.

As I followed Malik through a dark, narrow alley in the Ghetto and into a dingy, little bar with sticky floors and sour air, I thought about how I'd let the rage and need for destruction take over my body. The power I'd held—my absolute indestructibility behind that power—part of me started thinking of ways to get it back. I shoved those thoughts aside. I did *not* want that to happen again. Or did I?

No. I definitely didn't.

I shook my head to get the images out even as the need grew. Two men—the only customers in the place besides Meir—stared at me from across the room, each of them playing with a bulbous, silver charm hanging from their necks. I wondered for a fleeting moment what their screams would sound like.

"Not now," Malik said.

I looked around, startled, like I'd just woken up. In fact, I did feel like I was drifting between reality and fantasy. My mind struggled to focus on the present. Meir and Malik were staring at me. Meir's wrinkles creased with worry. So they'd been talking about me and I hadn't even noticed. I wondered what Meir had said. Had he asked why I looked half-crazed? If so, would Malik tell him about the dead woman and her burnt shop? I hadn't wanted Meir to know this part of me. I'd resolved to keep it from him when I'd first discovered this strange ability. But now, perhaps he needed to know. It was getting out of control. I was hurting people... killing them.

I needed to leave. I needed to turn myself in. I needed to die. They'd been right to lock me away. I was dangerous—perhaps the most dangerous person in the galaxy... in the universe. Who knew how many civilized planets there were? Dozens, hundreds maybe—and for some reason the number four-hundred-and-two popped into my head. Maybe it was a shadow of a memory from my life before *Sho'ful*. It didn't matter, though. What mattered was that all those planets had their criminals, their sickos—but I was the worst.

Meir stiffened as I stared back, anxiety growing on his face. He nodded once, and I knew then that Meir would hold Malik to his word. He'd demand the information that would condemn me in his eyes, and then he would no longer love me. "Let's go," he said.

We left the poorly lit bar, leaving its two patrons and one bartender in silence. The speeder stood halfway down the alley, hidden in the shadows between the walls of buildings on either side of the narrow street. Our footsteps echoed off the cobblestone pavement as I followed closely behind Meir and Malik.

Malik pulled out a white shirt and a pair of green pants for Meir and I turned my back to give him privacy. I wanted more than anything to scream and run away, but I stayed because I knew Malik would never let me get far. Even at this moment, I could feel his eyes on my back. He... knew. Maybe he could see it in my eyes—my dead, cold eyes.

One of them cleared his throat, and I turned to get into the speeder with my gaze shifting everywhere but on them. I climbed in the rear with Meir's discarded Tarmean uniform and leaned away from the two of them with my head resting against the seat.

Fluffy white clouds skittered across the soft, blue backdrop of sky. It was funny to think that just a few days ago I'd lain on the floor of my prison cell imagining this very image. Now I was experiencing it for real and dreaming of getting back into the clutches of my captors. It was amazing how reality could change my perspective on things. Never in all my ten years with the Mamood had I thought *I* was the greater evil.

Malik started the engine and the electromagnet purred to life. I barely noticed the smooth ride past the squat, stone buildings and then the glittering spikes. I should've been fascinated and on the edge of my seat like I'd been before, but so much had changed. I had changed. There was no longer only *a* threat of destruction. I was *the* threat, burning as I went.

I closed my eyes. I didn't want to think about it anymore. I didn't want to see the beauty I longed to consume.

I didn't open my eyes again until I felt the speeder slow to a stop. And even then, I didn't want to wake up to reality, but someone was talking to us and my curiosity was stronger than my depression.

Two men wearing polished silver armor and lavish red plumes atop glistening helmets stood on either side of the speeder. I sat up with my back ramrod straight. Though we hovered several feet above the ground, these men towered over us. They were giants—probably close to twice my height—and they spoke to Malik with the same thick accent as Lastrini had.

"Orsili?" one of them said. "Let's see your papers."

Malik dug through a pocket in his robe and pulled out the papers the guards had given us. Outwardly, he looked calm, but I'd watched him enough to know by his clenched jaw and too-innocent eyes that he was nervous.

We were stopped in front of a massive wooden gate. The stone walls on either side towered several stories into the sky. The structure looked ancient, but sturdy, not anything like the delicate towers that spotted the plains for miles around it.

The man on my left, closest to Malik, narrowed his eyes at us. "These papers say nothing about the Old City."

Meir shrugged. "Ranen Orsili is a good friend of mine and I was hoping to get a chance to see him for a few hours before our papers ran out." The man still looked skeptical. "I lived here with him for a short time a few years back. You may remember me. Meir Groff."

The man on my right pulled out some kind of palm device and waved it in front of Meir's face. After a few seconds, he nodded. "He's in our records."

The man on my left nodded as well and they both stepped away from the speeder, signaling us to move forward.

"What was that about?" I asked when we'd cleared the gate.

Meir twisted his body to face me. "The Old City is strictly for Ladeshians. Outsiders are prohibited in most cases—even other Soltakians. My friend, Ranen, has a lot of clout, though." He chuckled. "He is the Emperor's cousin, after all."

My eyes widened. The mystery behind Meir seemed to be getting more spectacular with each passing moment. But I narrowed my eyes at him. He'd said something that confused me, and I remembered Malik had used the term earlier that day, too. "What's a Ladeshian?"

"The ruling class of people on Soltak, the conquerors, the ones to unite the planet under their rule. They primarily live in their royal cities—Co'ladesh, Bri'ladesh, Fa'ladesh, and Eo'ladesh." He shook his head. "They obsess over their traditions, refusing even to make the common tongue their primary language. Did you notice their accents?"

I nodded.

He smiled and nodded his head to the left and right. "Look around you. The Ladeshians are one of the most advanced cultures in the galaxy, but you wouldn't guess it by looking at their homes."

I followed his gesture. Limestone and marble palaces dotted green acres on either side of a blue-stoned street. There was no hint at modernization like there'd been in the New City.

"Each one of these is thousands of years old, passed on from generation to generation. Some of them have been updated with a few modern comforts, but most of the occupants refuse even to install modern plumbing because it's not how their ancestors lived."

I thought about that for a minute and sympathized with them. I liked the idea of that sense of belonging to something, relating to those who lived thousands of years before. Maybe their actions seemed overzealous to some, but they retained a sense of who they were, not even giving in to other people from their own planet.

I envied them. I wished I had such a connection.

We traveled in a circle now, following the steady incline up the hill. Each house we passed loomed larger and more lavish than the last. Eventually, green hedges and stone walls hid the estates altogether. The blue-stoned streets reflected the sun's rays into my eyes with blistering intensity. I wiped away the stinging tears.

"There it is." Meir pointed to a three-story limestone palace on green lawns that encompassed most of the block, just below the very top of the hill.

Malik turned the speeder up the winding drive past towering trees with pink and white blossoms. Vines of lavender flowers covered the palace's white walls.

My hands ached to reach out and touch them. I inhaled, hoping to get a hint of their scent.

The speeder stopped in front of a set of wooden double doors. The surrounding windows were dark with the curtains drawn closed.

Finding the doors unlocked, we followed Meir inside, stepping into a large, open foyer packed from floor to ceiling with books and maps and little doodads that weren't familiar to me. A gust of wind came in behind us and sent thick layers of dust flying through the air. The place didn't look like it'd been occupied in a long time.

"Perhaps we've come at a bad time," Malik said.

My eye caught some subtle movement at the end of the foyer just behind sweeping, curved stairs. A dark figure, hunched and limping, slid out of the shadows. He growled at us and shouted, "Onan orsk azoori!"

Meir took a step forward with a broad smile on his face and his arms extended. "Oni latuli."

The figure halted. "Meir?"

My savior threw his head back and laughed. "It's good to see you, Ranen!"

Ranen came forward to greet his friend, hurrying despite his limp. Impatient, Meir closed the distance and swooped him up into a bear hug. I'd been wrong—Ranen hadn't been hunched over, he was just very short. His feet dangled at least a foot in the air as Meir pulled him up into his arms. When he'd been set back onto the ground, I was surprised to see even I dwarfed him. Considering how all the other Ladeshians had towered over me, I'd been expecting to meet another giant, not this gimpy little man.

He smacked Meir on the back and said in the thick, slurred accent I'd been growing accustomed to, "It's been too long, my friend. Far, far too long. Tell me, what brings you to me now, after all these years?"

Meir turned his bright, excited eyes to me. The deep look of adoration made my skin warm. I didn't deserve such a friend. "We need your help."

Ranen raised his eyebrows. "Of course." His voice turned grave. "Come, follow me." He waved his arm over his head dramatically in an awkward gesture. But as he did it, his short-sleeved tunic hiked up and revealed a mark on his arm. I might not have noticed it if it hadn't been for the fact that it appeared to be glowing.

I had this deep urge to find out what it was, but Ranen didn't give me a chance to ask before he turned and beckoned us to follow him down the hall and through an opened door to a large, gloomy parlor. While he drew back the curtains, Ranen motioned us to a small sitting area by one of the windows. The sudden light was staggering. "There. Much better." Ranen rubbed his hands together as he brushed past me to sit down.

I lowered myself onto the sofa by Meir while Malik sat on the edge of the chaise. The layer of dust disturbed by my weight flew out around me in a whoosh. I held my hand in front of my mouth and nose. It was too late. The back of my throat tickled, and I coughed.

"Ahh..." Ranen sank into his own chair, apparently undisturbed by the filth around him. He smiled at us, his eyes flickering first to Meir, then Malik, and finally resting on me. When they did, they widened in horror. Ranen's skin turned bone white and he leaned toward me. I ducked into Meir's arm.

Ranen started muttering to himself, seemingly unable to form a coherent sentence. I felt the tingling in my blood as my body registered the possibility of danger. I fought it back, clenching my jaw as I subdued it.

He wiped his hand over his face and some semblance of calm replaced the horror. "I wait no longer," he whispered. "The Destructor has come."

The shock hit me like a hammer. "What?" I murmured.

Ranen's gaze swept past me now. He talked slowly, to no one in particular. "To those who wait, the Destructor will come. In the year of decision, those who hide will show their faces."

"What?" Meir repeated my sentiment.

Ranen's eyes focused on me again and then dropped to my chest. They lingered there for a moment and I sank even deeper into Meir's protective arms. Ranen didn't seem to notice. He dropped his head into his hands with a groan and fell forward on the seat with his forehead resting against his knees.

"Ranen, what's wrong?" Meir's voice turned gruff as he pulled me tighter, almost roughly against his side.

I glanced at Malik. He glared at me and I could only guess at what he was thinking. He'd seen what I was capable of. Cold calculation filled his eyes as Ranen's words registered. This Mamood would no longer be led by honor.

Ranen started muttering to himself again. "I don't know what to do. I'm not ready for this. But the prophecy…" He groaned again. "Of all the Orsilis who could have prepared the warrior for battle, it had to be me."

The weight in my stomach turned to pure lead, sinking me down into the couch. *Warrior? Battle?*

I wanted to throw up.

Meir cupped his hand against my jaw and stroked his thumb along my cheek. He pressed his lips against my head for a moment, and then leaned forward. "Ranen, snap out of it! What are you talking about?"

The tiny little man raised his head and glared at me before turning to Meir. He gave a tentative smile. "Forgive me, my friend, for my poor behavior. Would you like something to eat or drink? I'm sure you are tired after such a long journey."

"Ranen…" Meir growled.

Ranen gulped. He turned back to me with piercing eyes. "I'd like to… talk to you… alone."

My eyes widened. There was no way I'd let myself be alone with this man.

"It isn't going to happen," Meir said.

Ranen sighed and sank back into his seat. "Fine." He sighed again. "I don't really know where to start. It's complicated."

"I want to know how you heard that name." My tongue was thick and heavy, like my body had decided I'd reached my limit on what I could handle and was now determined to keep me from asking any more questions. But this man had knowledge I knew deep down I needed. "Why did you call me the Destructor?"

Meir pulled away and looked down at me with questioning eyes. I ignored him as I stared at Ranen. There wasn't time to worry about his reaction. Later, after I knew what everything meant, I'd let his hate for me sink in.

Ranen studied me, weighing my resolve. I was sure he wondered just how much information I could handle. Little did he know I'd already been bombarded with more than enough to change me forever. Anything he said now would be nothing compared to what I'd already learned about what I was capable of. Still, I needed to hear it. Apparently, the look on my face was enough to convince him because he squared his shoulders and leaned toward me.

"The Orsilis were chosen by El thousands of years ago to identify the Destructor and inform him—her—of her mission. He sent a servant, Elysia—our mother—to mold the Ladeshian clan in preparation for the help the Destructor would need. She was an Auri, like you."

Meir went completely still—cold.

Ranen smiled and his eyes glazed over for a moment. "She taught us how to fight, how to build our glorious cities, and how important it was to cling to what she had given us." His gaze turned dark. "She warned us, though, that we would be alone for many, many years. The Auri had been warring with each other for centuries. Rebels had gone off on their own to rule the weaker peoples across the universe, pretending to be gods. Elysia's own son was the first Aurume—the Child of Auru—gifted with the ability to control the three elements of fire, water, and air. Before him, races had formed amongst the Auri—the Firestarters, Watergatherers, and Windbringers. They each wanted to rule the others, so El sent one who could rule them all. The Aurume visited us, the Ladeshians, on occasion after his mother died to make sure we were prepared. But after him, no one came. There was a new, unbreakable law in Auru: no contact with outside worlds." He paused, contemplating.

I wasn't ready for him to stop talking, though, so I urged him on. "And what is the Destructor's mission?" The other important detail—the one about me being an Auri, whatever that was—could be broached later. I needed to know as much as possible on this front first.

He looked at me in confusion. "To kill Manoo." His tone added the "of course."

My jaw dropped. This man wanted me to kill a *god*? Was he crazy? I glanced at Malik again. He continued to glare at me. In fact, his whole body seemed to have frozen in place since Ranen had opened his mouth. I still didn't have the guts to look at Meir, but I felt his eyes on me, too.

"Kill… Manoo." I had a hard time wrapping my mind around that idea. It was too much, too crazy. Sure, I'd envisioned it for one fleeting moment once, but that didn't mean I was even remotely capable of carrying it out. The man must've lost his mind.

"It's the whole reason for your existence." He was talking quickly now. "El promised to send Manoo's destructor, and you are she. There is no reasoning around it."

"And just how am I supposed to do it?" I shook my head to keep his words from seeping in and turning me into a certified crazy like him. He actually thought what he said made sense.

"Well..." he drawled. "I assume you're a Firestarter. El had said Manoo would be destroyed by Fire, since it was Fire that Manoo chose to use as a servant." He cocked his head. "Have you ever used your ability before? Do you know which element you control?"

I froze the muscles on my face into an emotionless gaze so no one would see the terror surging inside of me. I refused to answer him. There was no way I was going to tell him—in front of Meir, no less—that not only could I control fire, but the desire to do so built with each moment that passed.

But it was Malik who spoke up. "I've seen her use fire... and air."

I whipped my head around at him—the traitor. Oh, he'd seen plenty and he was about to see a lot more.

Meir's arms tightened around me.

"Fire *and* air?" Shock and fear saturated Ranen's tone. "You're the Aurume? The *Aurume*?"

Grudgingly, I ripped my gaze—my burning hate-filled gaze—away from Malik and turned back to the now-shaking little Ladeshian.

"Do you have any idea what this means?" Ranen stood up and started pacing in the little sitting area, growing more hysterical with each step. "The Auri are surely on the warpath now. I'd heard rumors of sightings over the last few years, but I thought they were nothing—just the ravings of the same lunatics who think unicorns live outside their doors." He stopped in front of me and grabbed me by the shoulders. "They'll come here. They'll find you, but you must not go with them. You *must* stay here."

"Enough!" Meir shoved Ranen's arms away and stood in front of me, facing Ranen. "I don't want to hear anymore!"

"Meir..." I grabbed his arm, hoping to calm him down.

"Ranen, you're my best friend, but I can't sit by and let you scare Ella like this." He spoke through his clenched teeth. "Don't you dare tell her what she *has* to do. Or we'll leave."

Ranen looked ready to argue, but with his teeth clenched just as tightly as Meir's, he nodded.

Meir yanked me off the sofa and dragged me out of the room, away from Ranen, away from Malik, away from everything I couldn't stand to face.

CHAPTER ELEVEN:
SHADRA

Meir led me through the second floor of the house to a rather large bedroom that was just as dusty and grungy as the rest of the place. What with being royalty and all, I would've thought Ranen would be able to afford a maid. Malik had stayed with Ranen in the parlor. It had looked like the two of them were eager to talk.

Meir left me alone so he could find room for himself, and so I'd decided to try for a bit of sleep. It'd been quite a few hours since I'd slept, so I was pretty glad to have a moment of peace.

But as I lay on the covers on my bed, sleep eluded me. My mind and body were far past the point of exhaustion, but too many thoughts ran through my head.

Cailen had said something to Olorun about the Auri. Ranen said I was Auri, but not only one of them; I was the Aurume, the Child of Auru, the leader.

Great.

But where were my wings? Or was I gimpy, like Ranen? And what about this ability to control *three* elements? I'd only used two. Should I expect another explosive episode?

I groaned and pressed the heels of my palms against my temples. I was never going to get any sleep. I turned and buried my head in my pillow in a futile attempt to drown out the noises in my mind. It didn't work. They just wouldn't stop.

Someone knocked on my door.

I barely lifted my head from the pillow as I told whoever it was to come in. I wasn't even sure they could hear me, but after a few moments, the door opened and Malik walked through. I sat up.

He looked worn, like he'd been up for days. He ran his fingers down his face, stretching the skin. "May I sit?"

I moved a little to give him room. He sat next to me and then lay down with his hands covering his face. I didn't say anything; I figured he would talk when he was ready.

After a few minutes, though, he still hadn't said anything and I began to worry. I leaned down to look closely at his face. I didn't think he was asleep, but it was hard to tell with his hands in the way. He must have felt me hovering because he moved his hands and looked at me with sad, tender eyes.

"What's wrong?" I said.

He took in a deep breath and then let it out slowly. He smiled. "I was just thinking about something Ranen said."

"Oh."

"But I came here to talk to you about something." He shook his head. "Well actually, I came here to guard you *and* talk to you."

"Guard me?"

He raised an eyebrow at me. "Don't think I haven't noticed those little wheels turning in your head, Ella. I know you're still planning on turning yourself in."

I bit my lip. Why did Malik have to notice everything? "So you're just going to stay in my room from now on? I hope you don't mind the floor."

He chuckled. "No, I don't mind the floor—I've slept on worse." He became serious. "I wouldn't have to do this, though, if I trusted you to do the right thing."

"I'm *trying* to do the right thing," I whispered.

"No, you're trying to do the stupid thing." He propped himself up on one elbow and I leaned away, uncomfortable with the sudden closeness. "Just what do you think is going to happen if I let you do what you want?"

"I know what's going to happen." My chin may have gone up an inch or two as I said that. "I know they're probably going to kill me. I *want* that to happen. You of all people should understand."

He rolled his eyes.

"How can you so easily disregard a human life?" I leaned away from him, itching to be as far away as possible. Where was his honor now? "I *killed* that woman, Malik. How can I go on living knowing there's something inside of me that enjoys hurting people?"

His face hardened. "You don't enjoy it. If you did, I would've agreed with you. But look at how you're beating yourself up,

Ella. You just need to control what's inside of you, not get yourself killed."

I looked down at my hands, away from his watchful eyes. "I don't think I can control it. I've tried, but it's too strong." I looked up. "What if I hurt Meir? How many more people have to die because I chose to leave *Sho'ful*?"

"Don't blame yourself because you wanted a life and the Kofra has done everything in his power to stop that." He shook his head, disgusted. "But answer my question: what do you think is going to happen to you if you go to them?"

I narrowed my eyes at him. I thought I *had* answered that question—I was going to die.

"They won't just kill you," he said, reading my confusion. "You're Shadra. Only one other person in the history of the Fiefdom has been named Shadra, and the ceremony is specific." He shrugged. "Every Mamood knows the story of the Destructor; the one destined to kill Manoo. Of course we know it—we know it better than the Praeori. They say Manoo is terrified of his coming judgment, of the one powerful enough to kill him. He thought he'd found him with the first Shadra. I guess you gave him reason to doubt that assumption." He smirked. "But Manoo's not human; he's spirit. So, the one who can kill him must be utterly destroyed in order to make Manoo safe."

"*Utterly* destroyed?" I felt my pulse quicken.

"The story goes that Manoo will possess the Kofra, strap you down with spiked restraints digging into your neck, wrists, and ankles, and eat you alive. First, he has to cut symbols, spells to trap your soul, all over your body and let your blood leak out— slowly, because you *must* stay alive through as much of it as possible, and then he'll eat you one piece at a time, saving your heart for last."

All the blood drained out of my head. I don't know how I didn't pass out, but I was close to it because the room spun and I swayed. Malik reached his hands out to grab my shoulders and prop me up. I prayed for the numb bliss of unconsciousness, but it didn't come. Instead, I was forced to play Malik's words over and over again in my mind.

Eat me alive. Destroy my soul.

What kind of world had I broken into? How could anyone stand to live like this?

Malik's arms wrapped around me and I felt him pushing me down to lie against the mattress. As soon as my head touched the pillow, I was out.

A thick, steel door stood between me and my predator, but as claws scraped against the cold metal, it didn't seem enough to protect me.

Thud.

Hinges creaked under the weight of the hound as it slammed its body into the door.

Thud.

The room shook under the weight of the beast. I cowered in the corner, my knees pressed against my chest.

Clang.

One of the hinges broke loose and fell to the floor. The hound's savage digging at my door intensified.

Thud. Scratch. Thud.

I pressed myself against the wall. Despite the darkness, I knew the hound would find me. It would never cease in its bloodlust.

Crash.

The door burst open. Red eyes stared back at me from the void.

I screamed as it lunged for me. Foamy lips and sharp teeth wrapped around my neck while razor-sharp claws tore at my belly, spilling my innards.

Flames erupted around me and consumed the beast. Its ear-piercing howls filled the room and spread outward, splitting the void.

I clutched my head and screamed. The flames had vanished and the hound's death throes had ceased—only the memories remained. But still, I screamed. When I finally realized I was in a room in Ranen's home, and not on *Sho'ful*, I clamped my hand over my mouth.

A nightmare. So now even my dreams weren't a refuge.

I whipped my head around, scanning the room for Malik. He wasn't there. I waited to hear footsteps outside my door—surely someone had heard me—but no one came.

I moved my hand away from my mouth and grabbed the back of my moist neck. The room was too dark—I hated it. I didn't ever want to live in the dark again. I leaned over the side of my bed and fumbled with the floor lamp.

Precious light flooded my room. I wrapped my arms around my waist and held tight to control the spasms rocking through my body. Sweat poured out of my limbs, cooling my skin. The goose bumps made my hair stand on end.

I'm not on Sho'ful. I'm not on Sho'ful. I had to say this at least twenty times before my pulse steadied and my breathing calmed. It'd all been so real, though. I could still feel the hound's teeth pressing into my neck, the flames that had burned…

I ripped my covers off and swung my legs over the edge of the bed.

There was no going back to the Mamood—I knew that now. I wasn't brave enough to do what I probably should. Let the universe burn; I wasn't going to become some ego-bloated god's tasty little snack. But if I wasn't going to sacrifice myself, that meant I had a destiny to fulfill. Sure, the details were a little fuzzy and I didn't exactly know what Manoo had done to warrant destruction, but I could guess. If the Mamood god was anything like his followers, he deserved to die. But Manoo wasn't going to give up, I knew that more now than ever before. He would follow me wherever I was. That meant I had to be prepared.

And at that point, I wasn't even close. I could barely hold down my food, walk up a flight of stairs—or across a completely flat surface—without tripping, let alone control the power inside me. How was I going to go up against someone who made heroes a lot more foreboding than me huddle in the shadows in terror? Manoo wasn't someone to take lightly, nor were his followers.

I needed some fresh air. The stuffy room with its clouds of dust hovering in the air weighed me down and I couldn't stand it anymore. I'd had enough of closed spaces and the idea of a nice walk in Ranen's gardens cheered me. I jumped out of bed and rushed out of the quiet, sleeping house. How long had I been out? My aching and rumbling stomach wasn't a good indicator for the passing of time. I'd grown too used to the feeling. The house had been dark before I'd fallen asleep—though it'd been early afternoon—but as I walked through the echoing halls, the oppressive quiet hinted at a late hour.

It wasn't until I stepped through the front entrance and into the chilly night that I realized just how late it had gotten. My eyes instinctively went up. Soltak's moon—an odd shade of green—hung in the center of the sky. So I'd been asleep for a while, then. It didn't feel like I'd been out for more than five minutes.

I stumbled down the front steps and dug my bare feet into the soft, cool turf. I moaned.

There was something odd about the air that I couldn't quite place. The cool breeze brought goose bumps up on my flesh, but my blood was warming, tingling in my limbs. The feeling was vaguely familiar, but I couldn't remember where or when I'd experienced it before. I took a deep breath, letting the air saturate every cell in my body.

I suddenly had this crazy urge to run, not out of fear or a sense of danger, but because I knew that I could. The soft grass beneath my feet called to me and I knew that running across Ranen's rich, green lawns would be the most splendid thing I'd ever done.

I took off and hit a wall. There was nothing in front of me—I wasn't blind—but the air around me constricted and kept me in place. I tried twisting myself out of it, but the wall surrounded me.

I panicked.

My blood started doing something I recognized immediately: tingling. I welcomed it, let it take over my body. I released it before it had a chance to burn and bright blue points of light dotted my vision. The wall around me was one solid blue light, tight and bound together. Rather than breaking it apart, I formed my own wall in the tiny space in front of me and pushed at the solid blue light.

Thunder and lightning ripped through the air as my wall tore at the other wall. I ignored the intense heat and turned to face a cloaked stranger, hiding in the dark.

I ordered the scattered blue lights into a funneled chaos and directed it at him. He stood his ground, untouched. New lights formed in my vision. These I recognized, too. They were red. I swept my hands through the air, calling the red lights to form around my palms. Flames danced around my fingertips. The stranger took a step back and brought his own hands up in defense.

"Ella, stop," he said.

My power stuttered and the tempest died out. I recognized the voice. Cailen pushed his hood back and stepped into the green glow of the moon.

Chapter Twelve:
Questions

"Cailen?" I blinked twice, afraid I was staring at a mirage. My lips stretched into a natural smile and my heart fluttered. Cailen was here. He was real. He was standing right in front of me, although the wings I'd remembered seeing weren't visible. And he felt like home, though I'd never realized I knew what that felt like.

He smiled back at me, his white teeth gleaming against his pale skin.

And then a sudden, irrational anger surged through me. "Why did you leave?"

His face hardened. "It wasn't my plan to leave you there, but something happened and we were called back to my ship."

"What happened?"

Cailen frowned and spoke slowly. "Our King died."

"Oh," I murmured. "I'm sorry." I blushed. My anger seemed very silly now. I shouldn't have felt so slighted because he hadn't taken me with him. It wasn't fair. Not everything could always be about me. "I didn't know."

Anger flashed across Cailen's face for an instant, but he shook it off just as quickly and smiled at me. "How could you have known?"

With a single step, he closed the small distance between us and wrapped his arms around my waist. I curled up against his chest, letting the warmth pass through me, saturate me, make me stronger. An electric current hummed between us, vibrating every cell in my body. There was just something about being around him, something I couldn't put my finger on. Everything about it felt good, but more than that, it felt *right*—like I wasn't really living unless he was there with me.

That tingling sensation I had come to dread swelled in my body, but this time it wasn't at all sinister. Instead of scorching my blood, it seemed to pass through it to Cailen, leaving only pleasant, intoxicating heat.

Cailen's broad hands clenched my back, pressing me closer to him. It wasn't enough for me. I needed more.

I looked up to stare into his eyes and was not at all surprised to see his warm, almost burning, gaze looking down at me. My breath caught as I realized what was about to happen.

He lowered his face to mine and brought his hand up to cup my cheek while his other hand maintained its unbreakable hold around my waist. With the tip of his nose, he caressed my other cheek, moving up and down slowly, teasingly.

I held my breath, waiting for what I knew was going to happen, what I wanted to happen.

With just a slight tilt of his head, Cailen's lips pressed against mine. They were soft and tender at first, moving carefully with my own. But as the electric current crashed through us, I felt his need rise. He pressed me tighter to him and his kissing became urgent, almost rough.

His hand moved from my cheek to the back of my neck, pinning me to him. There it twisted into my hair and formed into a fist.

Every cell in my body hummed. I never wanted it to end. I ached to think it had to. No, it wouldn't end—I'd make sure of it. Except...

I ripped away from him, gasping for air. Stupid, ridiculous air. When I tilted my head back up, searching for his lips, they were gone.

Cailen pulled away, chuckling.

I sighed. So much for never ending.

He brushed my hair away from my face. "I've missed you so much."

I scrunched my nose, giddy and drunk with it all. "How did you find me again?"

"The same way we found you the first time." He laughed.

I waited for more, but he didn't finish. "You're going to have to explain a little better than that."

"I wonder how much you can handle, though."

My heart dropped into my stomach, and I turned away. "Trust me. I've gone through a lot these last few days." My voice shook. "I doubt there's anything that will surprise me anymore."

Cailen was instantly anxious. He grabbed my hand to turn me around and stroked my face. "What's wrong? What happened?"

His concern surprised me and sent the tears pouring—stupid, traitorous tears. I wiped them away before they could run down my cheeks, but I knew my eyes were red and swollen and there was no hiding *that*. "It's nothing." My voice broke and I knew he'd hear the lie.

"Ella, tell me."

I shook my head.

His hand cupped my cheek. "Please."

That electric current coursed through my blood at his touch again. It charged my blood and made my head swim. I couldn't think, much less feel anything but the current of pure warmth pulsing in my veins. He wrapped me in his strong, capable arms. I tucked my face into his chest and released the stress of the past three days in the downpour of my tears. His cloak was soaked within a matter of seconds. "I don't know who I am anymore. So much has happened and I don't know how to deal with it." I didn't know why I trusted this boy, who was by all rights a stranger. I didn't know why I felt completely and utterly at home—safe—with him. Maybe because, deep down, I knew he wasn't a stranger. He was the boy who'd stayed with me in my memory throughout all the years of my captivity.

Cailen didn't say anything. He just rubbed circles on my back and pressed his cheek against the top of my head. His silence comforted me. I knew I could talk to him, tell him everything. "When I left *Sho'ful*, I thought… well, I didn't know what to think. To be honest, I didn't put much thought into my escape, but I definitely did *not* think I'd start shooting fire and air out of my hands, and that some crazy little man would say I'm some prophesied Destructor, or that I'd have to worry about not killing people when sometimes that's all I want to do…" I let the words trail off. Something was wrong. The muscles in Cailen's arms tightened around me and I was immediately ashamed. I'd admitted to being a monster, the worst kind.

He grabbed my shoulders and pushed me away just a little. One of his hands rested under my chin and tilted my face up to look at him. His tight, narrowed eyes studied me for what seemed like forever. I grew uncomfortable under his gaze and tried to pull away, but his hand under my chin would not let me go. Eventually his green eyes softened and he smiled.

I exhaled. I hadn't realized until then I'd been holding my breath.

Cailen released me and backed away. He left me feeling slightly dizzy from the lack of oxygen and intense inspection, and completely alone and isolated with the distance he put between us.

His eyes flickered to my chest. "I'd like to talk to this 'crazy little man.'" All trace of his smile was gone, replaced with a cold, uncaring stare.

"Oh... well..." I shook my head to clear my thoughts. "I think he's sleeping." I gestured toward the house with its dark windows. I was a little confused and very overwhelmed. The abrupt change in Cailen's demeanor was staggering. He was being... careful, as if he knew I was a bomb about ready to go off. "At least, I didn't see him when I was in the house."

Cailen nodded. "It's late."

"Would you like to come in and wait until the morning?"

"I didn't want to stay that long. And..." He let the thought drift off without finishing.

"Oh." I didn't know what I'd expected, but the disappointment surging through me right then knocked the breath out of me.

"I need to get you home, but I *need* to know what this man knows."

My heart thudded against my chest and my lips pulled up into a wide grin. Cailen wanted me to go with him? But then I thought about Meir and a weight sank into my stomach. I couldn't just leave him.

Cailen frowned and continued, "I guess waiting until the morning won't hurt, if..." he paused and his eyes turned on me, penetrating me, "...if I have your permission to stay and talk to him."

"Of course," I whispered. "I have a *lot* of questions for you, too." And he was going to answer every one of them.

He shook his head and frowned. "Don't you think you should get some sleep?"

"I slept the whole day away." I shrugged, trying to ignore how deeply his sharpness dug.

I don't think my attempt at lightheartedness fooled him because his eyes softened and he reached—slowly, with control—out to brush his hand against my cheek. The electricity at his touch made my head swim. "Okay," he smiled, "I'll answer *some* of your questions."

I led him through the house back to my room. He walked silently beside me, his eyes roving the dark corridors. He stopped once, when we were at the top of the stairs, to look back down at the messy foyer with its books and doodads. After a few seconds, he just motioned for me to continue leading him without a word or explanation. My room was at the end of the second floor corridor on the right of the house. The door stood wide open with all the lights on and pouring out into the hallway. I only remembered turning on the lamp and I had thought I closed the door.

Malik stepped out of the room, the glow from the lights darkening his silhouette. "I leave for a couple of minutes to go..." his eyes flitted to Cailen behind me "...to the bathroom and you decide to escape," he growled. "Didn't you listen to a damn thing I said earlier?"

Cailen stiffened and put one foot forward to stand between Malik and me. I grabbed his arm and moved around him.

"Malik, calm down." I hurried through the words. "I only went out for some fresh air. If I was really escaping, would I have come back?"

He wasn't paying attention to me anymore. He and Cailen stood like two frozen statues, glaring at each other. Even without touching him, I felt the electricity shooting out of Cailen, but it wasn't the same as before. It was sinister, and no longer directed at me.

"Cailen, stop." I grabbed his shoulders and tried to force him to bend down to look at me. When he tilted his head to look at me, his green eyes were burning. "Malik is a friend. He's *my* friend." As I said the words, I realized they were true. How did *that* happen? How did I go from wanting to kill this guy to actually liking him in just two days?

Shock and horror mingled with Cailen's rage. He spoke through clenched teeth. "A Mamood is your friend?"

I ducked my head. "Well, kind of... yeah."

He took a deep breath and returned his raptor gaze to Malik. "What kind of friend growls at a lady?"

I laughed out loud and even I could hear I was on the verge of becoming hysterical. "Oh, that's just Malik. I tick him off a lot."

Malik chuckled behind me. I fought the urge to relax, though, until I saw Cailen's shoulders drop and his eyes returned to mine.

He exhaled through his nose with his lips pursed. "I'm sorry for overreacting. Let's go into your room. You have questions for me."

"Yes," said Malik. I turned to see his arm extended toward the bright room and a huge grin on his face. "Let's."

So now Malik wanted to be the funny man. I didn't know a Mamood could have a sense of humor, though I failed to grasp just what was so funny about humiliating me. Cailen bristled, but otherwise said nothing as he brushed past the dark man in his robes. I followed behind with my eyes to the floor and blood pooling in my cheeks.

When I walked through the doorway, the huge room felt much smaller than before. I rushed to my unmade bed and sat down with my legs crossed. I didn't exactly know my motivation behind the move. Maybe it was because my mind was running wild with the assumptions I was afraid were going through Cailen's head, and I wanted to hide the messy sheets. Surely he wouldn't actually think that Malik and I...

But when I saw Cailen's face turn a deep burgundy, I knew that he could, and he did. Malik plopped onto the bed beside me and laughed. I whipped my head around and glared at him. The thought of burning him from the inside out flashed across my mind like a dark specter.

With my hands pressed against my temples to force the image out, I jumped off the bed before I did anything too rash and sat down on the floor in front of the fireplace. Cailen took his cloak off, set a bag that'd been strapped across his back onto the floor, and sat next to me. With our backs to Malik, I allowed myself to calm down. I wasn't going to let the Mamood get to me like that again.

The bed creaked behind me and Malik let out a contented sigh as I stared at the empty, and surprisingly clean, fireplace, waiting for my muscles to loosen and the tingle to subside. Cailen seemed content to wait by my side. I caught him sneaking glances my way two or three times, and I was consumed with wonder about what he was thinking.

Calmer, I took a deep breath and looked up at him. He was staring down at me, his green eyes shimmering. There was a hardness to his features that made me think he was still being careful, like he suddenly didn't know how to act around me.

After a while, though, he smiled. "Have you decided against the interrogation?"

I rolled my eyes. That was a good, blasé reaction. I couldn't let him know just how much he was getting to me. "Not exactly." I looked down at my hands. "I'm just trying to decide where to start."

"Start with the simplest and work your way up from there."

Though I desperately wanted to know why he'd come looking for me in the first place, I decided the how was the easiest to answer—it was also the one he'd avoided earlier. "How did you find me?"

His jaw tightened. "I thought I said start with the simplest."

"That is simple!"

"Pick a different one... for now. I'll answer this one later, when you know more."

He was definitely keeping something from me, I was sure of it now. He shifted away from me, making the gap between us wider.

I huffed. It may not have been the most mature thing to do, but I was getting annoyed. "Fine. What happened outside? Why did you attack me?"

He laughed. "I wasn't attacking you, Ella. You were going to run away from me and I didn't feel like chasing you."

"I wasn't running away from you! I didn't even know you were there."

His eyebrows drew down and he frowned. "You mean you didn't feel—" He scooted away another inch and looked away.

"Didn't feel what?"

"Next question."

"You haven't even answered any of the first ones yet!" This was getting ridiculous. He was being too evasive and I wasn't in the mood for it. I wanted answers.

"Cailen, look..." I gritted my teeth and pressed my fists against my thighs. "I already know I'm an Auri—whatever that is—so you can stop with these half-answers that lead to nothing. That little man I told you about only told me enough to make me go crazy with questions, so I would appreciate it if you were straight with me."

He held my gaze, studying me. All he would find was my firm resolve to know the truth.

He sighed. "How much did he tell you about the Auri?"

I smiled. Finally! He didn't look too eager to give away any information, but at least he was willing. "He said we could control the elements: fire, air, and water." I looked down. "He said that one of us could…" I coughed "…control all three."

His eyes darkened. "And?"

"And…" I gulped. I knew where he was going with this. Cailen had seen me using two of the elements earlier that night. He already knew what I supposedly was. "He said that the one who could do all three was the leader, the Aur-something."

"Aurume."

"Yeah, that's it!" I smiled again, trying to lighten his mood. It didn't seem to work.

Cailen closed his eyes. "I didn't want you to know any of this yet. It's too much to throw at a person all at once."

"Like I said, I've gone through a lot these past three days. It was actually a relief to get *some* answers."

He considered this for a second, and then let it go. "What else did he tell you?"

"That was it." Annoying, but true.

"So that's where your questions for me come in, I take it." Cailen chuckled. It was beautiful, perfect, and sent the electricity humming.

It was hard for me to think past the numbness in my head, so I just nodded.

"All right." He shook his head with a smirk. "If you think you can handle it, I'll give you your answers."

"Thank you."

A playful growl escaped his lips and he inched closer to me. "Auri are pretty good at finding each other because we know what we're looking for, and," he raised an eyebrow, "we're not like other humans."

Malik scoffed.

I rolled my eyes at the both of them. "I kind of guessed the being different part already."

He ignored me. "We emit a certain radioactive signature all the time, though it's stronger when we use our ability. We couldn't find you for years because some type of shielding must've been blocking your signature, but we picked it up three days ago."

"*Sho'ful*," I murmured.

"What?"

"I was on *Sho'ful*." I bit my lip. "It was a prison ship."

"Hmm… interesting." He didn't sound very interested; he sounded mad. "Well, when we picked up your signature, we went straight for the planet you were on, but you were gone by the time we got there. It was very dangerous for us to enter the Mamood-controlled territory because we knew their sensors would pick up our ships, but we didn't know how long our chance would last, so we ignored our law and followed you."

"So why didn't you take me with you when you found me?"

His teeth snapped together. "Stupid rules made years ago stopped us. I would've broken them if I'd known what Olorun and Leor were doing."

"What rules?" And why would they apply to *me*?

Cailen stared at the empty fireplace for several minutes. I was about to prod him—thinking he'd chosen to ignore me—but he turned back to me and said, "Do you remember what I told you about our King?"

"That he died." I reached out to comfort him when he lowered his eyes to his lap. "I'm so sorry, Cailen. I can see how upset you are. Did you know him personally?"

He looked up again and guilt, or fear, stared back at me. "Ella… the King… he was your father."

I gasped. "My father?" And then it all clicked together. All the clues that should've been terribly obvious from the moment I'd heard them rushed to the forefront of my mind. I was an Aurume, the one who could control all three elements, the only one who could rule the Auri. The King was dead—my father was dead.

"How many Auri are born with the ability to control the three elements?" I whispered.

His voice was grave. "Only one every generation. And only to your family."

"Only one." I swallowed the lump in my throat. "Great."

"That's why we couldn't take you. As the ruling Aurume, we need your express permission to transport you. And with that man waking up, we were in danger of being discovered." He growled. "Stopped by our own stupid rules."

"Uh-huh."

Cailen was clearly too caught up in his own self-loathing to see that I was falling into hysterics. My body bent over as I clutched at my waist. I gasped at the air, but not nearly enough entered my lungs.

"Ella?" Malik's anxious voice came from close behind me. "What's wrong with her?"

A pair of arms wrapped around my middle and pulled me up so I was standing. If it weren't for those strong limbs carrying my weight, I would've fallen back to the floor.

"Shh...It's okay," Cailen whispered in my ear. He muttered something under his breath, too low for me to hear.

Was everything okay, though? At that moment, not even close. The expectations kept piling up around me. I wondered if whoever was in charge was having a good laugh at my expense. It made me angry to think my life had become a joke. As if one surprise weren't enough, let's keep adding it up to see how long it takes Ella to really go nuts.

But at that moment, my mind could think with more clarity than it ever had before. It surprised me, actually, the way all the details fell into place and how I began to think through them. I didn't *have* to be any of these things—Shadra, Destructor, Aurume—and I didn't have to run away from them, either. I could do what I wanted; it was in my control. And suddenly, I knew that I *could* do them—that they weren't too much for me.

A thick headiness swept over me and I felt with perfect understanding the strength I possessed. The monster inside me hungered for Manoo's demise. Nothing else mattered.

My breathing slowed and my legs took some of the weight off Cailen's arms. I took in a deep breath and raised my gaze to him. He stared down at me, his green eyes anxious and flicking across my face.

"I'm fine," I said. It was truer then than ever before. Peace coursed through my blood, mingling with the numbness already there. The electric current from Cailen's touch pulsed through me like oxygen, strengthening my muscles and healing me from the inside out. I *was* fine, more than fine—I was strong.

CHAPTER THIRTEEN:
CAILEN

"So tell me more," I said as we sat back down on the floor and Malik returned to lying on the bed. Even before Cailen could answer, the Mamood's soft snores and heavy breathing filled the room.

Cailen's eyes narrowed. "Are you sure you can handle more? Don't you want to space this out?"

I laughed without humor. "I'm hoping the big stuff is out in the open now. Everything else is just filler, unless you have some more bombshells to throw at me."

He smirked. "No more bombshells."

"Good."

"So what else do you want to know?"

The one thing I really wanted to know was what was up with his attitude. Why was he being so cold and aloof all of a sudden? And why had he kissed me—my heart stuttered just thinking about it—if he was going to treat me like a pariah two seconds later? But I wasn't brave enough to ask those questions. Not yet. So I decided to keep it simple—and impersonal. "Tell me about the Auri—their history."

"*Our* history," he clarified.

I nodded sheepishly. It was going to take some time to get used to the idea that I belonged to anyone, especially anyone so magical, so straight out of a dream.

He pursed his lips, thinking. After several minutes, he folded his hands in his lap and leaned forward. "The story goes that El, Himself, taught us how to manipulate the elements. He was the one to give us our wings. Before that, we were just regular old humans. This was thousands of years ago, long before anyone in the galaxy even knew there were other planets and other humans living on them." He smiled at me. "The Auri were the ones to change all that."

"How?"

He shrugged. "We were pretty technologically advanced at the time of the transformation, but we weren't anywhere close to developing ships capable of traveling deep into space. Transporting took away the need. With a thought, we could travel from one point in space to another.

"Being explorers at heart, we wasted no time in our search for more life. What we found shocked us. The first explorers came home with tales of other *humans* living on dozens of lush, fertile planets.

"Oh, the plans those first ones had," he said wistfully. "We were to reach out to the other civilizations, make peace, and offer them our aid." He paused. "From what the first explorers had seen, those other humans had not yet reached our level of technology. We were to be heroes."

His face darkened and he continued in a low, foreboding voice, "The wars hadn't started yet, but the tension was already palpable. The Auri had separated into three distinct groups: the Salames, the Sylmes, and the Undinmes."

"What were they?" I whispered. Cailen's solemn tone was catching.

"Most know them better as Firestarters, Windbringers, and Watergatherers."

"Oh." I remembered Ranen talking about the wars among the three races. He had sounded nearly as solemn as Cailen did now. Those days must've been horrible.

Cailen looked past me with his eyes glazed over. He was somewhere else, thinking of things I couldn't imagine. "Our governments crumbled under the increasing tension and millions died even *before* the official Firestarter attack. Poverty and crime chipped away at our society and exploration was officially halted. How they thought they could have prevented people from transporting, I can't imagine." He shook his head in disgust.

"When the Firestarters *did* attack there was hardly anyone left, and those were mostly..." he cleared his throat and looked away, "...children. In a way, the coup saved us," he continued quickly. "The Firestarters were ruthless in their bid for power over the other two Auri races. They enslaved the Watergatherers and Windbringers and controlled their populations. But at least there was some order.

"Generations passed and eventually the slaves revolted. The wars had started again." He sighed. "By this point, thousands of Auri had escaped their bondage and were living on other planets. Some Firestarters who weren't in power had left, as well. Though most tried to blend in and live alongside the regular humans, some pretended to be gods and ruled whole planets. There's one in particular who committed such travesties and led so many astray, her name has become reviled among the Auri." Cailen shuddered, and then spit out the name like it was a curse. "Morgan. She began the Order of Fae'ri."

"Fae'ri?"

"It's from our ancient tongue. 'Fae' is the word for idols, or gods. Fae'ri directly translates to 'Auri gods' in the common language."

"Oh." I didn't know what else to say to that. Part of me—maybe a shadow of a memory—cringed just hearing the name.

"Eventually," he continued after a short pause, "we were saved from ourselves." Light sparkled in his eyes. His sudden change in emotion was catching and sent little flutters of expectation in my stomach. "El sent us the Aurume: the Child of Auru—Elsden. He was the first Auri ever with the ability to manipulate all three elements."

"Ranen told me about him." I smiled like I was in on some special secret.

"Yes, Elsden—the son of Elysia the Watergatherer and Zuruk the Firestarter. No one thought such a union could be possible—with Firestarters being so... temperamental, you see. At first, most thought Elsden's abilities came from his mixed parentage, but when his brother was born only a Firestarter, they knew El must've had something to do with it.

"Everyone loved him and he rose to power easily. None of the three races had any qualms about listening to his orders." He paused. "It took years to gather all the Auri from across the many galaxies, but eventually he did and he instituted the new law of isolation. Everyone agreed and swore never to transport off the planet. Those who broke their vow were hunted down and killed swiftly—an example to others.

"With transport so limited, our pursuit of technology resumed. Eventually, we were able to build our spaceships and travel the more conventional way—all under the Aurume's permission, of course. We still didn't reveal ourselves to other humans," he shrugged, "but we watched from a distance, gathering information and increasing our knowledge."

I sighed. It was all so sad, not magical like I'd thought. Their gift from El had become a curse in so many ways, much like His gift to me: the Destructor—the one powerful enough to stop Manoo. Perhaps others would've given up everything to have such power—not me. I could already feel the monster breaking my will to be good. Who knew how much longer I could fight back the darkness rising inside me?

Several minutes passed before I noticed Cailen had stopped talking. I'd become too swept away with visions of rogue Auri using their abilities to dominate the universe. How could anyone have fought against them? Would they even have wanted to? These beautiful, unstoppable beings who could appear out of thin air—their claims of divinity would have been easy to believe.

"And so it was peaceful after that? After Elsden?" I needed to know the monster could be beaten.

"For the most part, yes." Cailen pursed his lips. "No one's ever forgotten the wars or the devastation they caused, but there are some who pop up every few generations who believe we should reclaim our hold on other humans, reclaim our godhead."

"That's disgusting." *And yet...*

"Yes, it is."

I tried to imagine what it would've been like to grow up on Auru, to have the horrors of the wars drilled into me, or to be raised to believe I was something greater than *other* humans. I couldn't. For as long as I could remember, I thought I *was* a regular human being—not something great, or special. Not something even close to being as amazing as Cailen.

But Cailen did grow up on Auru. He had a life there that didn't include me. It felt like my life had just barely begun and Cailen was already an important part in it. There had been no life on *Sho'ful*, only a hint of existence. I'd been alive, but not living.

I needed to know more about Cailen. I needed to live vicariously through his memories to reclaim some hold on my Auri self.

"Tell me about you. What was it like growing up on Auru? What did you do there?"

He laughed out loud, his eyes sparkling. "That's a lot of questions."

Warm blood flooded my cheeks. I looked away for a second, but turned back to him with pleading eyes.

"Hmm…" He pursed his lips. "You want to know about me… It's a long story," he warned.

"We've got all night and I'm not even close to being tired."

Cailen chuckled. "You know, you haven't changed a bit. You were always so curious when you were little, too."

"Really?" I crinkled my nose. The idea that Cailen had any memories of me from so many years ago was strange, and sweet. I liked that there was someone out there who actually knew me—the me before the Mamood.

He sighed and leaned back on his elbows. "Exactly the same." He smiled. "You even wrinkled your nose like that whenever I said something you particularly liked."

"You're changing the subject. We're supposed to be talking about you." I bit the inside of my cheek to rein in the giggles that threatened to burst past my lips.

"Ah, that's right. Well, after you were—" his eyes darkened "—taken… my father enrolled me into the training academy in Freor. I begged him to, actually. It's an elite facility located in the eastern Firestarter territories. Those who actually manage to live through the training have every door open to them, every top post at their disposal." He shrugged. "I was the right age—eleven—so he made some contacts and I was tested. The tests were grueling—meant to find the best out of those who only *thought* they were good enough—and I passed. My mother was furious for obvious reasons."

I bit my lip and cocked my head. Cailen saw my look of confusion and clarified. "Very few people actually live through the training. Out of my graduating class, for example, over two hundred started with me and only four were left eight years later."

"That's awful!" I felt my face turn down in horror. "Why would they even have such a place?"

"It's a part of who we are, Ella. The Firestarters, especially. They're obsessed with the art of war, and always have been." He smirked. "The fainthearted do *not* try to get into this particular academy. There are other military academies whose failures simply go home as such. At the one I went to, they die." His face turned smug as he continued, "I was the first Windbringer in over a century to graduate."

I choked back the bile building up in my throat. "It just seems so wrong."

"The ones who sign up know what they're doing. They know they probably won't live."

"They're children, Cailen!" My hands shook at my side. "How can they know?"

His green eyes went flat. "I knew."

I opened my mouth to say something, but nothing came out.

"Anyway, after eight years of intense training in deserts—the hot *and* the cold kind—at the edges of volcanoes, in places so remote and deadly that half the class died in them alone, I graduated and took over command of the battleship, *Aurora*. That was two years ago, and I've been looking for you ever since."

I really looked at Cailen for the first time then. Though I knew time had passed, it was hard to differentiate the man from the boy I remembered. Yet, as he told me his story, I became increasingly aware of his sheer physical size. He wore a sleeveless shirt that stretched tight against the broad planes of his chest. The curves of his muscles wrapped around his limbs in perfect proportion to his height. There was something different about him, though, that I hadn't noticed before. I couldn't figure out what it was, and it nagged at me.

I tore my eyes away from his chest… his arms. "Why you? Surely there was someone looking for me before you, so why did you take over?"

Cailen leaned back all the way and put his hands behind his head. "That one's not so easy to answer."

I waited with my knees curled up against my chest. After several minutes, it was clear he wasn't sharing any more than that. I decided now was the right time to ask my most pertinent question. I bit my lip and leaned forward so he was forced to look at me. "Why are you here? And why are you acting so careful, like you're afraid? What is it you're not telling me, Cailen?"

He stared at me for an immeasurable moment, motionless.

"You've got another bombshell for me, don't you?" I whispered. The truth of it slapped me in the face. He didn't even have to answer me, I already knew.

Cailen nodded.

"But you're not going to tell me." It wasn't a question. It was clear on his face the time for answers was over.

He shook his head.

I fumed and stormed off to the other side of the room. I needed space between us, and the huge bed acting as a barrier helped me to keep my head. I hated the secrets, the lies. He had said no more bombshells and here was another one not an hour later, one he was determined to keep from me.

Malik was passed out on the bed—my bed—still snoring softly, and completely oblivious to my mini-tantrum. For some reason, that made me even angrier. It was totally childish and ridiculous, but I didn't care. I stomped my foot on the floor and slumped to the ground, trying to make as much noise as possible. His heavy breathing didn't even stutter.

I took in a few deep breaths, trying to calm myself. There was no reason for me to be as angry as I was. No reason except that Cailen was keeping secrets from me. No reason except that I couldn't be alone in *my* room, lie down on *my* bed...

So it was totally ridiculous for me to behave in such a manner, fuming like a two-year-old. That little fact didn't stop me from doing it.

I twisted my body around to lie on my stomach with my chin resting in my hands. My two irritants were behind me. Neither one was easy to ignore. The electricity humming between Cailen and me didn't lessen with this little distance and Malik's raspy breathing grated against my ears. So I started humming to myself. It was a meaningless little tune that I composed on a whim, but it helped.

Eventually, I was able to look past my irritation. Cailen was being careful and secretive, distant, but maybe he was doing it for my sake. I couldn't imagine why or how he could think that attitude would help me, but I tried to understand. Thinking his feelings were indifferent, or even malevolent, wasn't helpful; I refused to travel down that line of thought. And if he was doing it for my sake, what secret was he keeping that would be so awful? Weren't the other ones bad enough to make anything pale in comparison?

I shook my head. This was something big, and it involved Cailen directly. He'd been willing, if not eager, to answer my questions until I asked him why *he* was the one searching for me, and what he was keeping from me. As soon as that question was out, he'd shut up.

I growled, and then took a deep breath.

I knew what I had to do. There was one key detail missing that would connect everything together. I was sure of it. Cailen had all the knowledge, so I would have to be sneaky and pry it out of him. The last thing I needed was for Cailen to close up on me again. Begging him to tell me would never work. I'd already gotten a firsthand glimpse into how stubborn he could be. This was a secret he would never willingly tell me.

Chapter Fourteen:
Decision Time

A salty and absolutely mouthwatering aroma drifted down the hall toward me as I found my way to the kitchen the next morning with Cailen trudging behind me. He wasn't overly excited about spending the morning with Meir, Ranen, and Malik. In fact, his balled fists and clenched jaw were enough to set me on edge right along with him. Though I'd apparently given my permission the night before for him to break the Auri law of no contact with other peoples, he'd explained that years of holding that law sacred made him feel like a traitor for breaking it now. I had tried to reassure him that everything would be fine and that, in fact, *I* had been the first one to break it, but he waved that off as something I couldn't have helped.

It was rather comforting to know that some of his edginess and distance the night before could be attributed to his unease around Malik. Still, I knew that wasn't the only explanation and I intended to stay by his side to find out the truth.

I pushed open the kitchen door and dropped my gaze to the floor with a hint of a smile on my lips. Red-hot embarrassment flooded my cheeks as I realized that standing right behind me was a guy—a very cute guy. Meir was staring at me and by his eager and slightly possessive expression, I could tell Malik had already informed him of our newest guest.

Cailen stepped even closer behind me—I could feel his hot skin against my bare arms—waiting to enter. Ranen was wide-eyed and practically jumping where he sat. Clearly the man had issues. I shuffled forward, my eyes still on the stone floor, and took an empty seat next to Meir at the round, wooden table.

Ranen started shoveling some type of yellow, lumpy food onto a plate. "You look like you could use plenty of this." He chuckled.

"Thanks." I grabbed a fork to pick at my food. I wasn't going to make the same mistake twice. Sure, I was hungry, famished even, but I'd learned my lesson. I needed to pace myself.

He laid three strips of cooked meat—the source of the absolutely delicious scent that had led me to the kitchen in the first place—on my plate with some slices of bread. I grabbed one of the strips and nibbled. It sent my taste buds dancing, and I forgot about pacing myself.

Cailen sat between me and Malik and started loading up his own plate. His back was ramrod straight and his movements stiff.

Meir was still staring at me. I turned to him and smiled, hoping that would be enough to calm his anxiety. He gave me a hesitant smile in return. His eyes flicked from me to Cailen, and I could see the questions hiding under the surface of his erratic gaze.

I decided I needed to open up that line of conversation. There was no point in delaying the inevitable. I swallowed the food in my mouth, cringing as it scraped against my throat. "Meir, Ranen, this is Cailen. He's... uh..." I looked to Cailen for help. Was I allowed to call him an Auri in front of them? What was I supposed to say?

He smiled at me, and then extended his arm out to the two older men. "I'm an old friend of Ella's. And..." he continued slowly, with reservations, "I guess the head of the search party."

Ranen nodded. He pumped Cailen's hand with much more enthusiasm than was necessary and was slow to let go. Cailen tried to be subtle in his attempt to remove his hand from the crazy little man's grasp, but eventually he just had to yank it away.

Meir was... apprehensive. He accepted Cailen's offered hand, but dropped it again after one quick shake. "An old friend?" He raised an eyebrow and cocked his head.

I didn't think it was possible, but Cailen's body stiffened even more. He leaned away from me and set his fork down. I added this reaction to my list. I didn't think it was the detail I was looking for, but it was possibly related.

"Friend of the family, actually." Cailen's voice was rough and offered no opening for further explanation.

I cleared my throat. "He… uh… actually wanted to talk to you, Ranen." I peeked at Meir out of the corner of my eye. He angled his body toward me with one arm on the table and the other on his knee. I stuffed more food into my mouth and looked away.

Ranen's eyes brightened. "Of course, of course! I would be honored!"

Cailen gave a sharp nod. "Not here. Somewhere private."

I whipped my head around and glared at him. If he thought he was going to talk about me behind my back, he had another think coming.

He gave a reassuring smile. "Don't worry, Ella. I want you there, too, but," he looked from Malik to Meir, "I'd rather we didn't have an audience."

Malik chuckled, but Meir fumed. I sank down into my seat in some misguided attempt to escape my savior's heated glare. Though he was already a major part of my life, there were some things I preferred he stayed oblivious about. I guessed that whatever Cailen wanted to talk to Ranen about was one of those things. So, I didn't speak on Meir's behalf. I knew he wanted me to, but I couldn't. Eventually, his gaze cooled and he turned back to his half-empty plate of food. I'd need to talk to him privately at some point.

I started nibbling at my food again while everyone else wolfed theirs down. The room was almost oppressively quiet. As the minutes passed, the tension grew like a living thing around me. I stuffed one more bite of the lumpy, yellow food in my mouth and stood.

My wordless request to get the conversation started seemed to work. Cailen and Ranen stood up with me and I followed behind as Ranen lead us through the front foyer. He walked past the doorway to the large parlor we'd been in yesterday and opened the door to a paneled library with shelf after shelf of books behind glass casings. It was shocking how clean this room was. I'd come to expect the dusty mayhem present in every other inch of the enormous estate. Not a speck of dust dotted the furniture, though bright light poured in through the windows. Every book sat in its place, every piece of furniture pristine. A set of finely upholstered blue velvet sofas sat in perfect placement before a fireplace in the shape of a large cat's maw. Wisps of smoke curled up from the burnt and dying embers. A hint of the morning chill caused moisture to bead against the windows, still waiting for Soltak's sun to burn the cold away.

Ranen sat on one of the sofas and gestured for Cailen and me to take the other. Our bare arms brushed against each other as we sat in silence across from the Soltakian. A jolt of electricity hummed through my veins and Cailen inched away from me. I didn't understand the reaction. Whenever I felt the electricity between us that made my blood numb, all I wanted to do was move closer to him, touch him more. I dreamed of his arms wrapping around me, smothering me in the numbing haze. My head swam like someone had drugged me. Before I knew it, my hand was inching closer to graze his. I jerked it back and stuffed it under my leg.

Ranen's far-too-perceptive eyes narrowed in suspicion.

I couldn't be sure, but I thought Cailen shook his head an infinitesimal amount when Ranen turned his gaze on him. Before I could give it much more thought, Ranen leaned forward with his elbows on his lap and a broad grin spread across his face.

"Now talk," he said.

Cailen leaned forward as well, his shoulders tensing as his fists clenched. "What do you know of the Destructor?"

My breathing stopped. I couldn't tear my wide and horrified eyes away from Cailen. This is what he wanted to talk to Ranen about? How did everyone *know*?

"She's the one meant to issue El's judgment upon Manoo, ending the reign of evil in this universe once and for all."

Cailen's gaze hardened. "What else do you know?"

Ranen's eyes flicked to me for an instant. He gulped. "Well, it's not entirely certain if she, uh, lives through the experience."

My held breath came out in a whoosh. I struggled to find my voice, but my question was little more than a squeak. "What?"

Ranen readjusted himself on the couch and spoke quickly. "Well, there's some doubt on that point, you see. It's not really discussed much in the old prophecies. There may be a line or two in some of the more obscure papers about how 'under flame and smoke, the two will be consumed,' but that doesn't necessarily mean you... or if it does, that you will die."

"How could it not?" My squeaky voice somehow rose up an octave.

"Well, there are passages that indicate an accomplice for Manoo, and many scholars in my family theorized that perhaps he was the one the quote was referring to. Or!" He raised a finger, pausing to make sure I was listening. "It could have been referring to the man whom Manoo will possess during the rite of the Shadra... if it gets that far. Which we hope it won't because, well, the prophecies imply that there won't be much hope for you if it, um, goes along that path."

"Wait a second." I held up my hand. "This isn't a sure thing? I might not actually win against Manoo?"

Cailen's piercing gaze turned on me while Ranen fidgeted with his shirt sleeve. "Well...no." He sighed. "You see, this is the turning point. Either you win and evil is destroyed, or you lose and Manoo is allowed free reign for an unconfirmed number of years. Possibly forever." He brightened. "Though I can't imagine El would actually let that happen."

I stared at Cailen. He looked back at me with an unfathomable expression. I might not win, and even if I did, I probably wasn't going to live. This seemed like a sick mockery of my previous whim of self-sacrifice. It was one thing to give up my own life under my own power; it was quite another to know I had no choice.

"Everything must happen just so," Ranen continued. "Though no one really knows how that is supposed to be. Hopefully, though, we have a few years to prepare you before Manoo discovers who you are and names you Shadra. That's the catalyst. Once you're named, everything will be set in motion."

Could someone's heart stop beating and still keep them alive? Because it felt like every last cell and organ in my body had just frozen in place.

"How do you know Ella is the Destructor?" Cailen was speaking to Ranen, but he didn't tear his eyes from me.

"The locket—the red and orange flower symbol of the Destructor." Ranen's tone was wistful. "It was left by Elsden to be found by the Destructor alone. There are stories that El left a message for the One within its locked compartment."

Like a reflex reaction, my hand went up to the locket around my neck. "But I didn't find this," I said, staring at Cailen. "You did."

He shook his head...slowly. "No. You found it the day you were kidnapped. As soon as I saw it in your hands, I knew what it was and convinced you to give it to me." He looked away. "I was trying to protect you."

I didn't remember any of that, and suddenly I was angry. What had the Mamood done to me? Why couldn't I remember anything? I'd been seven, for crying out loud! I should have remembered *something*! "Why can't I remember?" I said that much louder than I needed to, but I didn't care. Fury broiled in my veins.

Cailen rubbed a path along my arm. "Ella, you went through a lot of trauma. Maybe your mind shut down to protect itself. You just escaped. Give it time."

Did that make sense? Maybe. I *had* been using my dreams to escape—I'd always known that. Maybe I'd subconsciously forgotten my past to keep it separate from my hellish present. Well, my dreams had been an escape up until last night. A shudder passed through me as I thought of the hound's jaws around my throat. I remembered my hand on the locket, so close to my neck, and dropped it to my lap. "Why did you give it back?" My voice was barely above a whisper.

"Because I had to live ten years without you, and I always blamed myself. I swore that if I found you, I wouldn't deny your destiny again."

So Cailen did care. He cared more than he wanted to let on. His face looked tender, sweet, and less guarded than usual. But an undercurrent of agony lay just underneath the surface. My heart swelled, almost painfully so, and I ached to wrap my arms around him.

However he felt, it was pretty clear he wanted distance between us, and I was far too timid to be the one to breach the wall he'd built. Besides, there was something far more important that needed to be clarified. Cailen and Ranen needed to know.

"Manoo's already named me Shadra," I murmured. "He did it right before I escaped."

Before I even had a chance to register their reactions, a ball of flames exploded from the maw of the fireplace, curling in waves and coming right toward me.

CHAPTER FIFTEEN: WAR

"No!" In one quick movement, Cailen stood up and thrust his hand against my chest, pushing me back. The sofa rolled on top of me.

I was stuck on my back with my body all curled in on itself. I tried to move, but the sofa pinned me down. Flames roared around me. I could barely hear Ranen's squeals of panic above the ear-splitting thrumming as the fire consumed and sucked at the air.

Something started grabbing me. Invisible fingers pulled at the sleeves on my dress, dragging me along the floor. I managed to straighten my legs out, so I kicked at the sofa and twisted my body around.

Smoke hovered inches above my head and scorching heat prickled the skin on my back. I rose to my knees and crawled away from the flames. Ranen was ahead of me, leading the way.

But where was Cailen?

I twisted my head around, squinting my eyes at the blast of heat. Cailen still stood in front of the fireplace. Flames swirled around him as tendrils ripped through his wall of air.

"No," I whispered.

My blood began to tingle and I knew it was only a matter of seconds before those roaring flames would have to bend to my will. If only Cailen could hold on that long.

A tendril of flames whipped out and smacked Cailen against the chest. He retreated a step, but held on. I crawled toward him, preparing myself for when the red points of light would appear in my vision.

Ranen wrapped his bony fingers around my ankle and yanked me away. I dug my nails into the wood floor, but he was too strong.

The flames rose above Cailen and slammed down on him. I knew in an instant that he couldn't recover from that kind of attack.

"No!" I sucked at the air, preparing to lunge away from Ranen's restraining fingers and toward the consuming flames. The smoke burned my throat.

Ranen had a grip on both my ankles and pulled me out of the room with one final heave. When I was clear of the doorway, he jumped up and pushed a keypad. A metal door slid closed in front of me, cutting off my vision of the burning flames as they consumed Cailen.

I clutched at my chest and screamed.

"Shh!" Ranen's face hovered inches above mine. "It's here for *you.*"

"I could've stopped it! I was so close! I could've saved him!"

Ranen shook his head. "No. That is Fire in there. You aren't strong enough yet."

I fixed my gaze on the smooth, silver door. "Cailen."

The keypad chirped and Ranen punched in some kind of code. The door slid open and as it did water poured out of the library, soaking me.

Two sets of footsteps pounded on the floor behind me. "What's wrong? What happened?" Meir's voice clenched with anxiety. It was nothing compared to the way my torn and bloody heart burned in my chest.

Someone's hands grabbed at me. I shrugged them away. I needed to see Cailen, if there was anything left of him. I rose to my feet and stumbled forward, too drunk with grief to figure out how to put one foot in front of the other.

The room was a disaster. Scorch marks rose up the walls like shadowy fingers. The sofas were burnt and blackened, the floor charred. And Cailen was... gone. I slipped on a puddle of murky water and my head slammed against the floor. I didn't even have the energy or the will to put my hands behind me to stop the fall.

Tears and pain eluded me.

"There's something over here," Malik said.

My head popped up. Behind the other ruined couch, he crouched over something—something green and blue. I crawled forward as fast as I could, not trusting my feet.

A green and blue cocoon—roughly Cailen's size—lay on the floor. I stroked it with careful, timid fingers. The electric shock that jolted through my bones nearly knocked me onto my back. It wasn't an unpleasant feeling. In fact, it was altogether mind-tingling and euphoric. My muscles jelled into a sweet, hazy mush.

I moaned.

Cailen's wings hadn't been there the night before or even that morning, but they were there now, wrapping him within their velvety folds.

I pulled at the folds where I guessed his head would be; they peeled away without much force. Cailen's face was black and blistered, his eyes shut tight. I choked back a gasp. Malik rubbed my shoulder and pulled me into a hug.

"Is he breathing?" I whispered. I didn't dare check myself.

Malik leaned slightly forward with me still in his arms. "Yes."

I let out a deep sigh of relief. If he was breathing, he'd be okay. Somehow, I was certain of that fact. And if he was okay, I could live on.

The storm of emotions all roiled underneath the surface of my cool exterior. Now that I knew Cailen was safe, I couldn't let Malik... or Meir... know the depth of my feelings. I was sure they guessed—I hadn't exactly hidden my pain from them just a few moments ago—but I would keep them guessing. At least, until I had any idea of what was going on.

"We need to get him on a bed," Meir said. "And maybe call someone to come over and look at him."

"No!" Ranen and I said at the same time. Whatever Ranen's reason for it, I didn't want anyone poking and prodding Cailen. I didn't understand exactly why, but it just seemed so... wrong.

Luckily, I didn't have to explain this because Ranen spoke up. "I'd like to wait a little while before the presence of the Auri becomes publicly known, my friend. We have no idea how anyone will react."

Meir nodded even though he looked a little unsure.

"Take him up to my room," I said. "I'll keep watch over him. If he gets worse, we'll call someone." I didn't mean what I said—there was no way I wanted anyone touching Cailen except me. And I hated lying to Meir. It felt like rot in my mouth. But telling him a lie was still easier than admitting there was something between me and Cailen. How could he possibly believe me? And how could I possibly explain something *I* didn't even understand? The only thing that mattered now was keeping him close to me. My instincts told me that I *needed* to stay by Cailen.

Ranen agreed—perhaps seeing the lie in my eyes—and Malik and Meir carried the velvety and beautiful, but prostrate form up the stairs and down the hall to my room.

Hours passed as I kept vigil by his side, with no change and no idea of when he would wake up. I was sure he was healing himself. Certain details had clicked into place early on in my watch. I remembered with perfect clarity the events that had taken place on the *Meridian* when he and two other Auri boarded the ship. I had been in severe pain and bleeding, but my wounds had healed almost instantly when Cailen had stood by me. I also remembered the command Cailen had given to one of the Auri about standing near Meir. At the time, I had thought it was to guard him. Now I understood that it was to heal him.

There was something about those wings—something special. Still, it had taken only minutes to heal Meir and me. So far, Cailen had been out for hours.

I didn't know what I'd do without him. There was something there between us, wholly undefined and perhaps indefinable. It wasn't dependent on how much time we'd spent together or how much we knew about each other. Perhaps we didn't even have a choice in the matter. But I knew beyond all reasoning that I belonged with him, and he with me. Whenever he was near me, I felt strong… and whole. Apart from him, I was weak and crippled, unable to even breathe without effort.

Someone tapped on my door. I caressed Cailen's form—luxuriating in the warmth that pulsed through my blood and heated my body—before leaving his side to answer the knock. Ranen stood in the hall holding a tray of food.

I gestured for him to come in, and then returned to my seat by the bed.

"How is he doing?" He handed me a sandwich before setting the tray down on the bedside table.

I rotated the sandwich in my hand, playing with it, studying it, trying to do anything but think about how much the answer to Ranen's question bothered me. "The same," I finally whispered.

"How are you doing?"

His question took me off guard. I took a bite of my food to delay the answer and give me a second to wrap my mind around it. "Worried, mostly." I didn't know how to explain the magnitude of the emotions coursing through me.

"Hmmm…"

"So what happened down there?" I remembered too clearly the moment in the foyer when Ranen said something had come for me. I needed that clarified now.

"The war has started."

I didn't say anything. Nothing could really surprise me anymore. I just nodded my head and took another bite of the sandwich—it was some kind of cold meat and I would've enjoyed it under different circumstances.

"In the first wars," he said, "Manoo enlisted the aid of Fire, and it chose to obey him. The results were devastating. Even after ten thousand years, many civilizations still suffer from the scars." He paused and I felt his eyes on me. I didn't turn my gaze from Cailen to look. "And Fire now serves him again."

"You talk like it's a person, something with a mind."

"It has a certain consciousness, just as the other elements do. It's limited, though, and unable to really think much for itself." He sighed. "Fire is chaotic. It is drawn to those who share the same purpose for destruction. Manoo is, therefore, its perfect master."

"I don't understand. If the elements can choose who controls them, then how can the Auri do what they do? I've used my power before. I've felt fire and air bend to my will; they had no choice."

"El put the Auri in charge of three of the elements. Only *He* controls Earth. Therefore, they must obey you. But Fire is rebellious. In order to control it when it doesn't want you to, you must be stronger. It's a battle of the minds, and no one knows fire better than Fire itself."

"Great." I sighed.

He chuckled. It was nice that he could find the humor in the situation, though I failed to grasp it myself.

"It's not as powerful as you think; it has its limits." He handed me another sandwich when he saw I'd finished the first. "From what Malik has told me, you can form flames out of the heat in the air. Fire can't do that. It needs at least a spark."

I shook my head. "That doesn't make any sense."

"Sure it does." He plucked a strand of hair from my head. I winced and glared at him. "This strand of hair carries your blue-print. Though it's there, and it's *yours*, you can't do anything with it. Put it in the hands of a geneticist, though, and an army of Ellas can be created."

"I guess I see your point… kind of." Fire had limits that I didn't. I needed to find a way to use those limits to my advantage. I couldn't see how, though. If I was right about what Ranen implied, Fire would still be able to take control the moment I put enough of the points of light together to make a flame.

And then I would be dead.

Ranen exhaled in a gust of air. "And now Manoo knows where you are."

I whipped my head around. "How do you figure that?"

"Fire wouldn't have been able to find you without his guidance." He pursed his lips. "Someone must have told him… someone who is working against us."

There was only one person I could think of who knew where I was going and who would be mad enough, hate me enough, to go to Manoo: Pallaton. Malik had been clear on that point.

Right then a siren pealed through the air just as the ground shook and debris pinged against my bedroom window. Engines roared in the sky above the estate.

Manoo had found me. The Mamood had found me.

Chapter Sixteen:
The Mamood are Coming

My wide and terrified gaze flicked to Ranen as another blast shook the palace. I dove for the floor and covered my head. The remnants of my sandwich scattered across the floor.

Meir burst into the room. "There are thousands of fighters outside! The streets are on fire and they destroyed the home next door!"

Engines vibrated the walls in another pass. I held my breath, waiting for the palace to explode around me.

Meir's big hands wrapped around my shoulders and lifted me up. I leaned into his chest and hid my face against his arm. I would've felt safe there with my savior if the weight of my own doomed destiny wasn't crushing in around me. As it was, despite the aura of warmth and strength still emanating from Cailen to me, I had trouble breathing.

More death, more destruction... because of... me.

"We need to get to the bunker." Ranen's clear voice rang through the air even above the mind-numbing roar of the fighters outside. A part of me noted with shock that he wasn't screeching and running around like I'd expected of him. He was perfectly calm and in control of himself as he grabbed one end of Cailen's wing cocoon. "Help me with him."

Meir rubbed my back once more and squeezed me tight before letting go. "Can you handle the weight?" he yelled above the noise.

Ranen patted his left hip and shrugged. "I'll manage. Be gentle with him, though." He nodded toward Cailen. "His wings look fragile enough to tear in half."

I grabbed Cailen's cloak and bag and went on ahead of them to hold the door open. Another blast shook the house, knocking me into the wooden frame. They brushed past me with the co-cooned form in their arms as I pressed my body against the door, both to give them room and to stay on my feet. Ranen's limp was worse as he struggled under Cailen's weight, but he kept up with Meir.

I stayed by their sides, pressing my hands against the smooth marble walls, as we moved through the back part of the house to the servants' quarters. At least, I assumed from the narrow, plain halls that they were intended for servants.

Ranen led us down steep, narrow stairs that opened into the pantry off the kitchen.

"Ella, get the door." I could barely hear Ranen's strained voice above the roar that seemed to get louder with each passing second, but I understood what he wanted when he nodded toward a wooden door at the end of the stuffed room.

I squeezed past them, knocking down jars and sacks of food along the way. The overcrowded room reminded me of something.

I spun around to face Ranen and Meir. "Wait! Where's Malik?"

Meir readjusted his load. "He went out for a run."

My breathing stopped. "He's outside?" I screeched.

"Don't worry." Meir grunted. "He knows how to take care of himself. He'll find his way back to us."

I stood there, dumbfounded and unable to pull my jaw up. What was Meir thinking? We needed to go and find him. How was Malik supposed to find this bunker Ranen was talking about? He would be stuck out there, unprotected.

"Ella, please!" Ranen sagged with his hands nearly to the floor. "The door."

I bit my lip and turned around. It felt wrong to leave Malik to fend for himself, but I knew there was very little I could do about it at the moment. Ranen strained under his load and, I was sure, was quite eager to get to safety before the walls of his home fell on top of us.

I grasped the knob—it was warm—and pulled the door open an inch. I peeked out to see what was going on before we made a run for wherever Ranen was going to take us. The black sky was lit up with thousands of fighters zooming past us like meteors. Warning sirens blared in my ears and heat scorched my skin. Ranen's lawn was on fire.

Fire.

My eyes popped wide and I slammed the door closed.

"What's wrong?" Meir grew anxious as he assessed my trembling body.

I turned my gaze on Ranen as I answered Meir. "There's fire everywhere."

Ranen gritted his teeth and dropped Cailen's legs. "Can you carry him yourself, my friend? I'm going to need my hands."

Meir set Cailen down and moved around to straddle his waist. With one quick heave and a grunt, he threw him over his shoulder.

"Follow me!" Ranen was ahead of us this time as I trailed behind Meir. "We need to get to the library!"

We picked up our pace and burst through the kitchen door. Pots and pans swung from hooks in the ceiling and clanged against each other with each sway of the palace from the explosions outside. Dust and debris fell in clouds around us. I clamped my hand over my nose and mouth to filter the air.

Sweat trickled down my neck to my spine as the room heated up. Following some kind of instinct, I turned my head around to look back at the door we'd just come through. It flew off its hinges and slammed into the wall just inches from me. I froze.

"Run!" Ranen screamed.

Fire rolled into the room in waves. The air shimmered and the pots melted and warped as the temperature spiked. The flames halted in their pursuit and turned this way and that, like a sentient being... looking for me. It froze and I was certain, somehow, that it was looking right at me. I forced my trembling foot to take a step back. The flames reared up and the roar that pierced the air—a sound filled with rage and hate—made me double over in pain.

And then it came for me. Like a rabid animal foaming at the mouth, it burned through the space between us.

A voice in my head screamed at me to run, to stand up, to do anything but sit there. I couldn't comply; my muscles refused to obey the logical side of my brain, the side that made sense. Instead, the side that was shut down in terror reigned supreme.

Don't move, it said. *Maybe it will be quick.*

My logical side had an argument for that, too. It wouldn't be quick. Manoo didn't want me dead... yet.

A broad hand clamped onto my arm and pulled me up. I obeyed without thinking, running to keep up with whoever had his grasp on me, running to put distance between me and the flames.

We ran through the foyer. I followed blindly behind, trusting the one who guided me. The already dark palace had filled with a thick haze of black smoke, blocking out all vision. I coughed and gasped, trying to force the burning smoke out of my lungs.

My right foot hooked around my left ankle and I stumbled to the floor. The flames roared right behind me. I felt the heat burn through my dress, scorching my skin.

The hand pulled me up again, but this time it pressed with urgency against my back as we continued running. We were losing ground. Sweat steamed off my skin and the precious oxygen that I tried desperately to fill my lungs with was sucked out of the air and replaced with smoke and fumes.

Flames licked my bare feet, burning my skin. I ran faster. We passed the stairway. Just a few more steps…

The hand on my back nudged me and I turned with it. We burst into the library. I kept running, but the hand slid away. I turned to find the one with me; he was nothing but a dark silhouette against the reddish glow of the flames. The door slid closed, blocking out the light. I could see nothing.

"This way." I couldn't tell if the voice was Ranen's or Meir's, though they sounded so different from each other. With my mind barely holding it together in the midst of panic, I wasn't even able to think clearly enough to care.

The hand pushed me to what I guessed was the back of the room before it forced me to pause and then slipped from my body again. There was a dull thud, like when heavy cloth is dropped on a hard surface, and then a shimmer of light.

"Get down there," he said.

I blinked my eyes, forcing them to adjust. Subdued light glowed below me, outlining a set of stairs. I shuffled my foot forward, feeling with my toes for the edge of the first step. The hand grabbed my arm to steady me.

The stairs were ice cold against my skin—uncomfortable after the blazing heat. And it was *hot* in the library. Although Fire seemed unable to get through, the room acted like an oven. I pulled my heavy hair off my neck and slung it over my shoulder. The difference in temperature was minimal, but refreshing.

I went down on tiptoes to avoid as much contact with the frigid metal steps as possible. Meir was at the bottom with Cailen slung over his shoulder, waiting for me. Soft lights glowed off the smooth walls in the narrow hallway. I looked behind me, expecting to see Ranen descending the steps. The olive-toned face and grey eyes that stared back at me made my breath catch.

"Malik!"

"Hey, kiddo." He smiled and brushed against me.

Kiddo? I crinkled my nose. When had Malik actually started liking me enough to use a term of endearment? And why was I practically giddy with excitement over it?

"Shh!" Ranen pushed his way between us and started up the stairs. "Not until the door is closed," he breathed. I whipped my head around. I hadn't even seen him down there.

The door latched with a harsh metallic clang. The tunnel felt eerily quiet after the sounds of the battle outside and the roar of the fire that had chased me through the house. My pulse pounded in my ears.

Ranen pushed past us again and waved us forward. "Follow me."

As we moved through the tunnel, lights along the walls swelled in brightness. Though they didn't do much to penetrate the darkness, I was relieved to be able to see anything at all.

Now that we were safe—at least as safe as we could be—the shocked and unthinking side of my mind decided to take a break. As a result, I was allowed to realize the enormity—and horror—of what was happening outside. Again, like a nightmare that wouldn't let me wake up, death and destruction nipped at my heels. And not just *my* heels. No, because that wasn't enough for them; everyone around me had to suffer, too... again. I couldn't even imagine how many people were suffering now. I'd seen the fighters weaving in and out of formation in the sky, hitting targets below them. I'd felt the shaking ground after each explosion. Co'ladesh was under attack because the Mamood had come for *me*.

We passed an arch in the otherwise seamless hallway. I was the last to step through and when I did, Ranen fingered a keypad on the wall. A thick, metal door slid down from the ceiling with a resounding thud. We passed a few of these before we finally stopped in front of a door that was closed already. Ranen froze with his hand half-raised. We all looked at him, waiting.

Finally, Malik said, "Ranen, what's wrong?"

Ranen shook his head, and then waved his hand in front of a glowing blue screen. The door slid open, revealing a room stocked with folded cots resting against the back wall, a table with four chairs, and piles and piles of fastened trunks. "The palace is destroyed," he said.

Meir shoved past him with Cailen, but I stayed by Ranen's side. "How do you know?"

He ignored me and crossed the length of the small room to another door. I glanced quizzically at Malik, who only shrugged before he went over to Meir to help him with a cot. Ranen was a strange man and I didn't need to waste my time worrying about all his quirky tendencies.

When the old Ladeshian returned with cans of food, I glanced into the room he'd gone into and caught sight of walls and shelves filled with food, clothes, blankets, and other necessities. Well, at least he knew how to prepare.

When Malik finished setting up the cot against the wall, Meir laid Cailen down. He pressed his hand against his lower back and stretched, and his spine cracked and popped.

I set up my own cot and slid onto the hard but strangely squishy fabric. How that worked, I still have no idea.

Something crashed to the floor, making me jump. A long stream of curses poured out of Ranen's mouth from the storeroom. I looked to Meir—maybe he knew what'd happened—but he just shrugged.

"Get out of here!" Ranen yelled. A tubby orange-and-white cat flew through the air past the storeroom door and landed lightly on its feet.

Suddenly, I didn't feel so safe. If some animal had found a way into Ranen's seemingly impenetrable underground bunker, what would stop Fire or the Mamood soldiers?

Meir laughed. "Still haven't gotten rid of this thing, huh?"

Ranen came out with a shallow bowl and set it on the floor. "There. Eat that. But leave our food alone!" He looked up at Meir with a worn expression. "I brought him down here a few weeks ago after he ripped a hole in my favorite chair. I guess I didn't think he would be so resourceful in finding my food."

Intrigued, I got up from my cot and went to sit by the cat, who was now happily devouring the hard little kibbles in his dish. I stroked his long fur and his throat started to rumble.

"What's his name?" I murmured.

"Fluffy Nuts."

Malik started coughing. "What?" he choked out between gasps.

"Fluffy Nuts." By Ranen's tone, I guessed he was just as confused about Malik's reaction as I was. "I named him that because of a condition he had as a kitten: elephantiasis of the testes." He tsked.

Malik was outright laughing by that point. Even Meir chuckled under his breath. I didn't get the joke. Though, I usually didn't get half of what Ranen was saying. Maybe if I did, I'd be laughing, too.

I shrugged it off, trying to ignore the fact that Malik was now practically rolling on the ground and choking on his guffaws, and continued to stroke the cat. I was amazed and delighted at how the simple gesture of running my hand down his soft back over and over again could calm my troubled mind. Fluffy seemed to enjoy it, too. Perhaps it was what I needed—a break from reality to enjoy one simple act of kindness for another living being.

I knew it couldn't last forever, though. One truth nagged at me from the back of my mind, threatening to overwhelm me: the Mamood knew where I was, and had come for me.

CHAPTER SEVENTEEN:
MESSAGE

I was sitting by Cailen's side... again. He still hadn't woken, although an entire day had passed since he'd been attacked in the library. Though my heavy lids drooped and I had trouble remembering to open them with each blink, I refused to leave his side. He needed me. I didn't know how I knew, but there was something inside me, convincing me I needed to be by him. Perhaps it was the pull that had been steadily building since he'd showed up.

Fluffy sat on my lap with his neck stretched out across my leg. My skin tingled with each steady rumble from his throat. I sighed. If only my life were as simple as this cat's. But it wasn't, and no amount of wishing or moping was going to make it happen.

I was probably going to die, and a lot of people were going to die with me. Self-sacrifice no longer seemed like a viable option. I had a vague notion Manoo wouldn't just send his soldiers home if I turned myself in. No, giving Manoo exactly what he wanted—my body on a marble slab—wouldn't save anyone.

Fighting Manoo, though, didn't sound like a viable option, either. There was no way I could win. Ranen had thought I *might* have a chance if I'd had years to prepare, but I didn't have years. I had days, if I was lucky—days to become stronger than Fire.

Impossible.

Meir's hand clamped down on my shoulder, a strong but gentle touch, already so familiar. I wondered what my future—my destiny—meant for him. He'd been so distant lately. Did I sicken him? Did he hate me?

As I stared up into his black eyes, I was sure his affection remained. But how could it? I was a freak—a freak whose only purpose in life was to kill and destroy. How could my savior—the preserver of life—ever find something to love in me again?

He smiled at me, and I smiled back. Everything clicked into place then. Love didn't make sense; it didn't need to. Love just was. He hadn't chosen me any more than I'd chosen him, but we were together and completely inseparable. I could be the worst person in the galaxy; Meir was already trapped. It made me sad. He deserved better.

I would *be* better.

Meir grabbed a chair from the table and pulled it up to Cailen's cot. He didn't say anything as he sat down, but I could tell he wanted to. There was some underlying tension he was trying to hide from me. I decided to give him a minute to organize his thoughts.

Fluffy was looking at me, wondering why I'd stopped petting him no doubt, so I scratched him behind the ears and pretended I couldn't feel the stress pouring out of Meir in waves.

Minutes passed in silence and I grew worried. Meir stiffened more and more, his limbs pulling tight. Anguish rippled across his face when he finally turned to me. Instinctively, I brushed my fingertips against his prickly cheek.

"I'm sorry for bringing you here," he whispered. "I never—"

"Shh..." I leaned my head against his shoulder. "Meir..." I paused, looking for the right words. "You saved me."

His jaw tightened. "I saved you from nothing." Meir pulled away from me, leaving my head to slide down to my chest.

"Don't say that."

He shook his head. "I never should have brought you here."

"You couldn't have stopped what's happening." I brought my hands down and stared at the lazy animal sprawled across my lap. "It started before we ever left Talia." At that moment, more clues I had missed fell into place. Obvious clues. Manoo naming me Shadra had been the catalyst. I'd had the dream just after overhearing the guards... my open cell door... the hole at the bottom of the ship... finding myself on solid ground rather than in lifeless space... the hands, the voice. Things had been set into motion that I couldn't stop. El had set things in motion.

El had set things in motion.

Of course! I was His tool, nothing more. And now He needed me. "It started before I left *Sho'ful*," I whispered.

Why, though? Why had I been on *Sho'ful* in the first place? How could El have allowed that to happen? If not for my imprisonment, I could've been trained, prepared. Now I was practically useless. I was stronger than *no one*, let alone Manoo. And more than that, I was out of control.

Meir brushed his thumb against my cheek and pulled it away again. My skin was cold and moist where he touched me—a tear. I looked up at him then and he had tears welling around his red-rimmed eyes, too.

"What can I do?" he said.

I half-smiled. "Just be here for me." There was no longer any chance of stopping the path of destruction, and my heart sank as I realized there never had been.

"I can do that." And he grinned that huge grin I loved so much—the one that creased his face in wrinkles.

I chuckled once, but then turned serious again. I was worried about him and I could see the tension around his eyes. "How are you doing... you know... with all of this?"

Meir's face smoothed as he grasped my question. "It's a little odd, I'll admit." He stroked his beard. "Imagine how you would feel if all your fairytales came to life."

Fairytales?

He must've read the confusion on my face. "Auri shouldn't actually exist. At least, that's what I'd always thought. I read about them in children's stories, but never did I imagine they were real." He sighed. "It's a little... troubling."

I nodded. Very troubling.

Cailen's cocoon moved. I froze. Blue and green waves rippled across his body as his wings curled away from him and flopped to the floor. His eyes were still shut. In my haste to lean over him and make sure he was all right, I nearly dropped Fluffy. The quick and nimble cat instead jumped onto Cailen's chest. He grunted under the sudden weight.

As I hovered over him, checking him to see if his burns were gone, it became immediately apparent that very little was left of his clothes. His shirt hung off of him in burnt shreds and his pants... were nearly just as bad. I blushed and turned away.

Out of the corner of my eye, I caught a subtle movement from Cailen's bed. His hand reached out to grab mine. Warmth shot through me like spiked adrenaline. My numb legs nearly gave out under me.

Careful to avoid any eye contact with anything below his waist, I faced him. He smiled up at me. I cupped his face in my free hand and kneeled by his side—Meir stood close behind me. Fluffy was kneading Cailen's chest with his big paws and burrowing his head against his neck.

"What is that?" Cailen's eyes strained to see what was snuggling with him.

I laughed. It felt so good to do. "It's Ranen's cat, Fluffy Nuts."

He coughed, just like Malik had done. "What?"

Malik was laughing again. I shook my head—boys were too hard to understand.

"Always making fun of my cat!" Ranen clearly couldn't find the joke, either. Maybe it was just Cailen and Malik who were weird. "He could barely walk!" He scooped up his cat and dropped a coarse, green blanket over Cailen's hips. I was exceedingly grateful.

Cailen unfolded the blanket and draped it over his nearly naked body. He sat up and looked around. "Where are we?" His voice was rough and I nudged Meir, pointing to the pantry.

I shrugged. "Ranen is apparently prepared for everything. He's got an underground bunker that looks like it could survive the end of the galaxy, though it can't seem to keep out a pesky little cat."

Cailen smirked. It was beautiful. My heart warmed and swelled beneath my chest, tickling my stomach.

Meir came back and offered Cailen a clear glass of water, which was received most graciously and consumed in a matter of seconds.

I glanced at Meir. I'd detected wariness from him the day before at breakfast and I wondered if it was still there. To my surprise, Ranen and Malik also hovered over us. Ranen was just as jumpy as ever, bumping into the cot with his hands fluttering in front of him, looking for something to do. Malik, on the other hand, stood off to the side with his arms crossed in front of him. He was looking at me. I pursed my lips and turned away.

"Would you like some food?" Ranen took the empty glass. "I'm sure you're famished."

Cailen stiffened, but then shrugged. I was sure he wasn't used to being taken care of. From what he'd told me of his training, it sounded like he'd dealt with a lot worse before and hadn't had an entourage of friends to pamper him afterward.

Ranen limped off anyway—to make him a sandwich, I guessed. I shook my head and laughed. The man was probably having the time of his life. The way he stared at Cailen was almost creepy. I had to remind myself Cailen was probably the first Auri anyone had seen in thousands of years. Wait, that wasn't right. *I* was the first Auri anyone had seen. Boy, that was going to take a while to get used to. Me, an Auri. What Meir had said only added to the creep factor. I guess after a few thousand years of no contact, a civilization of winged people was bound to fall into myth.

Winged people. I wondered where *my* wings were. Cailen's were so beautiful, draped behind him and flowing to the floor. I reached out to run my finger along the bright green edge. The electricity spiked and vibrated through my blood and bones. Cailen shuddered and whipped his wing away.

To say I wasn't hurt would be a bold-faced lie. The hazy euphoric tingling I had come to expect every time I touched him was immediately replaced and overshadowed by the overwhelming grief at knowing Cailen did not reciprocate my feelings. It threatened to crush me with each breath. I brought my hand up to my throat. I felt like I was choking.

Ranen leaned over me and handed Cailen a sandwich, just like I'd guessed. Cailen turned away from me and ate it.

"I wonder where your wings are, Ella." Ranen was looking down at me, curiosity written all over his wrinkled and pockmarked face.

I stared at him for a long time before I knew I could answer without my cracking voice giving me away. "I guess I'm just a gimp." *A freak, a monster, a wraith, take your pick.*

"Ha!" Cailen shook with laughter. There was no hope for me now; the tears I'd been struggling to contain threatened to pour out in torrents. I would've run away right then and there to hide in a corner if Cailen's face hadn't immediately softened when he saw my anguish. "You are anything but a gimp. You're... perfect."

My breathing stopped.

He brushed his fingers along my forehead to push a stray hair away. His fingers lingered on my face as he ran them down my jaw. The muscles along his neck and shoulders were drawn tight. "I didn't mean to laugh. I'm sorry."

"I forgive you," I said breathlessly. Yes, that was the best way to describe it because I was completely and entirely past the ability to breathe. I couldn't even remember where I was anymore.

Cailen took his hand away and chuckled. "But honestly, I was only laughing because you thought you didn't have wings!"

"Well, where are they?" Malik was the one to speak up this time. I'd come to realize he rarely spoke unless the subject matter was important.

I nodded emphatically, anxious to know the answer.

"They're the same place mine are when I don't need them." He reached out to stroke my back. "Beneath your skin."

Malik came up behind me and pushed my shoulders forward to round out my back. I didn't struggle. I was still too dazed at the idea that I actually had wings!

"Where?"

"You can't see them through the dress she's wearing now, but they run along her back on either side of her spine." Cailen shifted on his cot to show Malik while also trying to keep his body covered with the blanket.

"How do they fit?" Malik was no longer asking the questions I cared about. It seemed he was more interested in the mechanics of it all. I just wanted to see them.

I stood up and tugged on Cailen's arm. "I want to see them. Help me."

Cailen readjusted his blanket after I nearly pulled it off him in my haste. "Ella, like I said, you aren't wearing the right dress. Plus, I'm not exactly dressed for that kind of stuff myself." He looked around at Malik, Ranen, and Meir who had inched even closer during the last few minutes.

"Oh," I said.

He shook his head and rolled his eyes. "Did anyone happen to grab my bag?"

I smiled. "I did."

"Good. Would you bring it to me, please? I've got a few things in there for you, and a change of clothes for me."

I skipped over to my cot and grabbed the bag from under the makeshift bed. With a few coughs and whispers, Malik, Ranen, and Meir all dispersed to give Cailen some privacy. Due to the fact that there wasn't far to go, they just ended up lying on their respective cots. Ranen and Meir pulled out some reading material they'd found in the bunker, while Malik found a pair of weights to work his arms. Even Fluffy took the hint and left.

As soon as I handed Cailen the bag, he unzipped it and pulled out brightly colored clothes that shimmered under the harsh ceiling lights. He pushed them toward me.

"What are these?" I pinched some of the fabric between my fingers. It was lightweight and velvety soft.

"Those are your dresses." He smiled, and shrugged. "No one really knew your size. I'd told them you were pretty small, so we decided to recycle some of your mother's dresses from when she was a little younger than you. They're supposed to hang loose anyway, so even if they are a bit big, it shouldn't matter."

"My mother?" I whispered. Why was I so surprised? Shouldn't I have known I had one? The news of my father's death hadn't been painful because I'd forgotten his existence long ago, but... my mother. That was a completely different story.

Cailen nodded. "She misses you. Like you wouldn't believe."

"She... misses me?" Tears welled up in my eyes; I didn't even try to hold them back.

"I'll take you home right now." He ran his thumb along my brow. "It's where you belong."

I almost gave in. *Home.* I couldn't remember ever having a home. Even now the word seemed foreign to me. But I couldn't leave Meir; it was too painful to think about. And I couldn't run anymore. It was time for me to stand and fight.

I shook my head. "I can't go. Not now."

"We can prepare you, too, Ella." He gestured behind me. "Better than this man!"

I didn't bother to look to see Ranen's reaction. I spoke quickly before he had a chance to argue. "The Mamood are already here. I can't just leave the Soltakians. Not when they're dying because of me."

His eyes narrowed. "The Mamood are here?"

I'd forgotten he didn't know that part. I nodded.

Cailen growled. It wasn't like the playful sounds he'd been making two nights ago. This was deep and menacing. "Hurry up and get one of those dresses on. You're definitely going to need them now."

I snatched a jade and gold-colored dress from the pile and ran to the pantry, closing the door behind me. Though I didn't see how dresses were going to help me against the Mamood, I decided now was not the time to ask.

The blue dress lay around my ankles—I didn't bother to kick it away—as I pulled the silky jade dress over my head. The material cascaded around my body in waves. The back was entirely open, exposing the long mounds I now guessed were my wings. Gold designs shimmered along the fabric in curling loops and swirls. The front and back of the dress were clasped together at my shoulders with green, jewel-encrusted buttons, while the fabric cowled along my chest. The dress was loose, but not uncomfortable. In fact, it was so light and soft that I felt like I was wearing nothing at all on a breezy day.

I picked up the blue dress from the floor and walked out of the pantry. Every eye focused on me as I stepped through the doorway. Blood rushed to my cheeks and I looked at the floor.

Meir's and Ranen's awed gazes didn't surprise me. Meir always looked at me with deep devotion, and Ranen was so excited about our combined destiny that his shocked face was pretty much expected. Malik and Cailen were the surprising ones, the ones that made me look away in self-consciousness. The contrast in Malik's reaction from the first time he saw my face and now was enough to make my heart throb double-time. There was awe there that almost rivaled Meir's.

Although Cailen had been pretending to want distance between us since I'd opened my big mouth about all this Destructor business, I now could see the emotion roiling underneath. He wanted me. Actually, with the way he looked at me now, I was certain he *needed* me.

With my head down and my cheeks burning, I walked over to Cailen's cot just as he brushed past me with his blanket wrapped around his waist to take his turn to change. His wings were gone, hidden underneath his flesh. I threw my blue dress under my cot and grabbed the pile of clothes still on Cailen's bed. A green cloak—just like Cailen's—had been draped on top. I would've thought it was his if it hadn't been immediately apparent it was too small for him. I took the pile and put it on top of my own cot. There were seven dresses altogether, enough for one week.

"So, are you ready to let out your wings?" I jumped and pressed my hand against my heart at Cailen's voice. I hadn't even heard him walk up.

"What's wrong?" he said.

I took a few deep breaths before talking. "You scared me."

"Oh, sorry." He paused. "So, are you ready?"

"Absolutely." There was nothing I wanted more in that moment than having more proof of my connection to Cailen.

He smiled, but then grew serious. "I'm going to rub the seams along your back so you know where to work the muscles." As he said it, his hands started running along the length of the mounds on my back. "When you let your wings out, you *must not* flap them."

I cocked my head. "Why?"

"You'll transport."

"Okay, let's wait a second." Meir had jumped off his cot and taken two long strides toward us. He glared at Cailen and reached a hand out to grab me. "What exactly do you mean by transport?"

"I mean that the chemical in her wings will be triggered and begin the process of bending space. It's only dangerous your first time if someone isn't holding onto you and if you think about going anywhere hazardous to your health." Cailen smiled. "She'll be fine." He looked at me, every bit as serious as Meir. "You won't flap your wings."

I shook my head. "No."

"Good." He nodded his head once.

Meir didn't back away. Though Cailen hadn't moved to allow him to grab me, Meir looked like he was thinking about how he could take him down.

"Meir, I'll be fine. Cailen won't let me do anything stupid."

"Of course I won't."

Meir took a step back, but the expression on his face didn't change one bit.

I looked up at Cailen. "Okay, I'm ready."

His jaw and muscles tightened as he rubbed my back, almost as if he were preparing himself for an onslaught. "It's going to take a lot of concentration." His voice was tight and drawn. "You've only ever released your wings once before."

I wondered how he knew that particular bit of information. Sure, we'd known each other when I was young, but would he have known every moment of my life enough to be sure I had only released my wings once?

I shook the thoughts aside. I needed to concentrate. The blood in my veins along my back reacted to his touch, warming and prickling. I bit my lip and clenched my fists, trying to work every muscle in my body in the hopes of getting the right ones.

Something felt different. I felt the flesh pull away at two different points on my back. The feeling was similar to opening my eyes after a long, deep sleep. I kept pushing at those spots, straining against the effort.

I was close—so close. I could feel the seams widening and my wings pushing to get out.

And then I was almost knocked off my feet. Every hazy, electrical, tingly sensation I had ever gotten near Cailen exploded a thousand-fold. Those feelings had been nothing more than the prickles after a limb falls asleep compared to having that limb ripped open. And yet, that wasn't the best comparison because, though my body was in a form of pain, it was a good pain—the best pain of my life. My knees buckled and I fell face-first against the floor. I gasped for air and moaned.

Someone's hands were grabbing at me then. They weren't Cailen's—I would've known—and I almost screamed for them to leave me alone. I didn't want anyone to touch me in that moment but Cailen. I needed him then like I'd never needed anyone before. My body ached to have his arms wrapped around me, drawing me tight against him.

I moaned again.

"What's wrong with her?" Meir's hoarse voice brought me back down to reality. I couldn't hover above the clouds forever. I needed to focus and control the feelings raging through me. I would control them.

Blood rushed to my cheeks. I was suddenly humiliated, as if how I was acting should never be displayed in public.

I pushed myself up to my knees and ignored my pulsing, burning blood. Ranen, Meir, and Malik were all kneeling around me, anxiety etched into their faces. I looked past them, over their shoulders. Cailen was leaning against the wall on the opposite end of the room, as far away from me as possible. His eyes burned as they bored into mine.

Ranen gasped. I followed his shocked gaze down to the dangling locket around my neck. As it opened, a piece of paper fell out and landed on the floor.

"The message," Ranen whispered.

I picked up the paper and unfolded it. Three words stared back at me. Three words that answered every question I'd had since all of this had begun. Three words I should've known all along, but somehow hadn't. El had known I'd need to hear this. He'd known even thousands of years ago when He had Elsden prepare the message for me.

My heart pounded against my chest.

"What does it say?" Malik asked.

For a moment, I could say nothing. There was no reason to keep it a secret, but it felt so personal, like a message between lovers. The words were simple enough. They didn't hint at this privacy I overwhelmingly felt. But they answered *my* question, no one else's: *why is all of this happening to me?*

"For My purpose." The words were out before I could stop them. I didn't even feel my mouth open to whisper them. But they were there and now everyone knew them.

I was overwhelmed by the truth of the words and the release they brought. Death and destruction followed me around because El meant them to, to prepare and test me. I had been imprisoned on *Sho'ful* because El had plans for me. I'd needed to be there. The Auri had locked themselves up on their planet for thousands of years. Had I remained, I never would've known Manoo had named me Shadra. I never would've had reason to fear him, hate him. And as I gazed into Meir's fear-filled eyes I realized I never would've had something to fight for… to die for.

Every action had a reason behind it. I knew that now. And I no longer cared that I was probably going to die. No, I wouldn't offer my life to Manoo as I'd planned just days ago. Instead, I would offer my life to El.

CHAPTER EIGHTEEN:
LOST AND FOUND

Ranen's fingers lazily picked at that glowing mark on his arm as he stared at the opposite wall with glazed eyes. With everything that'd happened over the past few days, I'd forgotten about it. Seeing it again, though, piqued my interest.

After a few seconds his eyes caught mine and he dropped his hand.

"What is that?" I asked.

He waved his hand in the air as if to wave off my question. "It's a ComTat."

"A ComTat?"

"Communications Tattoo."

I pushed myself off my cot and sat next to him to see it better. The markings were fine and raised just slightly above the skin. Thin lines swirled around like paths in a maze, and some parts glowed more brightly than others. "Does it do anything?"

He raised his eyebrows and chuckled. "It communicates."

Okay, so that should've been pretty obvious to me. I tried to recover some sense of dignity. "But how?"

He fingered one of the larger swirls on the ComTat. "It picks up a signal and transfers the message through vibrations throughout my body's nervous system until the information is then translated in my brain."

"That's interesting."

He nodded.

"Is that how you knew about the palace?" It seemed so obvious now—the way he'd just frozen, like he'd been listening to something.

Ranen frowned and dug deeper at the ComTat.

"What's wrong?"

"I haven't heard anything for a while now." He dropped his hand to his lap. "It has me concerned."

I focused on the swirls and lines on his arm, unwilling to go there with Ranen. I refused to think the Mamood could have won so quickly and easily. The bluish glow emanating from the image swelled and receded along a constant path around the tattoo.

I followed its path so long, I'd memorized it long before Ranen opened his mouth again. "I think I'm going to take a nap." And with that, he turned away from me, hiding his arm under the length of his body, making it clear he wanted to be alone.

I stood up and went back to my own cot. Poor Ranen. Everything about him annoyed me—especially the fact that every time I looked at him I knew how I must appear standing next to Cailen: weak and broken, hardly the champion he'd have chosen. But still, I didn't want this for him. I didn't want this for anyone.

I sat down on my little bed. Before resting my head against the wall, I caught Cailen's gaze just as he looked away, hiding something from me. I thought I heard him mumble something like "white wings," and shake his head. So my wings were white, that didn't mean he had to be so horrified. And yet, he was definitely horrified. Since the whole embarrassing "event," I'd caught him sneaking glances a few times. Sometimes he looked so disgusted, I thought he was going to be sick.

I turned my back on him, crushed. We'd come so far since meeting I'd thought we really had a chance. Apparently not. I made the boy ill—not much hope for romance from that.

I closed my eyes, ignoring the gazes I felt coming from Malik and Meir. Neither one of them had stopped staring at me since the great reveal. I wasn't just Ella to anyone anymore.

"Time to go!"

My eyes popped open to see Ranen's previously sedentary body jump off the cot and scuttle around the bunker, picking up blankets, grabbing food.

"Go where?" Meir's voice was slow.

"The Block, of course. They're sending shuttles around now." It was impossible to miss the sound of relief in the old man's voice. Ranen opened a door, revealing stairs going up to a hatch along the ceiling. He stuck his head outside and called down, "We've lucked out. It rained all day today."

"What's the Block?" Malik said from just behind my shoulder. I tried to ignore the tingles that set off in my stomach.

Ranen looked back and gestured for us to follow him up the stairs. "It's a secure underground haven for Ladeshians and the military."

I grabbed my bundle of clothes as Meir pulled me with him. Fluffy ran past us and disappeared into the woods behind Ranen's house—at least, what was left of Ranen's house. Broken stone and burnt timbers littered the ground. Water sloshed under our feet. It'd rained a *lot*.

Black clouds hovered low in the sky, hiding the mountain peaks in the distance and threatening to dump their contents on the ground at any moment. Meir rubbed my cold shoulders and guided me around the burnt skeleton of the palace to the road. Dozens of people swarmed onto a vehicle. Under normal circumstances, I would have considered the shuttle quite large, but with all the people crowding inside and around it, it looked almost tiny. I wondered if there would be room for us, or if we'd have to wait for another one to come by.

Ranen sped up and I figured out this was it. We ran behind him and shoved our way through. Most of the people moved aside when they saw Ranen. It looked like even when lives were at stake, royalty couldn't be ignored, but a few parents with children clinging to their sides frowned, disinclined to lose their places.

We made it inside and wormed our way to the back. Many of the people were covered in blood, their clothes torn into shreds. I caught a few of them giving me wary glances and I realized I wore something quite literally fit for a queen—not to mention the fact that none of us had a scratch on us. Surely these people wondered why we'd been so lucky.

I was quickly reminded of my dislike of crowds. Hands and shoulders pushed against me, prodding for a way through. I recoiled away from them and sank into Meir's chest. He wrapped his arms around me and turned so I faced the window. I breathed in and out to calm the terror.

The shuttle lifted off the ground and moved out. I turned away from the staring eyes of the people left outside.

I turned to Ranen. "Are there other shuttles?"

"Not for them." He cocked his head toward the window and the crowd of people we slowly passed. "All the shuttles are moving in now. Those people will have to find safety elsewhere."

Bile lurched up into my throat. There were children in the crowd.

Minutes passed and my mind filled with thoughts of all those who had died—and those who *would* die. The Mamood cared nothing for their lives. I wondered how depraved someone had to be to stop caring.

I stared out the window as we passed the devastation. Most of the homes had been completely destroyed—only a few still had some standing walls. None were livable, though, and nothing offered protection.

A flash of color in the corner of my eye caught my attention. I twisted around to look at the near blind spot behind the shuttle. Another flash of color—a red beam—ripped through the sky much closer to us. My eyes widened as every last muscle in my body froze. More red beams—at least a dozen—touched the ground all around the Old City. In a flash of instinct, I knew what they were targeting: the shuttles.

I gasped.

Cailen ripped me away from Meir. "Grab onto me!" His green and gold wings burst out from his back, conforming to the crowded space.

I looked at Meir in horror just as a red beam sliced through our shuttle and he was knocked away from me. I struggled against Cailen to grab him, but he and everything else in the vehicle disappeared.

Chapter Nineteen:
Nothing

Light swirled around me, weaving in and out in a never-ending dance of color. Voices boomed then faded like thunder in a storm. Malik, Ranen, and I huddled together with Cailen's arms wrapped around us. The swirling light moved in time with his whooshing wings.

After a few seconds, the swirling colors solidified into recognizable shapes. Men and women in form-fitting silver suits stood around us in a wide silver tunnel. Most of them carried weapons and gawked at us. Some of them were pointing those weapons at our chests.

Cailen released his arms. Malik and Ranen stepped to either side while I pressed myself closer to him.

One of the silver-suited men in the back of the small crowd said, "It's a Mamood!"

At that point *all* the rifles came up.

A few clicks and the room started humming as the laser weapons warmed up.

I twisted around to grab Malik. I didn't know how I was going to protect him, but I knew I had to. Cailen's arms tightened around me, holding me in place.

At no signal I could detect, all the soldiers clicked the off buttons and lowered their weapons. A man in similar dress to the other Soltakians, but at least a head taller, stepped forward as everyone parted for him. I recognized him immediately and groaned—Commander General Lastrini.

Malik pushed his shoulders back and raised his chin a fraction of an inch.

The giant leered at the Mamood. "Well, well, well. I was wondering when we would meet again." His cold, ice-blue eyes turned to me. I sank deeper into Cailen's arms. "I would recognize that tiny little form anywhere. You must be his Tarmean companion." He turned back to Malik. "Now where's the other one? These two are not him."

My stomach twisted. Meir. He was… gone. No, not gone. He *couldn't* be gone. He was just still out there, but we'd find him and he'd be all right. El owed me at least that much. Yes, we'd find him. We had to find him.

But I'd seen the beam hit our shuttle.

I gasped for breath. No, he had to be alive. Not Meir! *Not Meir!*

Cailen's restraining arms no longer comforted. I needed to run from there. I twisted against his hold, but it remained firm.

"Shh," he whispered in my ear, so low only I would be able to hear. "Not now. We'll find him, but not now."

Not now. We'd find him, but not now. Yes, we'd find him. We'd deal with our problem at hand and then go look for Meir. I could wait, as long as it wasn't too long.

Lastrini stared at me, perhaps thinking I'd lost my mind.

If I couldn't get Meir back, I probably would.

With his eyes still on me, he turned his head in Malik's direction. "We found your dead friend hidden by the storage containers, along with the weapon that killed him." He shrugged and turned his gaze away from me. "Now I don't mind so much that you killed one of your own, but I do find it suspicious that so shortly after you sneak into Soltak, the Mamood—your people—decide to attack." He took one step toward Malik. "Now, why is that?"

Ranen—who had up until that point been standing slightly behind Cailen—stepped up to the Commander General. The confidence radiating off of the little man was almost comical. The other Ladeshian was at least two feet taller than him and twice as wide. I would've been scared for Ranen's well-being if Lastrini didn't immediately drop to one knee upon seeing him. The crowd of soldiers followed his example.

Ranen said something in what I assumed was Ladeshian and everyone returned to their feet. "This man is a friend. You have my word on that," he continued in the common tongue. It was nice that he thought to include us in the conversation. Perhaps Ranen wasn't so bad after all.

Lastrini eyed Malik with a wary glance as he returned to his feet. After a few moments of speculation, he put his hand out for the Mamood. Malik didn't take it. "Forgive my hasty and some- what rude interrogation. It is my responsibility to protect my troops and my emperor." He gestured toward Ranen. "Though I respect Master Orsili's judgment, I did not become leader of the entire Soltakian force by not gathering all pertinent information merely because someone has given me their word. I really must know your name and why you chose to sneak into Co'ladesh."

I don't know what came over me, but I ripped myself out of Cailen's loose hold and stared up at the enormous Ladeshian. "His name is Malik. He was only helping me escape the Mamood. We have a common enemy, General Lastrini. Please, we mean you no harm."

He glared. "And who might you be, Little Miss?"

Malik's teeth snapped shut and Cailen's hands were pulling me back.

"She is Ella," Ranen said. "She has been named Shadra by Manoo." He paused and folded his arms. "And she is an Auri."

Lastrini blinked twice, and then roared with laughter with all his soldiers laughing behind him. My face flushed and heated. His accent grew stronger with his sneer. "Shadra *and* Auri? Where are your wings? Your sparkly dust?" He turned to Ranen. "Come, come, Master Orsili. You take me for a fool. All mythical creatures aside, what would the Mamood have to fear from this little girl?"

What indeed? I wished I could laugh along with the Solta- kians, but part of me also wished I could wipe their smug little smiles off their faces. In fact, I would. A little concentration on my part and they wouldn't be smiling for much longer.

I focused on my back, hoping and praying I wouldn't be as incapacitated as the last time. That wouldn't be helpful to the no laughing thing.

My wings burst out from my back, shimmering with hints of color with each subtle movement. I smiled when the laughing stopped quite suddenly.

Cailen released his hands from my arms and stepped back. The electricity coursing through my blood was staggering, but not nearly as bad as the first time. At least I was able to stay on my feet.

Lastrini showed no emotion whatsoever. His cool demeanor infuriated me.

"What have you to say, General?" I fumed. "I am an Auri. Here are my wings."

"I am not above being proven wrong, Little Miss." He shrugged. "The galaxy is vast. So the Auri exist. What does that have to do with you being named Shadra?"

I opened my mouth to say something, but for the life of me, I couldn't think of anything quite right. What was I supposed to say? Manoo's afraid of me because I'm so badass? No. The seven-foot tall Ladeshian would never buy it, and with his demeaning glare that looked me up and down, I started to question it myself. Quite sure I'd done the exact opposite of proving my point, I pulled my wings back beneath the folds of flesh.

"That is a conversation best reserved for the Emperor's ears," Ranen said. "I'd like to speak with him as soon as possible."

"He is about to meet with the Bre'ha, but I am sure he would like you to be there as well."

"The Bre'ha?" Ranen's face turned a very bright shade of red. If I didn't think it was impossible, I would swear his eyes were about to pop right out. "The Mosandarians are here?"

"They're coming." Lastrini shrugged. "They sent their leaders ahead of them."

"If you are going to talk to the Emperor," Cailen said, "Malik and I will look for Meir."

I twisted my head around to glare at him. Cailen was crazy if he thought he was going anywhere without me. Meir was my responsibility, not his.

Ranen nodded and started to walk away when Lastrini stopped him.

"Who is this Meir?"

"A friend of ours," Cailen said. "We were on a shuttle when it was attacked. We were able to escape, but Meir was left behind."

"How did you escape?"

Cailen's eyes went flat and hard. "My wings."

Lastrini raised his eyebrows. "You are an Auri as well?"

Cailen nodded.

The Ladeshian and Auri glared at each other, weighing each other's strengths. Though Cailen was half a foot shorter than Lastrini, he didn't look the least bit intimidated.

"Interesting galaxy we live in," Lastrini mumbled. "Well, if your friend was left on the shuttle, as you say, then he is likely dead."

I gasped. Dead? No, this man had to be wrong. "I just received a report," he continued. "The Mamood evidently halted their attack to allow us a chance to gather survivors. When the shuttles were on their way here, they attacked again." He glared at Malik. "Apparently, that is a common tactic."

Malik stayed motionless. "Apparently."

Lastrini growled. "And even if there was a chance your friend was alive, I wouldn't allow any of you to leave. We're at war and the three of you," he looked pointedly at Cailen, Malik, and me, "are hereby detained in the Block until more information is available."

I shook my head and grabbed his arm. "No, please! You have to let us look. Please!"

The General's ice-blue eyes melted and he gently released my hands. "I'm sending out a recon tonight to look for survivors. Master Orsili will give me a description of this Meir and I'll order my men to look for him specifically. I can't promise any more than that."

Relief washed through me. "*Thank* you."

"Take me to the Emperor now." Ranen looked ready to tear someone in half. It would have been a terrifying expression if it were on any other person. "I want to know what he is planning to do."

Lastrini motioned to a few of the soldiers behind him. "Get these three some rooms—the boys can share—and post guards."

Both Malik and Cailen bristled. I wondered what they found more offensive—being called boys or being babysat.

I didn't care. They could wrap chains around my ankles—I wouldn't notice. Nothing would matter until Meir was back with me, safe.

Two soldiers walked ahead of us while three walked behind with their weapons up and ready. We didn't say anything to each other, not as we traveled down one hallway after the other, and not when I walked into my room. Cailen glanced my way right before he was herded off to the room next to mine, and I almost started to cry when I saw the look on his face. I don't know how I knew, but I was certain he thought Meir was dead.

I held it in until my door slid closed, and then I threw myself onto the bed and sobbed. Every last tear my body could produce was drained out onto the pillow long before I was done. I cried until my eyes burned and my throat grew hoarse. What little hope I'd clung to was ripped away every time I thought of Cailen's face.

Meir couldn't have survived. No one could have survived that kind of attack—no one, and certainly not Meir. Of course not. I'd known I'd kill him. I'd known it all along. And now my savior had been destroyed.

I didn't have anyone to die for anymore; he was already gone. I knew that now, and I realized I'd known it the moment we'd transported to the Block and Meir wasn't with us. I'd been too stupid to accept it at the time. A part of me was still deluded into thinking there was hope. But there was no hope, only death. The one I'd wanted most to live was... gone.

An eternity passed long before that dreaded knock pounded on my door. I'd prayed for death at least a hundred times by then. It didn't come.

I lifted my head off the pillow and wiped my eyes, though they were already completely dry. My body just wasn't equipped to handle that depth of pain. "Come in," I croaked.

A woman with dark hair drawn tight against her head into a long ponytail came into my room. With her first step, she was all business, but when her eyes grazed my face, she faltered. I guessed I probably looked pretty bad.

She cleared her throat. "Commander General Lastrini asked me to inform you that we found no survivors."

"His body?" I really didn't want to see it, but some morbid part of me thought it would be better if I at least knew there was *some* part of him still out there.

She shook her head. "The damage was pretty severe. Most of it burned away."

So the Mamood had left me nothing. Nothing.

Nothing... nothing... nothing...

I curled my legs up and rocked back and forth. Waves of darkness crashed in around me, and I drowned in them.

Black... black... black... nothing... nothing... nothing...

I didn't see the woman leave. It was a long time before I saw anything.

My eyes wouldn't close, not even to blink, but it didn't matter. The shape and hue of the room, the texture of the bed, all of it was meaningless. There was nothing there anymore—nothing substantial.

I was somewhere real, but my mind drifted somewhere between the real and the unreal—in no man's land. Thoughts eluded me. There was something important trying to dig its way through my subconscious, but I didn't know what it was. It fluttered out of reach just when I tried to grab it.

No matter—it couldn't be *that* important.

Not important, not in the land of nothingness. Nothing... nothing... nothing...

Meir.

I gasped and the waves of darkness drained out of me.

Meir... Cailen... Malik...

Meir. *Cailen. Malik.*

Meir's last few moments played across my mind as I remembered the red beam from the Mamood ship tearing through the shuttle, me reaching for him as Cailen dragged me away.

A cold chill passed through my veins as it hit me. They'd done this to him. Both of them with their stupid lies and secrets.

And then something so much more powerful than grief ripped me out of the last wisps of haze. Rage. Every last mistake ever made was perfectly clear in the forefront of my mind. With perfect clarity, I knew who to blame and for once it wasn't me.

And the ones responsible were going to pay.

I got up from my bed and walked to the door. I decided to ask for permission to leave first, but a "no" certainly wouldn't stop me—it would just make it inconvenient. So I knocked lightly to hide the overwhelming burn in the core of my being, the need to crush and destroy. They'd be more inclined to say yes if I didn't look ready to kill.

The door slid open and three armed men faced me with their weapons slung across their chests. I didn't smile. There was no point in overacting and I was sure they expected to see me looking like a mess.

"May we help you, miss?" The one on my right said.

"I'd like to talk to my friends, if you don't mind." I sniffed back a sob. "I'd like some comfort right now."

The man who'd spoken looked to his fellow soldiers for input. One of them looked wary, so I sniffled a little bit more to nudge him in the right direction. He nodded and they escorted me to the room down the hall. The guards at Malik's and Cailen's room didn't say anything—they already seemed to know—as one of them waved his hand in front of the blue-lit screen to open the door and let me in.

This time I thought a little smile might be appropriate, so I peered up at the one closest to me and laid it on thick, big doe eyes and all. One thing had become perfectly clear since my escape: people tended to sympathize with tiny little me. Well, sympathize away—the universe was going to burn tonight.

Cailen and Malik stood up when I came in. They looked angry, like they'd been fighting with each other. I didn't care.

The door slid closed and the façade fell away. The rush of my fury poured out of me in a thick cloud. I could taste it on my tongue, bitter and tangy. So I turned on them, my focus clearer than it'd ever been.

I'd come to a deeper understanding of how my ability worked since Cailen had showed me how to release my wings. When I'd been knocked off my feet that first time, I realized the source of the tingling had always been my wings. Which meant that now I knew how to call it at will.

Blue, green, and red points of light popped into my vision, filling the air and illuminating the inside of Malik's body, Cailen's body, everything. I commanded the blue points of light to form and rush at Cailen. They swirled together as he flew back against the wall, pinned there by the tempest.

Malik froze though I hadn't done anything to him... yet.

Cailen was the focus of my attention now. "Why didn't you transport us here from Ranen's bunker? Why did you wait?"

His eyes glazed over in concentration and I knew he was trying to take command of the air trapping him against the wall. He wouldn't win; air obeyed *me*.

"Why?"

"The law." He gasped. I knew the pressure I was throwing at Cailen was crushing him. The blue points of light wedged together, forming a solid, unbreakable wall. "We can't reveal—the Auri secret—except for—emergencies."

"You said you couldn't transport me without my express permission, but you did it anyway."

"I couldn't—just let you die."

"Liar!" The wind howled my sentiments, twisting through his hair and loose clothes, ripping the ends. "You don't care about me!"

"That's not true." His voice was strained as I squeezed the breath out of him. "I care for you—so much."

"You've done nothing but lie and keep secrets since you came here."

"—protect you."

I shook my head and eased up on the force of wind. He was still pinned against the wall, but I needed him to be able to breathe. "I want the truth. Every last bit of it."

"Please, don't. Not this way."

"Tell me!" I was tired of the evasions and in no mood to be crafty.

He pressed his lips together, contemplating. "Fine. Just... let me down."

I loosened the wall of air and let him slide to the floor. It didn't matter. I was still in control. "Now tell me why every time I touch you, I practically get electrocuted and I just want to be closer to you. And why you've been so distant. And don't tell me you don't feel it too, because I know you do."

He hung his head. "Yes," he whispered, "I feel it, too." He looked up with wary eyes. "We've been bonded, Ella."

I waited.

He sighed. "The chemical in our wings—drilium—is very, *very* potent, especially when we release our wings for the first time. Do you remember what I said about before the wars? About the survivors being mostly children?"

I nodded.

"If a young one releases his wings for the first time without another young one releasing her wings for the first time as well, that young one's drilium would suck the drilium from every other present Auri." His eyes flicked to Malik. "It would be like sucking the blood out of a human being."

I considered this for a moment. "So what does that mean?"

His eyes returned to mine. "Pairs are selected at a very young age. When those two young ones release their wings for the very first time, the drilium from both Auri react with each other, changing each other, infusing with one another, and become a matched set."

"And?" I could tell there was more.

"The drilium never forgets the bond. The pairs call to each other and when they're close, the chemicals react. But when they're apart, they grow weak. Bonded pairs can't live without each other." He half-smiled, but wiped it away almost immediately. "Only the strongest can survive the kind of separation we went through. If we hadn't been reunited, our bodies would eventually have become so weak they wouldn't have been able to support themselves."

So that was the secret. That was the *lie*. The hovering cloud of fury sank to the ground as the cold truth threatened to choke me. Every feeling I'd had for him—and whatever he felt for me—was completely contrived. He was only here because he didn't want to die, not because of some long-ago friendship we might've had. Not because he cared.

No wonder he'd wanted to keep it from me. He just wanted to string me along and keep me close because of his own selfishness.

"None of it was real," I murmured. For him or me. And that was the worst part; my own body had betrayed me.

"That's not true!" He tried to take a step forward, but I slammed him against the wall. "Ella, please listen to me. I was ecstatic when they told me we were to be bonded."

"Of course you were." My voice was dead. I couldn't feel anything for him anymore, not even hate. "Who wouldn't be overjoyed to be stuck with the Aurume?"

Horror crossed his face and I almost believed it. But then I remembered what a great liar he'd been. Like all the times he'd told me there were no more secrets, no more surprises.

"I never cared about that. *Never*. You were my best friend. Of course I wanted to be with you!"

"How can you expect me to believe a word that comes out of your mouth?" I leaned toward him. "You let Meir die. If you cared even an ounce for me, you would've known to protect him as vehemently as you protected me."

Cailen's face fell. "I didn't know. I didn't see."

I threw every bit of force I could muster at him. His head smacked against the wall and his body fell limp.

No, Cailen hadn't seen because he was too busy worrying about himself. I'd been a fool to ever trust him—a fool to ever trust anyone.

That's when I turned on Malik.

"Ella, don't."

Silly Malik—he actually thought he could calm me down this time. It might've worked in the past, but now I wanted *him* to suffer.

I ordered the gale to swirl around me. Cailen slumped to the floor. A cursory glance let me see he was still alive and healing slowly. No matter how angry I was with him, I wouldn't become the monster I feared.

Blood pooled around his head.

I turned to Malik. "You knew the Mamood would attack the shuttles."

"I knew it was a possibility." His voice stayed neutral.

"No!" I roared and threw the wind at him. He slammed against the wall just as Cailen had. A glimmer of fear skittered across his face for a second before he could replace it with his infuriatingly calm façade.

I wanted to see that fear again.

"More than a possibility! You knew it would happen!" He'd risked all our lives to keep his damn Mamood secrets. Now my savior—the only person who'd never let me down—was dead. A new idea crossed my mind—if he didn't want to admit to the murder he'd helped his people commit, I'd take the breath from his lungs as payment.

Terror twisted every smooth feature on Malik's face as I drew the air out of his lungs. He didn't hold back; he let me see it all. His face turned red, then blue. When his eyes rolled up and his head slumped against his shoulder, I let him go.

Though the monster raged just beneath the surface, I refused to let it take complete control. I wouldn't sink to their level and be responsible for their deaths.

I turned my back on Malik and focused the blue points of light against the door. Metal creaked and groaned against the strain, but after just a few seconds of fight, it gave up. The door flew away, ripping most of the wall away with it. It slammed into the wall across the hall and fell to the floor with a loud thud and a clang. The soldiers were in full panic mode as they brought their rifles up and pointed them at me. The air hummed as the weapons charged, but not quick enough to stop me. I shoved them away with a burst of air and turned back the way we'd come.

The soldiers outside my room started firing. I froze. They were too fast; I couldn't stop them in time. Red beams slammed into me. I cringed, waiting for the scorching pain. I felt only a tingling warmth, a tickle.

I looked down. The energy dispersed throughout my dress, crackling and fizzing out.

Interesting.

That gave me a new idea. Whatever material the dress was made out of, it obviously had special protective abilities. I wondered if the cloak did as well. Cailen had seemed to value the dresses. He said I'd need them, especially now the Mamood had arrived.

I pushed air at the three soldiers and barely noticed as they flew down the hall. I had something far more important to attend to. I blew the door away from my room and retrieved the cloak—it still lay on the bed where I'd thrown it earlier. I didn't really want to traverse the entire underground bunker. There was no way to tell how big it was—though I assumed it must have been massive if it could shelter the entire Soltakian military—and I had no way to know how to get out the conventional way, regardless. I did have another option available to me, though.

Transport.

The tingling in my blood submitted to my beckoning, urging the flesh to separate and release the wings beneath. My beautiful white wings burst forth, bold and iridescent, and I concentrated on Ranen's estate as I let them flap.

Swirls of grey and silver light intermingled and eventually gave way to green and black, rolling in and out like waves on the seashore. When I was sure I had reached my desired destination, I halted my wings and folded them back beneath my skin.

Soltak's green moon illuminated the black night, casting hazy shadows on the ground. Ranen's crumbled home stood as a perfect testament to my life: everything good, strong, and beautiful must eventually perish. Those red points of light I'd carefully ignored were now at the forefront of my attention. I drew only a dozen of the lights together—just a spark—and let the flame dance a few inches in front of me.

"Manoo!" I knew he would hear me. His servant, Fire, was certainly listening. "I'm here! I'm not running anymore! Come and face me!"

The spark flickered, and then twisted in the air and grew, swirling and morphing. The flames swelled in the shape of a ball for just a second before they twisted in on themselves and the form of a faceless man stood crackling in front of me. It threw its head back and laughed, deep and menacing. "Is this my Destructor? A little girl?"

My teeth snapped shut even as hints of terror started to percolate in my blood. "I am the one chosen by El."

"Then El must have a sense of humor. Or He has no idea what He's doing. You are not ready to face me... But I gladly accept the offer."

I waited, but he didn't move. "Then fight me! Don't just stand there like a coward!" Perhaps egging him on wasn't the best course of action, but I was beyond the ability to reason. This... thing... whatever he was... was responsible for Meir's death. There was nothing I wanted more than to make Manoo share in that fate.

"No."

"What?" My blood burned for release. I craved the destructive force required to bring him down like water. I shook my head and growled.

"I'm not going to fight you." The fiery form took one step closer to me and hissed. "I'm going to destroy you."

The flames erupted into waves and swirled around me, trapping me inside. I pushed at the lights, ordering them to bend to my will, but they did not obey. Fire was in control.

Fury boiled out of me and I screamed.

CHAPTER TWENTY:
BACK TO HELL

My captors kept me on a very tight leash. Literally. As soon as they were able to maneuver around the fiery cage that'd trapped me on Ranen's estate, they'd shackled my neck and wrists with some kind of energy bracelets—the same energy that'd buzzed through *Sho'ful*, making my muscles feel like mush—and hauled me onto one of their fighters. I was helpless—and infuriated—as Fire hovered just inches away, ready to burn me to the ground if I did anything to escape or fight back.

The Mamood Capital planet of Kalhandthar was exactly as I'd always imagined it to be: cold, hard, and utilitarian. The only thing remotely beautiful—and really, it was more gaudy than anything with its rotund pillars and red and gold mosaics—was Manoo's temple at the Kofra's palace.

We were greeted on the palace grounds by the Kofra himself in his burgundy and gold robes, a troop of Tarmean soldiers, and three massive hounds who stood like sentinels at the Kofra's side.

My stomach twisted. I knew beyond any doubt those were the same kind of hounds as the ones on *Sho'ful*. They were exactly as I'd always pictured them: big and mean with lots of teeth, and frothing at the mouth. As soon as the dozen or so of my captors escorted me down the ramp onto the palace lawn with rifles pointed at my head and chest, the hounds started howling and clawing at the ground to get at me. Inadequately-sized men held what appeared to be very flimsy chains around the hounds' necks.

Though terror made sweat bead on my skin, I didn't falter. There was no doubt in my mind Manoo and his followers would revel in seeing my fear, but I would not give it to them. I tried not to think about Ranen's warning that if I went down this particular path—sacrifice—I would lose. That line of thinking wouldn't help me keep my cool façade.

The Kofra glided up to me as soon as my party halted a few yards away from him. He was younger—a lot younger—than I would've guessed. Though I'd never known much about Mamood politics, I did know it centered around the Kofra. I'd always assumed he was some crumpled old man wasting away on his throne. The boy staring back at me with raptor eyes barely looked older than Cailen or Malik.

"Welcome." He dipped his head then spread his arms out toward the men behind him. "We've been eagerly awaiting your arrival."

I almost laughed at his absurd greeting. His expression remained innocent, as if he hadn't amassed his men to murder me, but was instead welcoming me to some quaint gathering of friends.

When I said nothing, he continued, "I hope you were treated well on your way here. I would hate to learn any of my people behaved rudely to one such as yourself." His words dripped like honey off the tongue. So sweet and pure, I was half-inclined to believe them.

But I remembered what the Mamood had done to Meir and his words lost their power. This Kofra was the enemy.

I glared back at his smug smile. "They let me sleep, but I can't say much good about them." I lifted my wrists. "They did put me in chains, after all."

He chuckled and looked adoringly at the men pointing rifles at me. "For their protection alone, I assure you."

I just shook my head. Ridiculous. What was going on in this man's head? Did he actually think I was the bad guy here? They deserved El's judgment.

Manoo, though, wasn't playing along. I'd hoped he would fight me on Soltak, ending it there, but coward that he was, he seemed insistent I just bow down and offer myself up as his tasty little meal.

The Kofra stepped to my side and wrapped his arm around my shoulders. His soldiers tensed and gripped their rifles. He didn't seem to notice their anxiety. "Come, let us get you prepared. We still have some time before the ceremony and you must gather your strength."

Instinctively, I looked to the sky. The afternoon sun hovered at eye level above the horizon, turning the clouds ablaze with bright reds and oranges.

With a wary eye, I watched him as he led me to his palace. There was something not quite right. I'd expected beatings and starvation, not these kind words. My presuppositions were being threatened, but I clung to them with all my strength. I needed the hate to boil in my blood in order to find the strength to do what needed to be done. If I wasn't careful, this man would undermine all my intentions.

His soldiers didn't leave his side. They marched in formation with the Kofra's hounds leading the pack as we left the grounds behind and traversed the wide, marble halls. Despite the man's seeming indifference and robust confidence, those under him were not so easily assuaged. It didn't seem to matter to them that I had at least two hundred rifles pointed at me and three hounds ready to rip my throat out the moment I made a wrong move. For a moment, I got a glimpse of what it meant to be the Destructor. Their fear was not determined or undermined by my petite and half-starved form; they knew I was something more underneath this physical mirage.

Something more, and yet not enough.

There wasn't a single moment when I deluded myself into thinking I could actually win; that wasn't the point, at least not for me. If Meir had to die because I was supposedly important enough to this "god," then I would at least cause him some discomfort. But it seemed I wasn't even going to get a chance to do that.

The Kofra guided me with his entourage behind us to an open room. Marble benches lined the walls, with a single table for two centered beneath an open skylight. The white walls glowed orange under the sunset. Tarmean soldiers broke formation and filed along the walls, never taking their rifles off me. The Kofra and I continued toward the table with the three hounds and their masters at our sides. One of the hounds snapped his jaws just a hand-width from my head before his master yanked him back.

I took a deep breath to calm my growing nerves and sat down at the offered seat, behind a plate of food. The Kofra sat across from me.

He gestured to the plate. "Please eat. You must be starving."

Ha! Starving! I'd been starving for the last ten years of my life and *now* a Mamood cared? He could watch me starve.

On second thought, the steaming meat and vegetables did look rather good, and I was pretty hungry. I wasn't doing it for him, though. There was just no point in suffering out of spite.

I cut off a slice of the meat and nibbled. So it was fairly delicious. He still wasn't going to get an ounce of my gratitude. I took a large bite and washed it down with a glass of water.

The Kofra smiled.

I paused and waved my hand over the table. The chain hanging off my wrist sent my goblet of water to the floor to shatter into dozens of little crystal pieces. "Why are you doing this? We both know you're just going to kill me anyway."

He raised his eyebrows. "True."

I waited.

"It's a strenuous ceremony for all parties. Manoo needs you to be at your strongest. It would serve no one if you died prematurely."

"Nice."

He cocked his head. "You seem angry."

"I wonder why." By the quizzical look on the Kofra's face, I guessed he really did wonder. Perhaps he lived a sheltered life where martyrdom was a daily norm. "I don't want to die."

"Hmm…"

"What?"

"You're not the only one who's going to die tonight, Ella."

It shouldn't have surprised me that he knew my name—he was the one to give my name to the *Sho'ful* guards, after all—but it did. "What do you mean?"

"I, too, am being sacrificed." He looked off to the side and smiled.

"Why?"

He turned his dark, brown eyes back to me. "A human body is too weak for someone as great as Manoo to dwell in without destroying it." He leaned across the table. "So you see, two will fall tonight so our great Lord may live to spread his light upon all of humanity."

"This doesn't bother you?"

"Of course not."

"Why?" The man was brainwashed. There was no other explanation.

"Tell me. You follow El, don't you?" he said.

"I guess… yes."

He smiled again like he was humoring a simple-minded child. "Do you think El loves you?"

"I would have to say He probably does. He saved me from the Mamood, after all."

The Kofra chuckled and shook his head. "Do you speak with him often?"

I knew why he laughed; I wasn't exactly saved at the moment. "He's talked to me a couple of times." I didn't know where the Kofra was going with this, but I was starting to get worried.

"Manoo speaks to me every day. He personally appointed me as his head priest to guide his children in our holy crusade." The Kofra placed his hand on mine as it rested on the table. "He spoke to me just before you arrived, encouraging me in my duty tonight. Has El said anything to you since you were recaptured? Do you know his plan?"

A lump formed in my throat. I swallowed past it, but it swelled and pushed until I could barely breathe.

"Do not be upset." He rubbed his thumb along my wrist. "El has remained absent for many years, content to let humanity degrade with no help and no guidance. That's the only rebellion Manoo is guilty of; he could not just stand by and watch us dwindle down to nothing, warring without end and to no purpose."

"But you brought death to an innocent nation. As we speak, your people are attacking and killing the Soltakians."

"We bring war only to the guilty, those who refuse to fall under Manoo's light. They were trying to protect you—his Destructor." He shook his head. "Can you imagine the evil that would be allowed to reign if we had allowed you to grow into your potential? Your very title gives evidence to the evil El endorses."

I ripped my hand away and leaned away from him. My veins went numb. Was he right? Was everything I'd come to believe a lie? I couldn't wrap my mind around it. The only truth I'd ever known was that the Mamood were evil. I'd embraced the title and duty of Destructor because it was something I'd wanted. Even now I recalled my joy as I'd burned the woman and her shop, as I'd nearly ripped apart the Delsa-Prime, and even as I'd attacked my own friends. I'd been happy, embracing the fury within me.

"You're not the hero in this story, Ella," he said, echoing my thoughts. "You're the villain."

I shook my head. No, it couldn't be true. I rose from my seat and backed away. The edges of my vision darkened. My chains rattled as I stuck my arm out, sure I was about to fall. All three hounds snapped their jaws and clawed at the marble floor. Every rifle hummed, ready to fire.

"No," I said. "No."

The Kofra waved them off and came to stand next to me. "It will be all right. Soon evil will be purged. Your willing sacrifice will be noted in our histories and honored for all time."

I searched his warm, brown eyes but found nothing false in them. He believed what he was saying. As I thought of all the people who'd still be alive if not for me—Meir, the shopkeeper, all the people killed in the raid as I'd used them like a shield—I found myself starting to believe it, too. I was the evil one, the one who craved destruction and death, the cause of so much suffering. I needed to die.

The boy wiped away a tear from my eye and smiled. "It's time."

CHAPTER TWENTY-ONE: LOVE

My gaze drifted upward to the skylight; nothing but deep blue night stared back at me. The sun had set and Manoo was ready. Perhaps I would've once taken this as a sign of Manoo's deception—performing his tasks only in the shadows—but with the Kofra's words still echoing in my ears and his raptor gaze still on me, I could not.

A soldier undid my chains, letting them clatter on the floor, before he grabbed my arm and led me away from the Kofra, out of the round room, past the hall, and through the palace's rear grounds to Manoo's temple. More soldiers formed rank around me. I didn't struggle, though with the energy bracelets gone I could've escaped if I'd wanted to. But at the moment, I didn't want to. I couldn't think enough to want to. Though I tried, my mind could find no argument against the Kofra. I was a murderer, a monster—not good, not a savior.

A Destructor.

Meir was dead because of me and no one else. My hands had let go of him in order to save myself. My evil had brought the Mamood to defend their right to live. And I'd blamed and hurt others for what was my doing all along. A hole formed deep within my soul, killing all sense of feeling. There was only the truth: I deserved to die. I didn't fight the Tarmean soldiers as they led me up marble steps to a flat platform at the top of the temple because I *wanted* to die.

Other people stood there, waiting off to the side in white robes. In the center of the platform a tall stone slab rose out of the floor. An empty trench surrounded the slab and ran off in a straight line toward the front of the platform, facing the city.

There it broke off into different directions, forming loops and swirls until all the narrow trenches led to a shallow, silver bowl.

Another Tarmean soldier broke rank to join my escort. Both dug their hands into my forearms and pulled me toward the slab. A roar that thudded through my bones erupted from the city as I came into view. Hundreds of thousands—perhaps millions— of torch-carrying people crowded around the palace for miles, screaming and jumping. I looked away, but the sound even made the stone beneath my feet rumble.

I couldn't pick out any words, but the message was clear: they were rejoicing over my impending death. The small crowd allowed to watch on the platform must have consisted of rather important people. Unlike those in the city, this crowd stood silent and motionless.

Did they have a better sense of the gravity of the situation? Did they understand how much I hated myself? Probably not. The twisting guilt in my stomach told me I deserved affection and sympathy from no one.

The Kofra stepped onto the platform from the left side, just behind the group of white-clad nobles. They bobbed their heads and parted for him. He'd changed out of his burgundy robes into a silver cloak that shimmered under the light of the moon.

Without even looking in my direction, he glided past me with his eyes glazed over and stopped in front of the silver bowl. The crowd in the city erupted into a new kind of frenzy, overshadowing the one from before. My arms twitched to bring my hands up to my ears, but my guards' fingers tightened. Even the small group just a few feet away betrayed their emotions by mumbling amongst each other.

The Kofra bowed his head and dropped something into the bowl. Flames erupted with a pop and everyone fell immediately silent. The hush over the city was even more bone-chilling than the thunderous roar. Something important was about to happen, and I had a feeling I didn't want to be there when it did.

No. I wanted this. I wanted the destruction to stop.

My guards' hands twisted around my arms, cutting off the blood. Pins and needles prickled down my limbs, but I didn't care. Something much worse was coming.

The Kofra fell onto his stomach and stayed completely still. No one breathed.

One, two, three seconds passed and then his body started to flop around as the Kofra's psyche battled Manoo's. Only one could win, and everyone knew who that was going to be.

And then it stopped, and Manoo in the Kofra's body turned to face me.

My breath caught in my throat. The eyes were completely different—still dark brown and intense, but no longer innocent. The one staring at me behind those eyes was filled with a knowledge and understanding of fury I could only ever imagine.

"Hello," he hissed. I didn't think it was possible to hiss a greeting, but Manoo managed it. Every subtle movement of the Kofra's body was twisted into something altogether ugly. I knew instantly that the boy behind the body was already dead.

Someone coughed in the city below us; the sound echoed off the walls until it faded and everything was once again silent.

Rather than wait for me to respond to him, Manoo motioned to the group of witnesses on the platform. One man stepped forward with a knife and silver cup. The man was hooded, his face was cast in shadow, but my stomach twisted as soon as he came up behind me and removed my cloak. There was something sinister and familiar about the way he moved.

Manoo dipped his finger into the cup. It sizzled as the scent of cooking meat wafted its way to my nose. He didn't even flinch.

I clenched my jaw, waiting.

After a pointed look from Manoo, the guard on my right straightened out my arm and held fast.

Manoo withdrew his finger from the now smoking cup and let it hover just above my arm. Already, I could feel the heat radiating above me, ready to scorch my flesh.

"First, I will write the ancient spells in oil, burning them into your flesh. After we have placed you on the altar, I will write them in your blood, binding your soul inside your body."

He pressed his finger onto my arm and swept it around. Every nerve ending in my skin screamed as the hot oil seeped in and cooked me. I screamed as I tried to pull away, but the guards' hold on me only tightened.

Time seemed to slow as I drowned in the pain. More times than I could count, I was nearly crushed with the blackness, but just as I was about to feel the sweet release of nonexistence, someone splashed water on my face to pull me out of it.

Manoo wouldn't let me die. He wouldn't even let me pass out. I needed to feel it all—every last drop of oil that burned its way through my skin down to my muscle.

Before long, my whole body was on fire, sizzling and popping. Even the cool night air offered no release. Every breeze on my skin only inflamed the pain, making it radiate down to my bones.

Someone was talking, though I'd long ago ceased to really pay attention. But this voice was burned into my brain the way the oil was burned into my skin: Manoo. He was giving instructions to the cloaked man behind me.

"I must cut off her left wing first," Manoo said to the man as he grabbed the knife. "Be careful not to let any of the precious drilium fall to the floor."

My head swam as my mind tried to reason through his words. One thing was for certain—I was about to feel more pain. But somehow I knew this pain would be different.

My wings. They were my only escape. In the back of my mind I knew if I ever really wanted to leave, I still had a chance. But if he took my wings, I'd be a victim in every sense of the word.

Did I want that? Was I really ready to sacrifice myself?

Yes. Yes, I was.

Someone's hands clamped onto my back and started forcing my skin to separate over my left wing. Pain ripped through, cutting and burning as it went. I clenched my jaw and tried in vain to hold back the tears as they spilled down my cheeks. Those same hands dug into the pocket of flesh and grabbed hold of my wing, prying it out against its will.

My knees buckled under the agony and I screamed. The burning had been nothing compared to this. This was excruciating, mind-numbing pain. My guards held me still, though I flailed to rip my arms away from them. Instinct warred against my resolve. My body didn't care what my mind had decided—it needed to protect my wings, my lifeblood.

This couldn't be right. If Manoo was so good, why did he have to torture me to death?

"Shh…" A velvet voice whispered in my ear. It wasn't Manoo, but it was a voice I knew well. Malik. My eyes widened as I choked on a gasp. "Hello, Ella."

Malik was here? *How* was he here? And why wasn't he stopping this?

"Malik," I muttered through my whimpers. "Help."

His thumb traced circles on my wing. "Meir sends his love."

Meir? No, Meir was dead. The Soltakian soldier had said he was dead. "No."

"Yes." His hot breath scorched my ear. "Did you really think I didn't care? That I helped you out of the goodness of my heart?" He shook his head. "I was just waiting for the perfect opportunity."

Malik not care? No. Malik was my friend. I couldn't think through the pain. Malik was making no sense.

Something sharp dug into the base of my wing and started slicing. Pain like ice shot up my spine, paralyzing me, and I screamed. I tried to fight against the hold on my arm to get them off me, to make it stop. I'd changed my mind. I didn't want this. The guards' hands constricted.

Malik chuckled with his lips pressed against my ear. "That's what Meir sounded like last night after I found him."

Again with Meir.

I shook my head. It was impossible. Meir had died yesterday afternoon.

"After I convinced Cailen to help me leave the Soltakian's pathetic excuse for a bunker, I found my father's 'dear friend'—the betrayer—nearly crushed under that transport in Co'ladesh, and barely alive," he continued. "I pulled him out, helped him regain consciousness… and then I tortured him." He chuckled. "The two of you were so trusting, so naïve. How easily you believed my little tale about honor. Didn't you know you'd destroyed me the moment you came onto my ship? Screw honor!" he hissed. "You're just a worthless little girl. But you know that, don't you, kiddo?" He chuckled his maniacal little laugh again. "I knew I'd won you over completely the moment I used that precious term of endearment. You just want to be loved. Well, now you get to know betrayal. You get to let it crush you." He paused. "And you get to die knowing Meir will join you very soon." I could hear the smile in his words.

Burning shards ripped down my throat as I struggled to swallow. Meir had been alive and Malik had *tortured* him? He'd used us; betrayed us all along. He might've been the one to tell Manoo where I'd been hiding. I'd been wrong about him. *Everyone* had been wrong! Red spotted my vision—not the red points of light, not yet.

This red was rage.

"He kept calling for you, too. I'd left him alive when I came here, but I'm sure Soltak has some predators in need of a good meal."

"No." My voice was dead, but everything in me was alive. "No!" I roared and smiled as those red, blue, and green points of light blotted out my vision.

I'd never seen so many points of light before. Every person in the crowd below me and on the platform with me transformed into multi-colored orbs. I saw how the blue lights pooled where their lungs should be, how the red lights skittered across their bodies as blood rushed through their veins, and even the green lights—the ones I'd never controlled before—made up the great mass of their insides. In the distance—so far away I allowed myself a moment of shock I could see it at all—past the millions of spectators I saw a great ball of red lights, compacted and churning.

I turned on my guards and expanded the green lights in their bodies. Chunks of flesh and blood exploded as water swelled and rushed out, pouring over the platform. The white-robed men at the side of the platform started to back away, but I twisted the blue lights at them and ripped their bodies apart.

Malik threw back his hood and glared at me head-on, challenging me. The night erupted into screams as those in the city realized what was happening. I didn't even know where Manoo was, but no one held my wing anymore—it dangled along my back, limp—so I assumed he'd run away. I would find him, though. First, I had to deal with Malik.

"Where is Meir?"

He smirked his annoying little smirk.

I pushed at the blue lights and lifted Malik off the ground. Knowing that would never be enough to scare him, I expanded the lights in his lungs, pushing the bursting point. "Where?"

Malik faltered then and I watched with satisfaction and a touch of sorrow as all his pride crumbled. His cheeks puffed out and reddened as the strain in his lungs grew. I could only imagine the agony he was feeling at that moment. He blew out, desperately trying to empty what I just filled back in. He gulped and pushed his sweaty hair away from his face. "The mountains," he gasped. "Outside Co'ladesh. Between the two great peaks, alongside the river."

"How close to death was he when you left him?"

"Very."

Very. I needed to hurry while I still had a chance. But I wasn't going anywhere until Meir's suffering had been avenged.

I took one last look into Malik's deep, black eyes—eyes I'd once cared for—and mourned his utter betrayal as I pushed at the blue lights, watching as he flew high into the air toward the city. I then joined the red lights in his veins, letting his insides smolder and burn through him until his body hit the ground.

I twisted my head around, looking for my next victim, the one who was most to blame. The one who would pay for everything he'd stripped from me—Malik, Meir, my freedom. The one who would finally know what it was like to beg for death.

Manoo.

He stood just a few steps away from me with the bowl of flames in his hands and a smile on his face.

"You can't win." He seemed so confident, so sure of his victory, but I knew something he didn't. Something El had known all along. And something I had just begun to grasp.

I laughed and took a step toward him. "Do you want to know what the funny thing is?"

Manoo scowled at me.

"Ranen told me how to beat you days ago and I just realized it now." I laughed again, enjoying Manoo's frustration. "He said Fire was drawn to those who craved destruction."

Manoo's eyes darted to the bowl of flames, and then back to me. Understanding dawned in his eyes. I'd felt him pushing at the flames, trying to control them, but they didn't obey his orders.

They obeyed mine.

"Isn't it appropriate then that El would appoint a Destructor to defeat you?" I released my right wing and spread both wings out to the sides, feeling the healing tingle where the knife had sliced into me and the oil had burned my skin. "I'm the only one who Fire would ever choose to obey over you."

Manoo growled and threw the bowl away, but I didn't care. I didn't need his little bowl, not when there was something far greater in my line of sight. The huge bright ball of compacted and churning red lights on the other side of Kalhandthar submitted to my orders.

Somehow, instinct told me I needed to draw the points of light to each other as tightly as they would go—compress them until there was nowhere else for them to go but out.

So I did.

And that's when it exploded.

The god stuck in a man's feeble body ripped at his silver cloak and roared. He charged at me with his hands curled into claws, reaching for my throat. I slammed him down with a wall of air and trapped him on the marble slab meant for my sacrifice.

The black sky burned away as waves of fire rolled across the planet. I couldn't see or hear the millions of people below us anymore. They were probably already dead. I knew I had only seconds before the planet was consumed. So I committed to memory Manoo's face twisted in agony and terror, and then flapped my wings with only one place in mind.

Lights swirled around me for just a moment before an intense, scorching heat slammed into my body. I was stuck in the nowhere-land between two places even as the chaos going on in Kalhandthar tried to pull me back. Some unseen force yanked at my wings, dragging them—and me with them—away from where I wanted to be, away from Meir. I flapped on, forcing the transport to happen though my wings felt like they were moving through heavy mud.

The lights stopped swirling around me. There was nothing but heavy, deep black, a black that made all darkness I'd ever known before seem like staring straight into the sun. This blackness pulled at me, nearly ripping my wings away from my struggling body.

I couldn't breathe. The force had sucked away all the air from around me, from my lungs themselves.

With my jaw and fists clenched, I forced my wings to move and kept Meir in the forefront of my mind. I *would* get to him.

Off in the distance, like at the end of a very long tunnel, I saw a faint glimmer of light. I reached for it and flapped harder. The force behind me weakened as I moved forward and transporting became easier. With a few more flaps, my wings seared in intense pain, but they moved. That was all I could ask for at that point.

My muscles felt like they were about to burst and my lungs burned for the air that was still beyond their reach. I flapped one more time and warm sunlight beat down on me. I was in the middle of a forest, next to a gurgling brook.

My body fell to the soft, squishy ground. I tried to pull in the sweet, cool air and gasped. It was as though my lungs had forgotten how to work. I could only wheeze and sputter through bare wisps of air—not nearly enough.

Meir. I needed to get to Meir. But I couldn't. There was nothing I could do. My body refused to move or even think about doing anything but getting oxygen.

There was no way to tell how long I'd been out. When I'd transported in, I could've sworn I'd felt the sun on my bare skin, but when I woke it was dark. That could mean hours… or days.

Thunder punched through the sky. I rolled over and looked through the trees at the twinkling stars. One of those worlds was gone—I could feel it. I'd destroyed more than just a planet and its sun. I'd ripped a hole into the fabric of space. That must've been the force that had sucked me out of my transport and nearly killed me. I didn't know how I could be so certain, but I felt the truth of it beyond a shadow of a doubt.

Light flashed and rippled across the atmosphere and another blast of thunder punched the air. The light fizzled out, leaving only the twinkling stars to take its place.

Wait—something was off.

I sat up and groaned as my sore, burning muscles rebelled. There was a clearing a few dozen feet away from me. I stumbled over to it, keeping my eyes toward the sky.

There were no clouds. How could there be a thunderstorm with no clouds?

Light and sound rippled through the sky again, only this time I was paying attention. This wasn't a storm with random flashes of lightning and rumbles of thunder. Each flash of light came at a perfect interval.

I waited for it to happen again, knowing just where to look. At the center of the flash of light, some kind of ship broke through the atmosphere. It wasn't a Mamood ship. Even from this distance I could tell. I was pretty sure it wasn't Soltakian, either. From what I'd seen of their speeders, they liked their machines sleek and streamlined. These ships were bloated and curved, like curtains in a windstorm. That's when I remembered Lastrini saying something about the Mosandarians coming.

I closed my eyes and sank to the ground. Would the Soltakians know the war was over now that Kalhandthar was destroyed? Would the Mamood soldiers stop killing? Too many people had died already. Soltakians, Mamood, Meir.

Meir.

How had I forgotten about Meir?

I whipped around in search of him, digging through the thick carpet of dead leaves and brush. Would Malik have hidden his body? If he had, it could be hours before I found him.

The light continued to flash in the sky above me, helping in my search. When the light didn't shine, the green glow of Soltak's moon shone hazily on the ground. Still, it wasn't enough.

"Meir!"

The only thing that answered was the soft, bubbling sound of water running past rocks.

The river!

I ran to the sound, letting my gaze scan from one side to the other. A dark lump barely stood out, but I knew instantly it was Meir.

As I made my first step to him, a black haze as thick as tar descended over me, blocking out everything except Meir. Warmth rushed to my head as the world spun. The flashing light was gone. The moon, gone. I looked around for something—trees, the river, anything—but there was only the blanket of pure darkness, so much worse than anything *Sho'ful* had had to offer.

Only the darkness... and Meir.

I went to him and gagged at what I saw. Half his face had been ripped clean off, and his guts spilled out around him with flies buzzing and laying eggs in the graying flesh.

No, Meir. No!

I threw myself to the ground and let the torrents of despair rip through every last part of me. My heart twisted in on itself. It squeezed and throbbed against my chest until I couldn't feel anything but the pain. I'd lost him again. That had been Malik's true betrayal: letting me hope.

As if bidden from the dead, a cackling sort of chuckle I recognized all too well echoed around me. I peered out from behind the curtain of my hair as terror clenched at me. I brought a shaking hand up to clear away some of the strands.

"Who's there?" My voice shook right along with my hand.

"You know who." Malik's voice skittered around me, some-times close, sometimes far away.

"You're dead."

Malik laughed again. His maniacal cackling poured into me, making all the blood in my veins freeze.

I screamed.

"Ella!" Something shook me and I thrust my arms out to do what little I could to protect myself. "Ella, stop!"

The darkness seeped away from my mind and Cailen's face loomed in front of mine. I gasped and wrapped my arms around him, anchoring myself to this sense of reality.

"You're shaking," he said.

I dug my head into his chest and clenched my jaw shut to stop my chattering teeth. I tasted blood and let my tongue roam around my mouth, searching. A chunk of skin hung off the inside of my cheek. I pressed my tongue hard against the hole, reveling in the sting. The sting was real. The sting was good.

"What happened?"

I shook my head in answer.

Something fluttered behind Cailen, and too soon the sting began to seep away. I pressed harder, desperate. I dug my hands into Cailen's shoulders and pressed tighter to him. I couldn't lose this hold. I couldn't go back to the darkness.

Cailen leaned away with one arm still wrapped around my waist. I whimpered and bit back the tears. Before I knew it, the world had disappeared again.

I screamed.

A whirlpool of light swirled around me, in and out. And I continued screaming.

Silver walls formed around us. Men and women in silver uni-forms froze. And even thought I knew we were back in the Block, I was still screaming.

"Shh." Cailen rubbed circles on my back and pressed his cheek against my head. "You're safe now."

Cailen had said that to me before and he'd been right then. Maybe he was right now. So I let my screams die out even as I clung tighter to him. I couldn't let go. I knew once I did, I'd be lost again.

He lifted his head from mine and said to someone behind me, "Take him to a room and get someone to keep an eye on him."

I looked up then, my curiosity warring with my terror. Two soldiers in silver suits picked up Meir's prostrate form—which had been lying at Cailen's side—and carried him past me. Despite all the warnings in my head, I looked. Meir's face was... still intact. In fact, it looked flushed and healthy. No guts trailed out of his torso. His chest rose and fell with steady breaths. The only thing wrong with him was his left leg—it was gone at the knee.

I shook my head to make some sense of everything. Meir had been dead; I'd seen it. And not just dead, but torn apart. This wasn't Meir. It couldn't be. The world started spinning again and I knew that, if I didn't lie down soon, I was going to puke.

As if hearing my thoughts, Cailen picked me up and carried me down the hall in the opposite direction from Meir. I rested my head against his chest and took deep breaths. When he placed me on the bed, I wrapped his shirt in my fists and pulled him down with me.

"Please stay."

"I'm not going anywhere."

"I'm so sorry." Tears welled up around my eyes as I remembered how I'd betrayed him even after all he'd done for me.

"We all make mistakes, Ella." His voice was low and sad. He turned to his side and settled deeper beside me. "So, what happened?"

"I killed them," I whispered. For some reason, I knew saying it louder would make it feel too real. "All of them."

"And Manoo?"

"I don't know." I turned my face away from him.

He sighed. It was the kind of sigh I imagined meant he didn't know how to break something to me, but he was going to, anyway. "The Mosandarians are here. And the Mamood war ships are still surrounding the planet." He put his finger on my chin and forced me to look at him. "The war is still on."

And just like that, a hole in my heart ripped open. Everything I'd done had been pointless.

"But you did good. You did what you were supposed to do." He smiled and kissed me on the cheek. The current of warmth pulsed through me from my face all the way down to my toes.

This was real. *This* was my reality, not the darkness.

I bit my lip and looked away. The darkness couldn't have been real. It *had* to have been a hallucination. Didn't it?

I looked back at Cailen and stared into his bright, green eyes, wondering if they were real. Malik had done nothing but lie to me, and Cailen—despite everything I'd accused him of—had always told the truth. His eyes were real.

END OF BOOK ONE

Keep reading for a sneak peek of:

FAE

THE SEQUEL TO ELEMENTAL

COMING IN 2013 FROM SPENCER HILL PRESS

CHAPTER ONE:
SURPRISES

I fell on my bed, laughing.

"I'm being serious," Cailen said, his eyes wide with innocence. "I'm terrified of water."

A new round of giggles burst from my mouth and shook my whole body. I dove face-first for the pillow. It was totally ridiculous. *Cailen*? The guy who'd entered into a training program with hundreds of other students and came out as one of only four survivors was afraid of something as benign as water? I dove deeper into the soft, down folds to snuff out the noise. When I turned to peek at him, I could tell by the sour expression on his face that he was not amused.

I howled with laughter again.

My chest started to hurt and I needed to rub at it just it so I could breathe. Several minutes and an achy stomach later, I'd finally reined it in enough to look at him again.

He sat across from me on the only chair in my bedroom. He leaned the chair to its limits, pressing its back against the wall, his arms across his chest. Not good.

With a giggly sigh, I sat up to face him. It took a few breaths, but I managed to put on a straight face.

"Are you done?"

I had to think about that. And since I could feel Cailen's irritation rolling off him in waves, I decided to say, "Yes." It was easy to forget sometimes that Cailen wasn't used to being mocked. When I did remember, though, the guilt poured through me. In Auru, he was someone important. But he wasn't in Auru and that was because of me. "I'm sorry."

He tipped the front legs back onto the floor and leaned forward with a smile. Forgiveness always came so easily with him. "It's your turn."

Ever since I'd returned to Soltak over three weeks ago, there'd been nothing to do but wait for the inevitable ground battle between the Soltakians—and their allies, the Mosandarians—and the Mamood. Entertainment was hard to find amongst the miles of military-controlled corridors that made up the underground Soltakian bunker. They called it The Block for a reason—flat, bland, and nondescript. And it wasn't like we could leave. I was firm on that point. There was no way I could leave the Soltakians alone to face a battle I'd created.

I'd already proven I had no problem getting blood on my hands.

So Cailen had suggested we try a truth game, played by trillions of people across the galaxy, to pass the time. Between dwelling on the impending doom, wandering around aimlessly, or finding out more about Cailen, the choice pretty much made itself.

Plus, Cailen and I agreed we needed time together. It still bothered me that I didn't know whether our feelings for each other were genuine or contrived. I figured that, as long as we tried to get to know each other, some day it might not matter if they turned out to be either, neither, or both.

The drilium bond wasn't ever going to go away. I could feel it now, buzzing through my veins, drawing me to Cailen. The want I had for him was unbearable sometimes, but I didn't give in and touch him. I wasn't ready for that yet. Not until I knew I *really* loved him.

I scrunched my nose and rubbed my eyebrow. What truth did I have to tell that he didn't already know? Ninety-eight percent of my life was lost in the oblivion of my failed memory. The rest I'd spent with him.

Well, there was that one secret. I shuddered as goose bumps prickled across my skin. That was one particular secret I wasn't ready to tell anyone. No one could know about my hallucination. Besides, I'd only had the one. Malik's ghost must have decided I wasn't worth haunting.

"My favorite color is green," I finally said. A blush spread across my cheeks when I remembered just why my favorite color was that particular shade. Looking into Cailen's green eyes, I thought back to the years I'd spent in *Sho'ful* thinking about them. They were the only things that'd stuck with me. Everything else was gone.

He half-smiled with a knowing look. "Is that why you've worn that dress three times this week?"

I looked down and stroked the silky folds of my green Auri dress. A smile crept onto my lips as I realized Cailen not only noticed, but remembered. "I don't have to answer that. It's your turn," I said as I peered at him through the strands of my hair.

He leaned back again and looked up at the silvery ceiling for a few seconds. Weariness and impatience prickled from him to me. "I'm tired of being trapped in here. How about we go up top?"

"You know it's dangerous outside."

He chuckled. There was no humor in it, though. "Yes. Dangerous."

There were several long, uncomfortable minutes of silence before I'd decided our game had come to an end and stood up to put on my cloak. "Will we get into trouble if we leave?"

He tore his gaze away from the ceiling and smiled a wolfish grin. "I really don't care." And before I could react, he jumped out of his chair and grabbed my wrist.

BETRAYED

A GUARDIAN LEGACY BOOK

Being one of
the Nephilim
isn't as easy
as it sounds.

June 2012

EDNAH WALTERS

MINDER

A GANZFIELD NOVEL BY

KATE KAYNAK

January 2013

Having poison running
through your veins and
a kiss that kills really
puts a dent in high school.

Kelly
Hashway

Touch of Death

PODs

A Novel

The end
of the world
is only the
beginning.

Michelle Pickett

Coming in June 2013

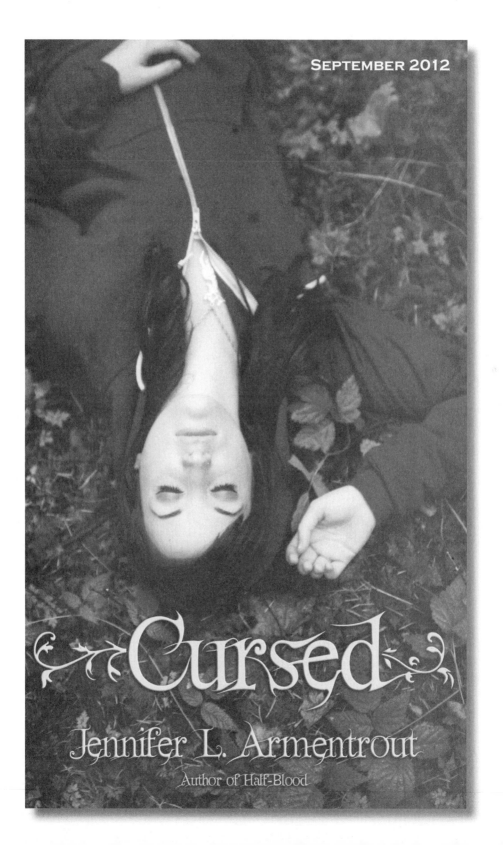

SEPTEMBER 2012

Cursed

Jennifer L. Armentrout

Author of Half-Blood

Acknowledgments

One would think that after writing a whole novel and going through all the edits, revisions, and headaches, writing a list of thank yous to acknowledge all those who'd helped me along the way would be easy.

But one would be wrong.

And since a picture speaks a thousand words, I'd thought about asking my publisher if I could start a new trend and provide a cartoon that adequately expressed the warm feelings I have for everyone. But then I remembered my skill at drawing ends at stick figures.

So writing it is.

First of all, I have to thank my parents. If you hadn't named me after a famous poet, I probably never would have connected the dots between the magical, beautiful words I loved to devour and the people who wrote them. It's probably a safe bet to assume I would have gone through the first few, impressionable years of my life thinking the words in books appeared out of thin air and that spark I'd first felt to write when I'd also first learned to read would never have occurred. So thank you. And thank you for also encouraging me in my craft, for never letting me settle for "good enough."

And thank you to my husband. Sometimes I wondered why I ever bothered to let you read my writing in the first place, but I'm glad I did. You taught me that I was looking for praise more than honest opinions. And boy did I make sure everything was perfect before I let you read anything again. That kind of support is invaluable and it prepared me for the real world of writing and publishing more than anything else could have.

I will never dare to put fluorescent lights on a spaceship again. Honestly, the idea does make me shudder now.

To my two little boys, thank you for being the most patient, forgiving, and quiet little children I ever could have hoped for.

To my high school English teacher, Mr. Russo, I thank you for pretending I actually had skill. Looking back now at what I wrote, I wonder how you didn't cringe. Oh, the adverbs. Those fickle little friends. But how I did love them. And the encouragement you gave me—despite the fact it probably wasn't warranted—pushed me forward in my pursuit of my dream. It was during my time in your class that I realized not only did I want to write, I wanted to do it for a living.

Also, thank you for showing me that writing didn't have to be all serious. I think I'd forgotten that fact by the time I hit my teens. I'll never forget our class iced tea and lemonade parties. Shadoobie, my friend. Shattered. Shattered.

To my betas, Victoria and Carol, thank you for putting up with me. I realize my rants and boohoo moments were pretty difficult to take sometimes. And I also realize I'm just about the most stubborn person when it comes to changing *anything* in my book, but you were patient and helped me to see the truth. I couldn't have gotten to the place I'm at today without the two of you.

Victoria, thank you especially for your astounding abilities. I am *still* in love with my cover and I consider myself very blessed for ever having met you. And I am so glad we both got over our shyness and decided to call each other and take our friendship past the online phase. I hope to meet you both in person some day. We can sip tea and eat crumpets!

Thank you to Kelly for taking the pictures of the very beautiful model on my cover. You got it just the way I'd always envisioned it.

And of course I can't forget all the wonderful people at Spencer Hill Press for giving me a chance and making me feel like a part of the family.

Kate, you are amazing. I still sometimes can't believe my good fortune. When I think about how I came to work with SHP, I just have to sit back and go "wow." And if it weren't for you and all the awesome support you showed me by reaching out to help me in my career, I don't know where I'd be today. When I met you in person for the first time, every good feeling I had about working with you was absolutely confirmed. Your energy and excitement was addictive. We need to get together more often.

And to Kendra, you are an editing ninja. You and Kate have saved me from certain humiliation. And while some writers might take it as a bad sign that they need two editors, I knew I was exceedingly lucky. Let's face it, I need all the help I can get. And you are awesome. Thank you for catching all that you did. I can honestly say that, after reading your edits and suggestions, I didn't need the few hours to think them over. They were so dead-on and perfect, I saw immediately how right you were. Thanks also to Kathryn Radzik, Danielle Ellison, Patricia Riley and Rich Storrs for copy-editing.

To Dan, Lisa, and Jennifer, thank you for welcoming me to the family. Your emails, Twitter support, and comments on my blog have been the highlight of many long, stressful days.

And finally, thank you to Adonai for blessing me with the skill to write. I realize that it most definitely didn't come about from my own doing. And thank you for sending all these people my way to help me become the writer I am today.

About the Author

Emily White lives in NY, wedged between two of the Great Lakes and a few feet of snow and ice. She's spent most of her life running away from the cold, and even spent a year in Iraq, but now contents herself with writing her characters into warm, exotic places in faraway galaxies. When not tapping away at her computer keys, she can be found reading, reading, and reading some more. And when she's not doing that, she's usually playing video games with her husband, peek-a-boo with her kids, or walking through her garden, wondering why the bugs insist on eating *all* her vegetables. Emily writes Young Adult Science Fiction.

emilytwhite.blogspot.com